The Hitchhiker's Guide to the Galaxy

Film Tie-in Edition

Douglas Adams was born in 1952 and created all the various and contradictory manifestations of *The Hitchhiker's Guide to the Galaxy*: radio, novels, TV, computer game, stage adaptations, comic book and bath towel. He lectured and broadcast around the world and was a patron of the Dian Fossey Gorilla Fund and Save the Rhino International. Douglas Adams was born in Cambridge, UK, and lived with his wife and daughter in Islington, London, before moving to Santa Barbara, California, where he died suddenly in 2001. After Douglas died the movie of *Hitchhiker* moved out of development hell into the clear uplands of production, using much of Douglas' original script and ideas. Douglas shares the writing credit for the movie with Karey Kirkpatrick.

Robbie Stamp was an executive producer on the *Hitchhiker's Guide to the Galaxy* movie and a close friend of Douglas Adams.

Also by Douglas Adams

The Hitchhiker series

The Hitchhiker's Guide to the Galaxy
The Restaurant at the End of the Universe
Life, the Universe and Everything
So Long, and Thanks for all the Fish
Mostly Harmless

The Hitchhiker's Guide to the Galaxy: The Original Radio Scripts
The Hitchhiker's Guide to the Galaxy Radio Scripts: The Tertiary, Quandary and Quintessential Phases

The Making of 'The Hitchhiker's Guide to the Galaxy'

The Dirk Gently series

Dirk Gently's Holistic Detective Agency
The Long Dark Tea-time of the Soul

The Salmon of Doubt

With John Lloyd
The Meaning of Liff
The Deeper Meaning of Liff

With Mark Carwardine
Last Chance to See . . .

By Terry Jones, based on a story/computer game by Douglas Adams
Starship Titanic

THE HITCHHIKER'S GUIDE TO THE GALAXY

FILM TIE-IN EDITION

DOUGLAS ADAMS

Afterword by Robbie Stamp

PAN BOOKS

First published by Pan Books 1979

Film tie-in edition first published 2005 by Pan Books
an imprint of Pan Macmillan Ltd
Pan Macmillan, 20 New Wharf Road, London N1 9RR
Basingstoke and Oxford
Associated companies throughout the world
www.panmacmillan.com

ISBN 0 330 43798 4

9 8 7 6

A CIP catalogue record for this book is available from
the British Library.

Typeset by SetSystems Ltd, Saffron Walden, Essex
Printed and bound in Great Britain by
Mackays of Chatham plc, Chatham, Kent

for Jonny Brock and Clare Gorst
and all other Arlingtonians for
tea, sympathy and a sofa

Contents

THE HITCHHIKER'S GUIDE TO THE GALAXY

Far out in the uncharted backwaters of the unfashionable end of the Western Spiral Arm of the Galaxy lies a small unregarded yellow sun.

Orbiting this at a distance of roughly ninety-two million miles is an utterly insignificant little blue-green planet whose ape-descended life forms are so amazingly primitive that they still think digital watches are a pretty neat idea.

This planet has – or rather had – a problem, which was this: most of the people living on it were unhappy for pretty much of the time. Many solutions were suggested for this problem, but most of these were largely concerned with the movements of small green pieces of paper, which is odd because on the whole it wasn't the small green pieces of paper that were unhappy.

And so the problem remained; lots of the people were mean, and most of them were miserable, even the ones with digital watches.

Many were increasingly of the opinion that they'd all made a big mistake in coming down from the trees in the first place. And some said that even the trees had been a bad move, and that no one should ever have left the oceans.

And then, one Thursday, nearly two thousand years after

one man had been nailed to a tree for saying how great it would be to be nice to people for a change, a girl sitting on her own in a small cafe in Rickmansworth suddenly realized what it was that had been going wrong all this time, and she finally knew how the world could be made a good and happy place. This time it was right, it would work, and no one would have to get nailed to anything.

Sadly, however, before she could get to a phone to tell anyone about it, a terrible, stupid catastrophe occurred, and the idea was lost for ever.

This is not her story.

But it is the story of that terrible stupid catastrophe and some of its consequences.

It is also the story of a book, a book called The Hitchhiker's Guide to the Galaxy – *not an Earth book, never published on Earth, and until the terrible catastrophe occurred, never seen or even heard of by any Earthman.*

Nevertheless, a wholly remarkable book.

In fact it was probably the most remarkable book ever to come out of the great publishing corporations of Ursa Minor – of which no Earthman had ever heard either.

Not only is it a wholly remarkable book, it is also a highly successful one – more popular than The Celestial Home Care Omnibus, *better selling than* Fifty-three More Things to do in Zero Gravity, *and more controversial than Oolon Colluphid's trilogy of philosophical blockbusters* Where God Went Wrong, Some More of God's Greatest Mistakes *and* Who is this God Person Anyway?

In many of the more relaxed civilizations on the Outer Eastern Rim of the Galaxy, the Hitchhiker's Guide *has already supplanted the great* Encyclopaedia Galactica *as the standard repository of all knowledge and wisdom, for though it has many omissions and contains much that is apocryphal, or at least wildly inaccurate, it scores over the older, more pedestrian work in two important respects.*

First, it is slightly cheaper; and secondly it has the words DON'T PANIC *inscribed in large friendly letters on its cover.*

But the story of this terrible stupid Thursday, the story of its extraordinary consequences, and the story of how these consequences are inextricably intertwined with this remarkable book begins very simply.

It begins with a house.

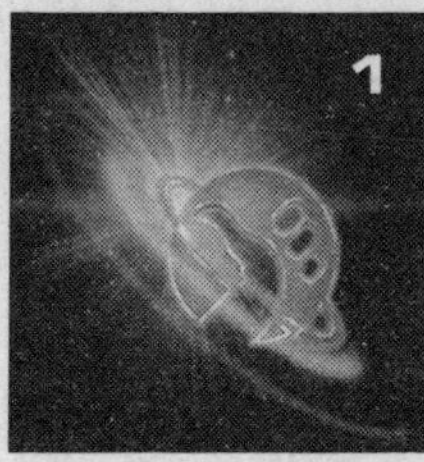

The house stood on a slight rise just on the edge of the village. It stood on its own and looked out over a broad spread of West Country farmland. Not a remarkable house by any means – it was about thirty years old, squattish, squarish, made of brick, and had four windows set in the front of a size and proportion which more or less exactly failed to please the eye.

The only person for whom the house was in any way special was Arthur Dent, and that was only because it happened to be the one he lived in. He had lived in it for about three years, ever since he had moved out of London because it made him nervous and irritable. He was about thirty as well, tall, dark haired and never quite at ease with himself. The thing that used to worry him most was the fact that people always used to ask him what he was looking so worried about. He worked in local radio, which he always used to tell his friends was a lot more interesting than they probably thought. It was, too – most of his friends worked in advertising.

On Wednesday night it had rained very heavily, the lane was wet and muddy, but the Thursday morning sun was bright and clear as it shone on Arthur Dent's house for what was to be the last time.

It hadn't properly registered yet with Arthur that the council wanted to knock it down and build a bypass instead.

At eight o'clock on Thursday morning Arthur didn't feel very good. He woke up blearily, got up, wandered blearily round his room, opened a window, saw a bulldozer, found his slippers, and stomped off to the bathroom to wash.

Toothpaste on the brush – so. Scrub.

Shaving mirror – pointing at the ceiling. He adjusted it. For a moment it reflected a second bulldozer through the bathroom window. Properly adjusted, it reflected Arthur Dent's bristles. He shaved them off, washed, dried, and stomped off to the kitchen to find something pleasant to put in his mouth.

Kettle, plug, fridge, milk, coffee. Yawn.

The word *bulldozer* wandered through his mind for a moment in search of something to connect with.

The bulldozer outside the kitchen window was quite a big one.

He stared at it.

'Yellow,' he thought and stomped off back to his bedroom to get dressed.

Passing the bathroom he stopped to drink a large glass of water, and another. He began to suspect that he was hung over. Why was he hung over? Had he been drinking the night before? He supposed that he must have been. He caught a glint in the shaving mirror. 'Yellow,' he thought and stomped on to the bedroom.

He stood and thought. The pub, he thought. Oh dear, the pub. He vaguely remembered being angry, angry about something that seemed important. He'd been telling people about it, telling people about it at great length, he rather suspected: his clearest visual recollection was of glazed looks on other people's faces. Something about a new bypass he'd just found out about. It had been in the pipeline for months only no one seemed to have known about it. Ridiculous. He took a swig of water. It would sort itself out, he'd decided, no one wanted a bypass, the council didn't have a leg to stand on. It would sort itself out.

God, what a terrible hangover it had earned him, though. He looked at himself in the wardrobe mirror. He stuck out his tongue. 'Yellow,' he thought. The word *yellow* wandered through his mind in search of something to connect with.

Fifteen seconds later he was out of the house and lying in front of a big yellow bulldozer that was advancing up his garden path.

Mr L. Prosser was, as they say, only human. In other words he was a carbon-based bipedal life form descended from an ape. More specifically he was forty, fat and shabby, and worked for the local council. Curiously enough, though he didn't know it, he was also a direct male-line descendant of Genghis Khan, though intervening generations and racial mixing had so juggled his genes that he had no discernible Mongoloid characteristics, and the only vestiges left in Mr L. Prosser of his mighty ancestry were a pronounced stoutness about the tum and a predilection for little fur hats.

He was by no means a great warrior: in fact he was a nervous worried man. Today he was particularly nervous and worried because something had gone seriously wrong with his job – which was to see that Arthur Dent's house got cleared out of the way before the day was out.

'Come off it, Mr Dent,' he said, 'you can't win, you know. You can't lie in front of the bulldozer indefinitely.' He tried to make his eyes blaze fiercely but they just wouldn't do it.

Arthur lay in the mud and squelched at him.

'I'm game,' he said, 'we'll see who rusts first.'

'I'm afraid you're going to have to accept it,' said Mr Prosser, gripping his fur hat and rolling it round the top of his head, 'this bypass has got to be built and it's going to be built!'

'First I've heard of it,' said Arthur, 'why's it got to be built?'

Mr Prosser shook his finger at him for a bit, then stopped and put it away again.

'What do you mean, why's it got to be built?' he said. 'It's a bypass. You've got to build bypasses.'

Bypasses are devices which allow some people to dash from point A to point B very fast whilst other people dash from point B to point A very fast. People living at point C, being a point directly in between, are often given to wonder what's so great about point A that so many people from point B are so keen to get there, and what's so great about point B that so many people from point A are so keen to get there. They often wish that people would just once and for all work out where the hell they want to be.

Mr Prosser wanted to be at point D. Point D wasn't anywhere in particular, it was just any convenient point a very long way from points A, B and C. He would have a nice little cottage at point D, with axes over the door, and spend a pleasant amount of time at point E, which would be the nearest pub to point D. His wife of course wanted climbing roses, but he wanted axes. He didn't know why – he just liked axes. He flushed hotly under the derisive grins of the bulldozer drivers.

He shifted his weight from foot to foot, but it was equally uncomfortable on each. Obviously somebody had been appallingly incompetent and he hoped to God it wasn't him.

Mr Prosser said, 'You were quite entitled to make any suggestions or protests at the appropriate time, you know.'

'Appropriate time?' hooted Arthur. 'Appropriate time? The first I knew about it was when a workman arrived at my home yesterday. I asked him if he'd come to clean the windows and he said no he'd come to demolish the house. He didn't tell me straight away, of course. Oh no. First he wiped a couple of windows and charged me a fiver. Then he told me.'

'But, Mr Dent, the plans have been available in the local planning office for the last nine months.'

'Oh yes, well as soon as I heard I went straight round to see them, yesterday afternoon. You hadn't exactly gone out of your way to call attention to them, had you? I mean like actually telling anybody or anything.'

'But the plans were on display . . .'

'On display? I eventually had to go down to the cellar to find them.'

'That's the display department.'

'With a torch.'

'Ah, well, the lights had probably gone.'

'So had the stairs.'

'But, look, you found the notice, didn't you?'

'Yes,' said Arthur, 'yes I did. It was on display in the bottom of a locked filing cabinet stuck in a disused lavatory with a sign on the door saying *Beware of the Leopard.*'

A cloud passed overhead. It cast a shadow over Arthur Dent as he lay propped up on his elbow in the cold mud. It cast a shadow over Arthur Dent's house. Mr Prosser frowned at it.

'It's not as if it's a particularly nice house,' he said.

'I'm sorry, but I happen to like it.'

'You'll like the bypass.'

'Oh, shut up,' said Arthur Dent. 'Shut up and go away, and take your bloody bypass with you. You haven't got a leg to stand on and you know it.'

Mr Prosser's mouth opened and closed a couple of times whilst his mind was for a moment filled with inexplicable but terribly attractive visions of Arthur Dent's house being consumed with fire and Arthur himself running screaming from the blazing ruin with at least three hefty spears protruding from his back. Mr Prosser was often bothered with visions like these and they made him feel very nervous. He stuttered for a moment and then pulled himself together.

'Mr Dent,' he said.

'Hello? Yes?' said Arthur.

'Some factual information for you. Have you any idea how much damage that bulldozer would suffer if I just let it roll straight over you?'

'How much?' said Arthur.

'None at all,' said Mr Prosser, and stormed nervously off wondering why his brain was filled with a thousand hairy horsemen all shouting at him.

By a curious coincidence, *None at all* is exactly how much suspicion the ape-descendent Arthur Dent had that one of his closest friends was not descended from an ape, but was in fact from a small planet somewhere in the vicinity of Betelgeuse and not from Guildford as he usually claimed.

Arthur Dent had never, ever suspected this.

This friend of his had first arrived on the planet Earth some fifteen Earth years previously, and he had worked hard to blend himself into Earth society – with, it must be said, some success. For instance he had spent those fifteen years pretending to be an out-of-work actor, which was plausible enough.

He had made one careless blunder, though, because he had skimped a bit on his preparatory research. The information he had gathered had led him to choose the name 'Ford Prefect' as being nicely inconspicuous.

He was not conspicuously tall, his features were striking but not conspicuously handsome. His hair was wiry and gingerish and brushed backwards from the temples. His skin seemed to be pulled backwards from the nose. There was something very slightly odd about him, but it was difficult to say what it was. Perhaps it was that his eyes didn't seem to blink often enough and when you talked to him for any length of time your eyes began involuntarily to water on his behalf. Perhaps it was that he smiled slightly too broadly and gave people the unnerving impression that he was about to go for their neck.

He struck most of the friends he had made on Earth as an eccentric, but a harmless one – an unruly boozer with some oddish habits. For instance he would often gatecrash university parties, get badly drunk and start making fun of any astrophysicists he could find till he got thrown out.

Sometimes he would get seized with oddly distracted moods and stare into the sky as if hypnotized until someone asked him what he was doing. Then he would start guiltily for a moment, relax and grin.

'Oh, just looking for flying saucers,' he would joke and everyone would laugh and ask him what sort of flying saucers he was looking for.

'Green ones!' he would reply with a wicked grin, laugh wildly for a moment and then suddenly lunge for the nearest bar and buy an enormous round of drinks.

Evenings like this usually ended badly. Ford would get out of his skull on whisky, huddle into a corner with some girl and explain to her in slurred phrases that honestly the colour of the flying saucers didn't matter that much really.

Thereafter, staggering semi-paralytic down the night streets, he would often ask passing policemen if they knew the way to Betelgeuse. The policemen would usually say something like, 'Don't you think it's about time you went off home, sir?'

'I'm trying to, baby, I'm trying to,' is what Ford invariably replied on these occasions.

In fact what he was really looking for when he stared distractedly into the sky was any kind of flying saucer at all. The reason he said green was that green was the traditional space livery of the Betelgeuse trading scouts.

Ford Prefect was desperate that any flying saucer at all would arrive soon because fifteen years was a long time to get stranded anywhere, particularly somewhere as mindbogglingly dull as the Earth.

Ford wished that a flying saucer would arrive soon because he knew how to flag flying saucers down and get lifts from them. He knew how to see the Marvels of the Universe for less than thirty Altairian dollars a day.

In fact, Ford Prefect was a roving researcher for that wholly remarkable book *The Hitchhiker's Guide to the Galaxy*.

Human beings are great adaptors, and by lunchtime life in the environs of Arthur's house had settled into a steady routine. It was Arthur's accepted role to lie squelching in the mud making occasional demands to see his lawyer, his mother, or a good book; it was Mr Prosser's accepted role to tackle Arthur with the occasional new ploy such as the For the Public Good talk, or the March of Progress talk, the They Knocked My House Down Once, You Know,

Never Looked Back talk and various other cajoleries and threats; and it was the bulldozer drivers' accepted role to sit around drinking coffee and experimenting with union regulations to see how they could turn the situation to their financial advantage.

The Earth moved slowly in its diurnal course.

The sun was beginning to dry out the mud that Arthur lay in.

A shadow moved across him again.

'Hello, Arthur,' said the shadow.

Arthur looked up and squinting into the sun was startled to see Ford Prefect standing above him.

'Ford! Hello, how are you?'

'Fine,' said Ford, 'look, are you busy?'

'Am I *busy*?' exclaimed Arthur. 'Well, I've just got all these bulldozers and things to lie in front of because they'll knock my house down if I don't, but other than that . . . well, no not especially, why?'

They don't have sarcasm on Betelgeuse, and Ford Prefect often failed to notice it unless he was concentrating. He said, 'Good, is there anywhere we can talk?'

'What?' said Arthur Dent.

For a few seconds Ford seemed to ignore him, and stared fixedly into the sky like a rabbit trying to get run over by a car. Then suddenly he squatted down beside Arthur.

'We've got to talk,' he said urgently.

'Fine,' said Arthur, 'talk.'

'And drink,' said Ford. 'It's vitally important that we talk and drink. Now. We'll go to the pub in the village.'

He looked into the sky again, nervous, expectant.

'Look, don't you understand?' shouted Arthur. He pointed at Prosser. 'That man wants to knock my house down!'

Ford glanced at him, puzzled.

'Well, he can do it while you're away, can't he?' he asked.

'But I don't want him to!'

'Ah.'

'Look, what's the matter with you, Ford?' said Arthur.

'Nothing. Nothing's the matter. Listen to me – I've got to tell you the most important thing you've ever heard. I've got to tell you now, and I've got to tell you in the saloon bar of the Horse and Groom.'

'But why?'

'Because you're going to need a very stiff drink.'

Ford stared at Arthur, and Arthur was astonished to find his will beginning to weaken. He didn't realize that this was because of an old drinking game that Ford had learned to play in the hyperspace ports that served the madranite-mining belts in the star system of Orion Beta.

The game was not unlike the Earth game called Indian Wrestling, and was played like this:

Two contestants would sit either side of a table, with a glass in front of each of them.

Between them would be placed a bottle of Janx Spirit (as immortalized in that ancient Orion mining song 'Oh, don't give me none more of that Old Janx Spirit / No, don't you give me none more of that Old Janx Spirit / For my head will fly, my tongue will lie, my eyes will fry and I may die / Won't you pour me one more of that sinful Old Janx Spirit').

Each of the two contestants would then concentrate his will on the bottle and attempt to tip it and pour spirit into the glass of his opponent – who would then have to drink it.

The bottle would then be refilled. The game would be played again. And again.

Once you started to lose you would probably keep losing, because one of the effects of Janx Spirit is to depress telepsychic power.

As soon as a predetermined quantity had been consumed, the final loser would have to perform a forfeit, which was usually obscenely biological.

Ford Prefect usually played to lose.

Ford stared at Arthur, who began to think that perhaps he did want to go to the Horse and Groom after all.

'But what about my house . . .?' he asked plaintively.

Ford looked across to Mr Prosser, and suddenly a wicked thought struck him.

'He wants to knock your house down?'

'Yes, he wants to build . . .'

'And he can't because you're lying in front of his bulldozers?'

'Yes, and . . .'

'I'm sure we can come to some arrangement,' said Ford. 'Excuse me!' he shouted.

Mr Prosser (who was arguing with a spokesman for the bulldozer drivers about whether or not Arthur Dent constituted a mental-health hazard, and how much they should get paid if he did) looked around. He was surprised and slightly alarmed to see that Arthur had company.

'Yes? Hello?' he called. 'Has Mr Dent come to his senses yet?'

'Can we for the moment,' called Ford, 'assume that he hasn't?'

'Well?' sighed Mr Prosser.

'And can we also assume,' said Ford, 'that he's going to be staying here all day?'

'So?'

'So all your men are going to be standing around all day doing nothing?'

'Could be, could be . . .'

'Well, if you're resigned to doing that anyway, you don't actually need him to lie here all the time, do you?'

'What?'

'You don't,' said Ford patiently, 'actually need him here.'

Mr Prosser thought about this.

'Well, no, not as such . . .' he said, 'not exactly *need* . . .' Mr Prosser was worried. He thought that one of them wasn't making a lot of sense.

Ford said, 'So if you would just like to take it as read that he's actually here, then he and I could slip off down to the pub for half an hour. How does that sound?'

Mr Prosser thought it sounded perfectly potty.

'That sounds perfectly reasonable . . .' he said in a reassuring tone of voice, wondering who he was trying to reassure.

'And if you want to pop off for a quick one yourself later on,' said Ford, 'we can always cover for you in return.'

'Thank you very much,' said Mr Prosser, who no

longer knew how to play this at all, 'thank you very much, yes, that's very kind . . .' He frowned, then smiled, then tried to do both at once, failed, grasped hold of his fur hat and rolled it fitfully round the top of his head. He could only assume that he had just won.

'So,' continued Ford Prefect, 'if you would just like to come over here and lie down . . .'

'What?' said Mr Prosser.

'Ah, I'm sorry,' said Ford, 'perhaps I hadn't made myself fully clear. Somebody's got to lie in front of the bulldozers, haven't they? Or there won't be anything to stop them driving into Mr Dent's house, will there?'

'What?' said Mr Prosser again.

'It's very simple,' said Ford, 'my client, Mr Dent, says that he will stop lying here in the mud on the sole condition that you come and take over from him.'

'What are you talking about?' said Arthur, but Ford nudged him with his shoe to be quiet.

'You want me,' said Prosser, spelling out his new thought to himself, 'to come and lie there . . .'

'Yes.'

'In front of the bulldozer?'

'Yes.'

'Instead of Mr Dent.'

'Yes.'

'In the mud.'

'In, as you say, the mud.'

As soon as Mr Prosser realized that he was substantially the loser after all, it was as if a weight lifted itself off his shoulders: this was more like the world as he knew it. He sighed.

'In return for which you will take Mr Dent with you down to the pub?'

'That's it,' said Ford, 'that's it exactly.'

Mr Prosser took a few nervous steps forward and stopped.

'Promise?' he said.

'Promise,' said Ford. He turned to Arthur.

'Come on,' he said to him, 'get up and let the man lie down.'

Arthur stood up, feeling as if he was in a dream.

Ford beckoned to Prosser who sadly, awkwardly, sat down in the mud. He felt that his whole life was some kind of dream and he sometimes wondered whose it was and whether they were enjoying it. The mud folded itself round his bottom and his arms and oozed into his shoes.

Ford looked at him severely.

'And no sneaky knocking Mr Dent's house down whilst he's away, all right?' he said.

'The mere thought,' growled Mr Prosser, 'hadn't even begun to speculate,' he continued, settling himself back, 'about the merest possibility of crossing my mind.'

He saw the bulldozer drivers' union representative approaching and let his head sink back and closed his eyes. He was trying to marshal his arguments for proving that he did not now constitute a mental-health hazard himself. He was far from certain about this – his mind seemed to be full of noise, horses, smoke, and the stench of blood. This always happened when he felt miserable or put upon, and he had never been able to explain it to himself. In a high dimension of which we know nothing the mighty Khan bellowed with rage, but Mr Prosser only trembled slightly and whimpered. He began to feel little pricks of water behind his eyelids. Bureaucratic cock-ups, angry men lying in mud, indecipherable strangers handing out inexplicable humiliations and an unidentified army of horsemen laughing at him in his head – what a day.

What a day. Ford Prefect knew that it didn't matter a pair of dingo's kidneys whether Arthur's house got knocked down or not now.

Arthur remained very worried.

'But can we trust him?' he said.

'Myself, I'd trust him to the end of the Earth,' said Ford.

'Oh yes,' said Arthur, 'and how far's that?'

'About twelve minutes away,' said Ford. 'Come on, I need a drink.'

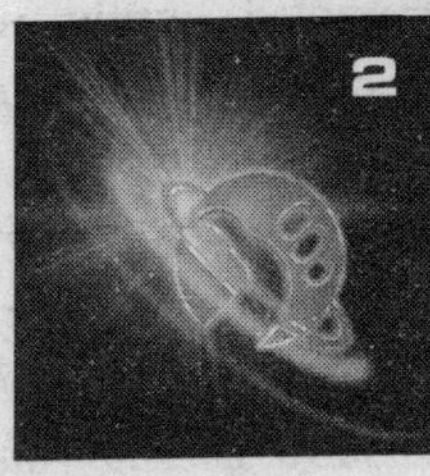

Here's what The Encyclopaedia Galactica *has to say about alcohol. It says that alcohol is a colourless volatile liquid formed by the fermentation of sugars and also notes its intoxicating effect on certain carbon-based life forms.*

The Hitchhiker's Guide to the Galaxy *also mentions alcohol. It says that the best drink in existence is the Pan Galactic Gargle Blaster.*

It says that the effect of drinking a Pan Galactic Gargle Blaster is like having your brains smashed out by a slice of lemon wrapped round a large gold brick.

The Guide *also tells you on which planets the best Pan Galactic Gargle Blasters are mixed, how much you can expect to pay for one and what voluntary organizations exist to help you rehabilitate afterwards.*

The Guide *even tells you how you can mix one yourself.*

Take the juice from one bottle of that Ol' Janx Spirit, it says.

Pour into it one measure of water from the seas of Santraginus V – Oh, that Santraginean sea water, it says. Oh, those Santraginean fish!!!

Allow three cubes of Arcturan Mega-gin to melt into the mixture (it must be properly iced or the benzine is lost).

Allow four litres of Fallian marsh gas to bubble through it, in memory of all those happy Hikers who have died of pleasure in the Marshes of Fallia.

Over the back of a silver spoon float a measure of Qualactin Hypermint extract, redolent of all the heady odours of the dark Qualactin Zones, subtle, sweet and mystic.

Drop in the tooth of an Algolian Suntiger. Watch it dissolve, spreading the fires of the Algolian Suns deep into the heart of the drink.

Sprinkle Zamphuor.

Add an olive.

Drink . . . but . . . very carefully . . .

The Hitchhiker's Guide to the Galaxy *sells rather better than* The Encyclopaedia Galactica.

'Six pints of bitter,' said Ford Prefect to the barman of the Horse and Groom. 'And quickly, please, the world's about to end.'

The barman of the Horse and Groom didn't deserve this sort of treatment, he was a dignified old man. He pushed his glasses up his nose and blinked at Ford Prefect. Ford ignored him and stared out of the window, so the barman looked instead at Arthur, who shrugged helplessly and said nothing.

So the barman said, 'Oh yes, sir? Nice weather for it,' and started pulling pints.

He tried again.

'Going to watch the match this afternoon, then?'

Ford glanced round at him.

'No, no point,' he said, and looked back out of the window.

'What's that, foregone conclusion then you reckon, sir?' said the barman. 'Arsenal without a chance?'

'No, no,' said Ford, 'it's just that the world's about to end.'

'Oh yes, sir, so you said,' said the barman, looking over his glasses this time at Arthur. 'Lucky escape for Arsenal if it did.'

Ford looked back at him, genuinely surprised.

'No, not really,' he said. He frowned.

The barman breathed in heavily. 'There you are, sir, six pints,' he said.

Arthur smiled at him wanly and shrugged again. He turned and smiled wanly at the rest of the pub just in case any of them had heard what was going on.

None of them had, and none of them could understand what he was smiling at them for.

A man sitting next to Ford at the bar looked at the two men, looked at the six pints, did a swift burst of mental arithmetic, arrived at an answer he liked and grinned a stupid hopeful grin at them.

'Get off,' said Ford, 'they're ours,' giving him a look that would have made an Algolian Suntiger get on with what it was doing.

Ford slapped a five-pound note on the bar. He said, 'Keep the change.'

'What, from a fiver? Thank you, sir.'

'You've got ten minutes left to spend it.'

The barman decided simply to walk away for a bit.

'Ford,' said Arthur, 'would you please tell me what the hell is going on?'

'Drink up,' said Ford, 'you've got three pints to get through.'

'Three pints?' said Arthur. 'At lunchtime?'

The man next to Ford grinned and nodded happily. Ford ignored him. He said, 'Time is an illusion. Lunchtime doubly so.'

'Very deep,' said Arthur, 'you should send that in to the *Reader's Digest*. They've got a page for people like you.'

'Drink up.'

'Why three pints all of a sudden?'

'Muscle relaxant, you'll need it.'

'Muscle relaxant?'

'Muscle relaxant.'

Arthur stared into his beer.

'Did I do anything wrong today,' he said, 'or has the world always been like this and I've been too wrapped up in myself to notice?'

'All right,' said Ford, 'I'll try to explain. How long have we known each other?'

'How long?' Arthur thought. 'Er, about five years, maybe six,' he said. 'Most of it seemed to make some kind of sense at the time.'

'All right,' said Ford. 'How would you react if I said that I'm not from Guildford after all, but from a small planet somewhere in the vicinity of Betelgeuse?'

Arthur shrugged in a so-so sort of way.

'I don't know,' he said, taking a pull of beer. 'Why – do you think it's the sort of thing you're likely to say?'

Ford gave up. It really wasn't worth bothering at the moment, what with the world being about to end. He just said:

'Drink up.'

He added, perfectly factually:

'The world's about to end.'

Arthur gave the rest of the pub another wan smile. The rest of the pub frowned at him. A man waved at him to stop smiling at them and mind his own business.

'This must be Thursday,' said Arthur to himself, sinking low over his beer. 'I never could get the hang of Thursdays.'

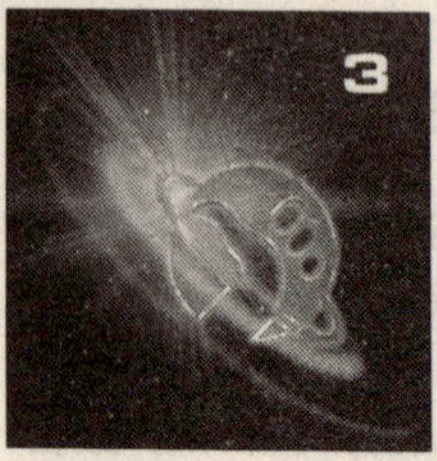

On this particular Thursday, something was moving quietly through the ionosphere many miles above the surface of the planet; several somethings in fact, several dozen huge yellow chunky slablike somethings, huge as office blocks, silent as birds. They soared with ease, basking in electromagnetic rays from the star Sol, biding their time, grouping, preparing.

The planet beneath them was almost perfectly oblivious of their presence, which was just how they wanted it for the moment. The huge yellow somethings went unnoticed at Goonhilly, they passed over Cape Canaveral without a blip, Woomera and Jodrell Bank looked straight through them – which was a pity because it was exactly the sort of thing they'd been looking for all these years.

The only place they registered at all was on a small black device called a Sub-Etha Sens-O-Matic which winked away quietly to itself. It nestled in the darkness inside a leather satchel which Ford Prefect habitually wore slung around his neck. The contents of Ford Prefect's satchel were quite interesting, in fact, and would have made any Earth physicist's eyes pop out of his head, which is why he always concealed them by keeping a couple of dog-eared scripts for plays he pretended he was auditioning for stuffed in the top. Besides the Sub-Etha Sens-O-Matic and the scripts he had an Electronic Thumb – a short squat black rod, smooth and matt with a couple of flat switches and dials at one end; he also had a device which looked rather like a largish electronic calculator. This had about a hundred tiny flat press-buttons and a screen about four inches square on which any one of a million 'pages' could be summoned at a moment's notice. It looked insanely complicated, and this was one of the reasons why the snug plastic cover it fitted into had the words DON'T PANIC printed on it in large friendly letters. The other reason was that this device was in fact that most remarkable of all books ever to come out of the great publishing corporations of Ursa Minor – *The Hitchhiker's Guide to the Galaxy*. The reason why it was published in the form of a micro sub-meson electronic component is that if it were printed in normal book form, an interstellar hitchhiker would require several inconveniently large buildings to carry it around in.

Beneath that in Ford Prefect's satchel were a few biros, a notepad, and a largish bath towel from Marks and Spencer.

The Hitchhiker's Guide to the Galaxy *has a few things to say on the subject of towels.*

A towel, it says, is about the most massively useful thing an interstellar hitchhiker can have. Partly it has great practical value – you can wrap it around you for warmth as you bound across the cold moons of Jaglan Beta; you can lie on it on the brilliant marble-sanded beaches of Santraginus V, inhaling the heady sea vapours; you can sleep under it beneath the stars which shine so redly on the desert world of Kakrafoon; use it to sail a mini-raft down the slow heavy river Moth; wet it for use in hand-to-hand combat; wrap it round your head to ward off noxious fumes or avoid the gaze of the Ravenous Bugblatter Beast of Traal (a mindbogglingly stupid animal, it assumes that if you can't see it, it can't see you – daft as a brush, but very very ravenous); you can wave your towel in emergencies as a distress signal; and of course dry yourself off with it if it still seems to be clean enough.

More importantly, a towel has immense psychological value. For some reason, if a strag *(strag: non-hitchhiker) discovers that a hitchhiker has his towel with him, he will automatically assume that he is also in possession of a toothbrush, face flannel, soap, tin of biscuits, flask, compass, map, ball of string, gnat spray, wet-weather gear, space suit, etc., etc. Furthermore, the strag will then happily lend the hitchhiker any of these or a dozen other items that the hitchhiker might accidentally have 'lost'. What the strag will think is that any man who can hitch the length and breadth of the galaxy, rough it, slum it, struggle against terrible odds, win through, and still know where his towel is is clearly a man to be reckoned with.*

Hence a phrase which has passed into hitchhiking slang, as in 'Hey, you sass that hoopy Ford Prefect? There's a frood who really knows where his towel is.' (*Sass: know, be aware of, meet, have sex with; hoopy: really together guy; frood: really amazingly together guy.*)

Nestling quietly on top of the towel in Ford Prefect's satchel, the Sub-Etha Sens-O-Matic began to wink more quickly. Miles above the surface of the planet the huge yellow somethings began to fan out. At Jodrell Bank, someone decided it was time for a nice relaxing cup of tea.

'You got a towel with you?' said Ford suddenly to Arthur.

Arthur, struggling through his third pint, looked round at him.

'Why? What, no . . . should I have?' He had given up being surprised, there didn't seem to be any point any longer.

Ford clicked his tongue in irritation.

'Drink up,' he urged.

At that moment the dull sound of a rumbling crash from outside filtered through the low murmur of the pub, through the sound of the jukebox, through the sound of the man next to Ford hiccupping over the whisky Ford had eventually bought him.

Arthur choked on his beer, leapt to his feet.

'What's that?' he yelped.

'Don't worry,' said Ford, 'they haven't started yet.'

'Thank God for that,' said Arthur and relaxed.

'It's probably just your house being knocked down,' said Ford, downing his last pint.

'What?' shouted Arthur. Suddenly Ford's spell was broken. Arthur looked wildly around him and ran to the window.

'My God, they are! They're knocking my house down. What the hell am I doing in the pub, Ford?'

'It hardly makes any difference at this stage,' said Ford, 'let them have their fun.'

'Fun?' yelped Arthur. 'Fun!' He quickly checked out of the window again that they were talking about the same thing.

'Damn their fun!' he shouted and ran out of the pub furiously waving a nearly empty beer glass. He made no friends at all in the pub that lunchtime.

'Stop, you vandals! You home-wreckers!' bawled Arthur. 'You half-crazed Visigoths, stop, will you!'

Ford would have to go after him. Turning quickly to the barman he asked for four packets of peanuts.

'There you are, sir,' said the barman, slapping the packets on the bar, 'twenty-eight pence if you'd be so kind.'

Ford was very kind – he gave the barman another five-pound note and told him to keep the change. The barman looked at it and then looked at Ford. He suddenly shivered: he experienced a momentary sensation that he didn't understand because no one on Earth had ever experienced it before. In moments of great stress, every life form that exists gives out a tiny subliminal signal. This signal simply communicates an exact and almost pathetic sense of how far that being is from the place of his birth. On Earth it is never possible to be further than sixteen thousand miles from your birthplace, which really isn't very far, so such signals are too minute to be noticed. Ford Prefect was at this moment under great stress, and he was born 600 light years away in the near vicinity of Betelgeuse.

The barman reeled for a moment, hit by a shocking, incomprehensible sense of distance. He didn't know what it meant, but he looked at Ford Prefect with a new sense of respect, almost awe.

'Are you serious, sir?' he said in a small whisper which had the effect of silencing the pub. 'You think the world's going to end?'

'Yes,' said Ford.

'But, this afternoon?'

Ford had recovered himself. He was at his flippest.

'Yes,' he said gaily, 'in less than two minutes, I would estimate.'

The barman couldn't believe this conversation he was having, but he couldn't believe the sensation he had just had either.

'Isn't there anything we can do about it, then?' he said.

'No, nothing,' said Ford, stuffing the peanuts into his pocket.

Someone in the hushed bar suddenly laughed raucously at how stupid everyone had become.

The man sitting next to Ford was a bit sozzled by now. His eyes weaved their way up to Ford.

'I thought,' he said 'that if the world was going to end we were meant to lie down or put a paper bag over our head or something.'

'If you like, yes,' said Ford.

'That's what they told us in the army,' said the man, and his eyes began the long trek back towards his whisky.

'Will that help?' asked the barman.

'No,' said Ford and gave him a friendly smile. 'Excuse me,' he said, 'I've got to go.' With a wave, he left.

The pub was silent for a moment longer and then, embarrassingly enough, the man with the raucous laugh did it again. The girl he had dragged along to the pub with him had grown to loathe him dearly over the last hour, and it would probably have been a great satisfaction to her to know that in a minute and a half or so he would suddenly evaporate into a whiff of hydrogen, ozone and carbon monoxide. However, when the moment came she would be too busy evaporating herself to notice it.

The barman checked his throat. He heard himself say:

'Last orders, please.'

The huge yellow machines began to sink downwards and to move faster.

Ford knew they were there. This wasn't the way he had wanted it.

Running up the lane, Arthur had nearly reached his house. He didn't notice how cold it had suddenly become, he didn't notice the wind, he didn't notice the sudden irrational squall of rain. He didn't notice anything but the caterpillar bulldozers crawling over the rubble that had been his home.

'You barbarians!' he yelled. 'I'll sue the council for every penny it's got! I'll have you hung, drawn and quartered! And whipped! And boiled . . . until . . . until . . . until you've had enough.'

Ford was running after him very fast. Very very fast.

'And then I will do it again!' yelled Arthur. 'And when I've finished I will take all the little bits, and I will *jump* on them!'

Arthur didn't notice that the men were running from the bulldozers; he didn't notice that Mr Prosser was staring hectically into the sky. What Mr Prosser had noticed was that huge yellow somethings were screaming through the clouds. Impossibly huge yellow somethings.

'And I will carry on jumping on them,' yelled Arthur, still running, 'until I get blisters, or I can think of anything even more unpleasant to do, and then . . .'

Arthur tripped, and fell headlong, rolled and landed flat on his back. At last he noticed that something was going on. His finger shot upwards.

'What the hell's that?' he shrieked.

Whatever it was raced across the sky in its monstrous yellowness, tore the sky apart with a mind-buggering noise and leapt off into the distance leaving the gaping air to shut behind it with a *bang* that drove your ears six feet into your skull.

Another one followed and did exactly the same thing only louder.

It's difficult to say exactly what the people on the surface of the planet were doing now, because they didn't really know what they were doing themselves. None of it made a lot of sense – running into houses, running out of houses, howling noiselessly at the noise. All around the world city streets exploded with people, cars slewed into each other as the noise fell on them and then rolled off like a tidal wave over hills and valleys, deserts and oceans, seeming to flatten everything it hit.

Only one man stood and watched the sky, stood with terrible sadness in his eyes and rubber bungs in his ears. He knew exactly what was happening and had known ever since his Sub-Etha Sens-O-Matic had started winking in the dead of night beside his pillow and woken him with a start. It was what he had waited for all these years, but when he had deciphered the signal pattern, sitting alone in his small dark room, a coldness had gripped him and squeezed his heart. Of all the races in all the Galaxy who could have come and said a big hello to planet Earth, he thought, didn't it just have to be the Vogons.

Still, he knew what he had to do. As the Vogon craft screamed through the air high above him he opened his satchel. He threw away a copy of *Joseph and the Amazing Technicolor Dreamcoat*, he threw away a copy of *Godspell*: he wouldn't need them where he was going. Everything was ready, everything was prepared.

He knew where his towel was.

A sudden silence hit the Earth. If anything it was worse than the noise. For a while nothing happened.

The great ships hung motionless in the sky, over every nation on Earth. Motionless they hung, huge, heavy, steady in the sky, a blasphemy against nature. Many people went straight into shock as their minds tried to encompass what they were looking at. The ships hung in the sky in much the same way that bricks don't.

And still nothing happened.

Then there was a slight whisper, a sudden spacious whisper of open ambient sound. Every hi-fi set in the world, every radio, every television, every cassette recorder, every woofer, every tweeter, every mid-range driver in the world quietly turned itself on.

Every tin can, every dustbin, every window, every car, every wine glass, every sheet of rusty metal became activated as an acoustically perfect sounding board.

Before the Earth passed away it was going to be treated to the very ultimate in sound reproduction, the greatest public address system ever built. But there was no concert, no music, no fanfare, just a simple message. *'People of Earth, your attention, please,'* a voice said, and it was wonderful. Wonderful perfect quadrophonic sound with distortion levels so low as to make a brave man weep.

'This is Prostetnic Vogon Jeltz of the Galactic Hyperspace Planning Council,' the voice continued. *'As you will no doubt be aware, the plans for development of the outlying regions of the Galaxy require the building of a hyperspatial express route through your star system, and regrettably your planet is one of those scheduled for demolition. The process will take slightly less than two of your Earth minutes. Thank you.'*

The PA died away.

Uncomprehending terror settled on the watching people of Earth. The terror moved slowly through the gathered crowds as if they were iron filings on a sheet of board and a magnet was moving beneath them. Panic sprouted again, desperate fleeing panic, but there was nowhere to flee to.

Observing this, the Vogons turned on their PA again. It said:

'There's no point in acting all surprised about it. All the planning charts and demolition orders have been on display in your local planning department in Alpha Centauri for fifty of your Earth years, so you've had plenty of time to lodge any formal complaint and it's far too late to start making a fuss about it now.'

The PA fell silent again and its echo drifted off across the land. The huge ships turned slowly in the sky with easy power. On the underside of each a hatchway opened, an empty black square.

By this time somebody somewhere must have manned a radio transmitter, located a wavelength and broadcast a message back to the Vogon ships, to plead on behalf of the planet. Nobody ever heard what they said, they only heard the reply. The PA slammed back into life again. The voice was annoyed. It said:

'What do you mean you've never been to Alpha Centauri? For Heaven's sake, mankind, it's only four light years away, you know. I'm sorry, but if you can't be bothered to take an interest in local affairs that's your own lookout.

'Energize the demolition beams.'

Light poured out of the hatchways.

'I don't know,' said the voice on the PA, *'apathetic bloody planet, I've no sympathy at all.'* It cut off.

There was a terrible ghastly silence.

There was a terrible ghastly noise.

There was a terrible ghastly silence.

The Vogon Constructor Fleet coasted away into the inky starry void.

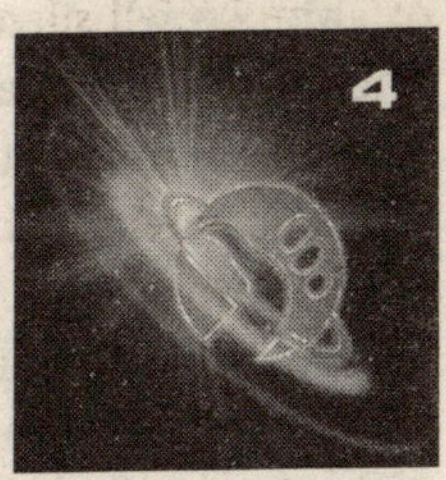

Far away on the opposite spiral arm of the Galaxy, five hundred thousand light years from the star Sol, Zaphod Beeblebrox, President of the Imperial Galactic Government, sped across the seas of Damogran, his ion-drive delta boat winking and flashing in the Damogran sun.

Damogran the hot; Damogran the remote; Damogran the almost totally unheard of.

Damogran, secret home of the *Heart of Gold*.

The boat sped on across the water. It would be some time before it reached its destination because Damogran is such an inconveniently arranged planet. It consists of nothing but middling to large desert islands separated by very pretty but annoyingly wide stretches of ocean.

The boat sped on.

Because of this topographical awkwardness Damogran has always remained a deserted planet. This is why the Imperial Galactic Government chose Damogran for the *Heart of Gold* project, because it was so deserted and the *Heart of Gold* project was so secret.

The boat zipped and skipped across the sea, the sea that lay between the main islands of the only archipelago of any useful size on the whole planet. Zaphod Beeblebrox was on his way from the tiny spaceport on Easter Island (the name was an entirely meaningless coincidence – in Galacticspeke, *easter* means small, flat and light brown) to the *Heart of Gold* island, which by another meaningless coincidence was called France.

One of the side effects of work on the *Heart of Gold* was a whole string of pretty meaningless coincidences.

But it was not in any way a coincidence that today, the day of culmination of the project, the great day of unveiling, the day that the *Heart of Gold* was finally to be introduced to a marvelling Galaxy, was also a great day of culmination for Zaphod Beeblebrox. It was for the sake of this day that he had first decided to run for the Presidency, a decision which had sent shock waves of astonishment throughout the Imperial Galaxy – Zaphod Beeblebrox? *President*? Not *the* Zaphod Beeblebrox? Not *the* President? Many had seen it as clinching proof that the whole of known creation had finally gone bananas.

Zaphod grinned and gave the boat an extra kick of speed.

Zaphod Beeblebrox, adventurer, ex-hippy, good-timer, (crook? quite possibly), manic self-publicist, terribly bad at personal relationships, often thought to be completely out to lunch.

President?

No one had gone bananas, not in that way at least.

Only six people in the entire Galaxy understood the principle on which the Galaxy was governed, and they knew that once Zaphod Beeblebrox had announced his intention to run as President it was more or less a *fait accompli*: he was ideal presidency fodder.*

What they completely failed to understand was why Zaphod was doing it.

He banked sharply, shooting a wild wall of water at the sun.

Today was the day; today was the day when they

---

* President: full title President of the Imperial Galactic Government.

The term *Imperial* is kept though it is now an anachronism. The hereditary Emperor is nearly dead and has been for many centuries. In the last moments of his dying coma he was locked in a stasis field which keeps him in a state of perpetual unchangingness. All his heirs are now long dead, and this means that without any drastic political upheaval, power has simply and effectively moved a rung or two down the ladder, and is now seen to be vested in a body which used to act simply as advisers to the Emperor – an elected governmental assembly headed by a President elected by that assembly. In fact it vests in no such place.

The President in particular is very much a figurehead – he wields no real power whatsoever. He is apparently chosen by the government, but the qualities he is required to display are not those of leadership but those of finely judged outrage. For this reason the President is always a controversial choice, always an infuriating but fascinating character. His job is not to wield power but to draw attention away from it. On those criteria Zaphod Beeblebrox is one of the most successful Presidents the Galaxy has ever had – he has already spent two of his ten presidential years in prison for fraud. Very very few people realize that the President and the government have virtually no power at all, and of these few people only six know whence ultimate political power is wielded. Most of the others secretly believe that the ultimate decision-making process is handled by a computer. They couldn't be more wrong.

would realize what Zaphod had been up to. Today was what Zaphod Beeblebrox's Presidency was all about. Today was also his two-hundredth birthday, but that was just another meaningless coincidence.

As he skipped his boat across the seas of Damogran he smiled quietly to himself about what a wonderful, exciting day it was going to be. He relaxed and spread his two arms lazily along the seat back. He steered with an extra arm he'd recently had fitted just beneath his right one to help improve his ski-boxing.

'Hey,' he cooed to himself, 'you're a real cool boy, you.' But his nerves sang a song shriller than a dog whistle.

The island of France was about twenty miles long, five miles across the middle, sandy and crescent-shaped. In fact it seemed to exist not so much as an island in its own right as simply a means of defining the sweep and curve of a huge bay. This impression was heightened by the fact that the inner coastline of the crescent consisted almost entirely of steep cliffs. From the top of the cliff the land sloped slowly down five miles to the opposite shore.

On top of the cliffs stood a reception committee.

It consisted in large part of the engineers and researchers who had built the *Heart of Gold* – mostly humanoid, but here and there were a few reptiloid atomineers, two or three green sylph-like maximegalaticians, an octopodic physucturalist or two and a Hooloovoo (a Hooloovoo is a super-intelligent shade of the colour blue). All except the Hooloovoo were resplendent in their multi-coloured ceremonial lab coats; the Hooloovoo had been temporarily refracted into a free-standing prism for the occasion.

There was a mood of immense excitement thrilling through all of them. Together and between them they had gone to and beyond the furthest limits of physical laws, restructured the fundamental fabric of matter, strained, twisted and broken the laws of possibility and impossibility, but still the greatest excitement of all seemed to be to meet a man with an orange sash round his neck. (An orange sash was what the President of the Galaxy traditionally wore.) It might not even have made much difference to them if they'd known exactly how much power the President of the Galaxy actually wielded: none at all. Only six people in the Galaxy knew that the job of the Galactic President was not to wield power but to attract attention away from it.

Zaphod Beeblebrox was amazingly good at his job.

The crowd gasped, dazzled by sun and seamanship, as the Presidential speedboat zipped round the headland into the bay. It flashed and shone as it came skating over the sea in wide skidding turns.

In fact it didn't need to touch the water at all, because it was supported on a hazy cushion of ionized atoms – but just for effect it was fitted with thin finblades which could be lowered into the water. They slashed sheets of water hissing into the air, carved deep gashes in the sea which swayed crazily and sank back foaming in the boat's wake as it careered across the bay.

Zaphod loved effect: it was what he was best at.

He twisted the wheel sharply, the boat slewed round

in a wild scything skid beneath the cliff face and dropped to rest lightly on the rocking waves.

Within seconds he ran out on to the deck and waved and grinned at over three billion people. The three billion people weren't actually there, but they watched his every gesture through the eyes of a small robot tri-D camera which hovered obsequiously in the air nearby. The antics of the President always made amazingly popular tri-D: that's what they were for.

He grinned again. Three billion and six people didn't know it, but today would be a bigger antic than anyone had bargained for.

The robot camera homed in for a close-up on the more popular of his two heads and he waved again. He was roughly humanoid in appearance except for the extra head and third arm. His tousled fair hair stuck out in random directions, his blue eyes glinted with something completely unidentifiable, and his chins were almost always unshaven.

A twenty-foot-high transparent globe floated next to his boat, rolling and bobbing, glistening in the brilliant sun. Inside it floated a wide semi-circular sofa upholstered in glorious red leather: the more the globe bobbed and rolled, the more the sofa stayed perfectly still, steady as an upholstered rock. Again, all done for effect as much as anything.

Zaphod stepped through the wall of the globe and relaxed on the sofa. He spread his two arms along the back and with the third brushed some dust off his knee. His heads looked about, smiling; he put his feet up. At any moment, he thought, he might scream.

Water boiled up beneath the bubble; it seethed and spouted. The bubble surged into the air, bobbing and rolling on the water spout. Up, up it climbed, throwing stilts of light at the cliff. Up it surged on the jet, the water falling from beneath it, crashing back into the sea hundreds of feet below.

Zaphod smiled, picturing himself.

A thoroughly ridiculous form of transport, but a thoroughly beautiful one.

At the top of the cliff the globe wavered for a moment, tipped on to a railed ramp, rolled down it to a small concave platform and riddled to a halt.

To tremendous applause Zaphod Beeblebrox stepped out of the bubble, his orange sash blazing in the light.

The President of the Galaxy had arrived.

He waited for the applause to die down, then raised his hand in greeting.

'Hi,' he said.

A government spider sidled up to him and attempted to press a copy of his prepared speech into his hands. Pages three to seven of the original version were at the moment floating soggily on the Damogran sea some five miles out from the bay. Pages one and two had been salvaged by a Damogran Frond-Crested Eagle and had already become incorporated into an extraordinary new form of nest which the eagle had invented. It was constructed largely of papier mâché and it was virtually impossible for a newly hatched baby eagle to break out of it. The Damogran Frond-Crested Eagle had heard of the notion of survival of the species but wanted no truck with it.

Zaphod Beeblebrox would not be needing his set speech and he gently deflected the one being offered him by the spider.

'Hi,' he said again.

Everyone beamed at him, or at least, nearly everyone. He singled out Trillian from the crowd. Trillian was a girl that Zaphod had picked up recently whilst visiting a planet, just for fun, incognito. She was slim, darkish, humanoid, with long waves of black hair, a full mouth, an odd little knob of a nose and ridiculously brown eyes. With her red head scarf knotted in that particular way and her long flowing silky brown dress she looked vaguely Arabic. Not that anyone there had ever heard of an Arab, of course. The Arabs had very recently ceased to exist, and even when they had existed they were five hundred thousand light years from Damogran. Trillian wasn't anybody in particular, or so Zaphod claimed. She just went around with him rather a lot and told him what she thought of him.

'Hi, honey,' he said to her.

She flashed him a quick tight smile and looked away. Then she looked back for a moment and smiled more warmly – but by this time he was looking at something else.

'Hi,' he said to a small knot of creatures from the press who were standing nearby wishing that he would stop saying *Hi* and get on with the quotes. He grinned at them particularly because he knew that in a few moments he would be giving them one hell of a quote.

The next thing he said though was not a lot of use to them. One of the officials of the party had irritably decided that the President was clearly not in a mood to read the deliciously turned speech that had been written for him, and had flipped the switch on the remote-control device in his pocket. Away in front of them a huge white dome that bulged against the sky cracked down the middle, split, and slowly folded itself down into the ground. Everyone gasped although they had known perfectly well it was going to do that because they'd built it that way.

Beneath it lay uncovered a huge starship, one hundred and fifty metres long, shaped like a sleek running shoe, perfectly white and mindbogglingly beautiful. At the heart of it, unseen, lay a small gold box which carried within it the most brain-wrenching device ever conceived, a device which made this starship unique in the history of the galaxy, a device after which the ship had been named – the *Heart of Gold*.

'Wow,' said Zaphod Beeblebrox to the *Heart of Gold*. There wasn't much else he could say.

He said it again because he knew it would annoy the press.

'Wow.'

The crowd turned their faces back towards him expectantly. He winked at Trillian, who raised her eyebrows and widened her eyes at him. She knew what he was about to say and thought him a terrible showoff.

'That is really amazing,' he said. 'That really is truly amazing. That is so amazingly amazing I think I'd like to steal it.'

A marvellous presidential quote, absolutely true to form. The crowd laughed appreciatively, the newsmen gleefully punched buttons on their Sub-Etha News-Matics and the President grinned.

As he grinned his heart screamed unbearably and he fingered the small Paralys-O-Matic bomb that nestled quietly in his pocket.

Finally he could bear it no more. He lifted his heads up to the sky, let out a wild whoop in major thirds, threw the bomb to the ground and ran forward through the sea of suddenly frozen beaming smiles.

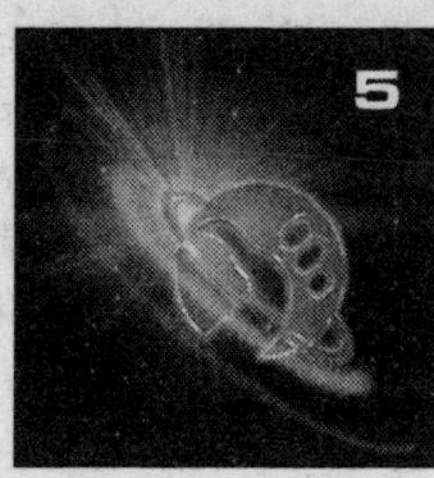

Prostetnic Vogon Jeltz was not a pleasant sight, even for other Vogons. His highly domed nose rose high above a small piggy forehead. His dark-green rubbery skin was thick enough for him to play the game of Vogon Civil Service politics, and play it well, and waterproof enough for him to survive indefinitely at sea depths of up to a thousand feet with no ill effects.

Not that he ever went swimming, of course. His busy schedule would not allow it. He was the way he was because billions of years ago when the Vogons had first crawled out of the sluggish primeval seas of Vogsphere, and had lain panting and heaving on the planet's virgin shores . . . when the first rays of the bright young Vogsol sun had shone across them that morning, it was as if the forces of evolution had simply given up on them there and then, had turned aside in disgust and written them off as an ugly and unfortunate mistake. They never evolved again: they should never have survived.

The fact that they did is some kind of tribute to the thick-willed slug-brained stubbornness of these creatures. *Evolution?* they said to themselves, *Who needs it?*, and what nature refused to do for them they simply did without until such time as they were able to rectify the grosser anatomical inconveniences with surgery.

Meanwhile, the natural forces on the planet Vogsphere had been working overtime to make up for their earlier blunder. They brought forth scintillating jewelled scuttling crabs, which the Vogons ate, smashing their shells with iron mallets; tall aspiring trees of breathtaking slenderness and colour which the Vogons cut down and burnt the crab meat with; elegant gazelle-like creatures with silken coats and dewy eyes which the Vogons would catch and sit on. They were no use as transport because their backs would snap instantly, but the Vogons sat on them anyway.

Thus the planet Vogsphere whiled away the unhappy millennia until the Vogons suddenly discovered the principles of interstellar travel. Within a few short Vog years every last Vogon had migrated to the Megabrantis cluster, the political hub of the Galaxy, and now formed the immensely powerful backbone of the Galactic Civil Service. They have attempted to acquire learning, they have attempted to acquire style and social grace, but in most respects the modern Vogon is little different from his primitive forebears. Every year they import twenty-seven thousand scintillating jewelled scuttling crabs from their native planet and while away a happy drunken night smashing them to bits with iron mallets.

Prostetnic Vogon Jeltz was a fairly typical Vogon in that he was thoroughly vile. Also, he did not like hitchhikers.

*

Somewhere in a small dark cabin buried deep in the intestines of Prostetnic Vogon Jeltz's flagship, a small match flared nervously. The owner of the match was not a Vogon, but he knew all about them and was right to be nervous. His name was Ford Prefect.*

He looked about the cabin but could see very little; strange monstrous shadows loomed and leaped with the tiny flickering flame, but all was quiet. He breathed a silent thank you to the Dentrassis. The Dentrassis are an unruly tribe of gourmands, a wild but pleasant bunch whom the Vogons had recently taken to employing as catering staff on their long-haul fleets, on the strict understanding that they kept themselves very much to themselves.

---

* Ford Prefect's original name is only pronouncable in an obscure Betelgeusian dialect, now virtually extinct since the Great Collapsing Hrung Disaster of Gal./Sid./Year 03758 which wiped out all the old Praxibetel communities on Betelgeuse Seven. Ford's father was the only man on the entire planet to survive the Great Collapsing Hrung Disaster, by an extraordinary coincidence that he was never able satisfactorily to explain. The whole episode is shrouded in deep mystery: in fact no one ever knew what a Hrung was nor why it had chosen to collapse on Betelgeuse Seven particularly. Ford's father, magnanimously waving aside the clouds of suspicion that had inevitably settled around him, came to live on Betelgeuse Five, where he both fathered and uncled Ford; in memory of his now dead race he christened him in the ancient Praxibetel tongue.

Because Ford never learned to say his original name, his father eventually died of shame, which is still a terminal disease in some parts of the Galaxy. The other kids at school nicknamed him Ix, which in the language of Betelgeuse Five translates as 'boy who is not able satisfactorily to explain what a Hrung is, nor why it should choose to collapse on Betelgeuse Seven'.

This suited the Dentrassis fine, because they loved Vogon money, which is one of the hardest currencies in space, but loathed the Vogons themselves. The only sort of Vogon a Dentrassi liked to see was an annoyed Vogon.

It was because of this tiny piece of information that Ford Prefect was not now a whiff of hydrogen, ozone and carbon monoxide.

He heard a slight groan. By the light of the match he saw a heavy shape moving slightly on the floor. Quickly he shook the match out, reached in his pocket, found what he was looking for and took it out. He ripped it open and shook it. He crouched on the floor. The shape moved again.

Ford Prefect said: 'I bought some peanuts.'

Arthur Dent moved, and groaned again, muttering incoherently.

'Here, have some,' urged Ford, shaking the packet again, 'if you've never been through a matter transference beam before you've probably lost some salt and protein. The beer you had should have cushioned your system a bit.'

'Whhhrrrr . . .' said Arthur Dent. He opened his eyes.

'It's dark,' he said.

'Yes,' said Ford Prefect. 'It's dark.'

'No light,' said Arthur Dent. 'Dark, no light.'

One of the things Ford Prefect had always found hardest to understand about humans was their habit of continually stating and repeating the very very obvious, as in *It's a nice day*, or *You're very tall*, or *Oh dear you seem to have fallen down a thirty-foot well, are you all right?* At first Ford had formed a theory to account for this strange behaviour. If human beings don't keep exercising their lips, he thought, their mouths probably seize up. After a few months' consideration and observation he abandoned this theory in favour of a new one. If they don't keep exercising their lips, he thought, their brains start working. After a while he abandoned this one as well as being obstructively cynical and decided he quite liked human beings after all, but he always remained desperately worried about the terrible number of things they didn't know about.

'Yes,' he agreed with Arthur, 'no light.' He helped Arthur to some peanuts. 'How do you feel?' he asked him.

'Like a military academy,' said Arthur, 'bits of me keep on passing out.'

Ford stared at him blankly in the darkness.

'If I asked you where the hell we were,' said Arthur weakly, 'would I regret it?'

Ford stood up. 'We're safe,' he said.

'Oh, good,' said Arthur.

'We're in a small galley cabin,' said Ford, 'in one of the spaceships of the Vogon Constructor Fleet.'

'Ah,' said Arthur, 'this is obviously some strange usage of the word *safe* that I wasn't previously aware of.'

Ford struck another match to help him search for a light switch. Monstrous shadows leaped and loomed again. Arthur struggled to his feet and hugged himself apprehensively. Hideous alien shapes seemed to throng about him, the air was thick with musty smells which sidled into his lungs without identifying themselves, and a low irritating hum kept his brain from focusing.

'How did we get here?' he asked, shivering slightly.

'We hitched a lift,' said Ford.

'Excuse me?' said Arthur. 'Are you trying to tell me that we just stuck out our thumbs and some green bug-eyed monster stuck his head out and said, *Hi, fellas, hop right in, I can take you as far as the Basingstoke roundabout?*'

'Well,' said Ford, 'the Thumb's an electronic sub-etha signalling device, the roundabout's at Barnard's Star six light years away, but otherwise, that's more or less right.'

'And the bug-eyed monster?'

'Is green, yes.'

'Fine,' said Arthur, 'when can I go home?'

'You can't,' said Ford Prefect, and found the light switch.

'Shade your eyes . . .' he said, and turned it on.

Even Ford was surprised.

'Good grief,' said Arthur, 'is this really the interior of a flying saucer?'

Prostetnic Vogon Jeltz heaved his unpleasant green body round the control bridge. He always felt vaguely irritable after demolishing populated planets. He wished that someone would come and tell him that it was all wrong so that he could shout at them and feel better. He flopped as heavily as he could on to his control seat in the hope that it would break and give him something to be genuinely angry about, but it only gave a complaining sort of creak.

'Go away!' he shouted at a young Vogon guard who entered the bridge at that moment. The guard vanished immediately, feeling rather relieved. He was glad it wouldn't now be him who delivered the report they'd just received. The report was an official release which said that a wonderful new form of spaceship drive was at this moment being unveiled at a government research base on Damogran which would henceforth make all hyperspatial express routes unnecessary.

Another door slid open, but this time the Vogon captain didn't shout because it was the door from the galley quarters where the Dentrassis prepared his meals. A meal would be most welcome.

A huge furry creature bounded through the door with his lunch tray. It was grinning like a maniac.

Prostetnic Vogon Jeltz was delighted. He knew that when a Dentrassi looked that pleased with itself there was something going on somewhere on the ship that he could get very angry indeed about.

Ford and Arthur stared around them.

'Well, what do you think?' said Ford.

'It's a bit squalid, isn't it?'

Ford frowned at the grubby mattresses, unwashed cups and unidentifiable bits of smelly alien underwear that lay around the cramped cabin.

'Well, this is a working ship, you see,' said Ford. 'These are the Dentrassi sleeping quarters.'

'I thought you said they were called Vogons or something.'

'Yes,' said Ford, 'the Vogons run the ship, the Dentrassis are the cooks, they let us on board.'

'I'm confused,' said Arthur.

'Here, have a look at this,' said Ford. He sat down

on one of the mattresses and rummaged about in his satchel. Arthur prodded the mattress nervously and then sat on it himself: in fact he had very little to be nervous about, because all mattresses grown in the swamps of Squornshellous Zeta are very thoroughly killed and dried before being put to service. Very few have ever come to life again.

Ford handed the book to Arthur.

'What is it?' asked Arthur.

'*The Hitchhiker's Guide to the Galaxy*. It's a sort of electronic book. It tells you everything you need to know about anything. That's its job.'

Arthur turned it over nervously in his hands.

'I like the cover,' he said. '*Don't Panic*. It's the first helpful or intelligible thing anybody's said to me all day.'

'I'll show you how it works,' said Ford. He snatched it from Arthur, who was still holding it as if it was a two-week-dead lark, and pulled it out of its cover.

'You press this button here, you see, and the screen lights up giving you the index.'

A screen, about three inches by four, lit up and characters began to flicker across the surface.

'You want to know about Vogons, so I enter that name so.' His fingers tapped some more keys. 'And there we are.'

The words *Vogon Constructor Fleets* flared in green across the screen.

Ford pressed a large red button at the bottom of the screen and words began to undulate across it. At the same time, the book began to speak the entry as well in a still, quiet measured voice. This is what the book said.

'Vogon Constructor Fleets. Here is what to do if you want to get a lift from a Vogon: forget it. They are one of the most unpleasant races in the Galaxy – not actually evil, but bad-tempered, bureaucratic, officious and callous. They wouldn't even lift a finger to save their own grandmothers from the Ravenous Bugblatter Beast of Traal without orders signed in triplicate, sent in, sent back, queried, lost, found, subjected to public inquiry, lost again, and finally buried in soft peat for three months and recycled as firelighters.

'The best way to get a drink out of a Vogon is to stick your finger down his throat, and the best way to irritate him is to feed his grandmother to the Ravenous Bugblatter Beast of Traal.

'On no account allow a Vogon to read poetry at you.'

Arthur blinked at it.

'What a strange book. How did we get a lift, then?'

'That's the point, it's out of date now,' said Ford, sliding the book back into its cover. 'I'm doing the field research for the new revised edition, and one of the things I'll have to do is include a bit about how the Vogons now employ Dentrassi cooks, which gives us a rather useful little loophole.'

A pained expression crossed Arthur's face. 'But who are the Dentrassi?' he said.

'Great guys,' said Ford. 'They're *the* best cooks and the best drinks mixers and they don't give a wet slap about anything else. And they'll always help hitchhikers aboard, partly because they like the company, but mostly because it annoys the Vogons. Which is exactly the sort of thing you need to know if you're an impoverished hitchhiker trying to see the marvels of the Universe for less than thirty Altairian dollars a day. And that's my job. Fun, isn't it?'

Arthur looked lost.

'It's amazing,' he said and frowned at one of the other mattresses.

'Unfortunately I got stuck on the Earth for rather longer than I intended,' said Ford. 'I came for a week and got stuck for fifteen years.'

'But how did you get there in the first place, then?'

'Easy, I got a lift with a teaser.'

'A teaser?'

'Yeah.'

'Er, what is . . .'

'A teaser? Teasers are usually rich kids with nothing to do. They cruise around looking for planets which haven't made interstellar contact yet and buzz them.'

'Buzz them?' Arthur began to feel that Ford was enjoying making life difficult for him.

'Yeah,' said Ford, 'they buzz them. They find some isolated spot with very few people around, then land right by some poor unsuspecting soul whom no one's ever going to believe and then strut up and down in front of him wearing silly antennae on their head and making *beep beep* noises. Rather childish, really.' Ford leant back on the mattress with his hands behind his head and looked infuriatingly pleased with himself.

'Ford,' insisted Arthur, 'I don't know if this sounds like a silly question, but what am I doing here?'

'Well, you know that,' said Ford. 'I rescued you from the Earth.'

'And what's happened to the Earth?'

'Ah. It's been demolished.'

'Has it?' said Arthur levelly.

'Yes. It just boiled away into space.'

'Look,' said Arthur, 'I'm a bit upset about that.'

Ford frowned to himself and seemed to roll the thought around his mind.

'Yes, I can understand that,' he said at last.

'Understand that!' shouted Arthur. 'Understand that!'

Ford sprang up.

'Keep looking at the book!' he hissed urgently.

'What?'

'Don't Panic.'

'I'm not panicking!'

'Yes, you are.'

'All right, so I'm panicking, what else is there to do?'

'You just come along with me and have a good time. The Galaxy's a fun place. You'll need to have this fish in your ear.'

'I beg your pardon?' asked Arthur, rather politely, he thought.

Ford was holding up a small glass jar which quite clearly had a small yellow fish wriggling around in it. Arthur blinked at him. He wished there was something simple and recognizable he could grasp hold of. He would have felt safe if alongside the Dentrassi underwear, the piles of Squornshellous mattresses and the man from Betelgeuse holding up a small yellow fish and offering to put it in his ear he had been able to see just a small packet of cornflakes. But he couldn't, and he didn't feel safe.

Suddenly a violent noise leapt at them from no source that he could identify. He gasped in terror at what sounded like a man trying to gargle whilst fighting off a pack of wolves.

'Shush!' said Ford. 'Listen, it might be important.'

'Im . . . important?'

'It's the Vogon captain making an announcement on the Tannoy.'

'You mean that's how the Vogons talk?'

'Listen!'

'But I can't speak Vogon!'

'You don't need to. Just put this fish in your ear.'

Ford, with a lightning movement, clapped his hand to Arthur's ear, and he had the sudden sickening sensation of the fish slithering deep into his aural tract. Gasping with horror he scrabbled at his ear for a second or so, but then slowly turned goggle-eyed with wonder. He was experiencing the aural equivalent of looking at a picture of two black silhouetted faces and suddenly seeing it as a picture of a white candlestick. Or of looking at a lot of coloured dots on a piece of paper which suddenly resolve themselves into the figure six and mean that your optician is going to charge you a lot of money for a new pair of glasses.

He was still listening to the howling gargles, he knew that, only now it had somehow taken on the semblance of perfectly straightforward English.

This is what he heard . . .

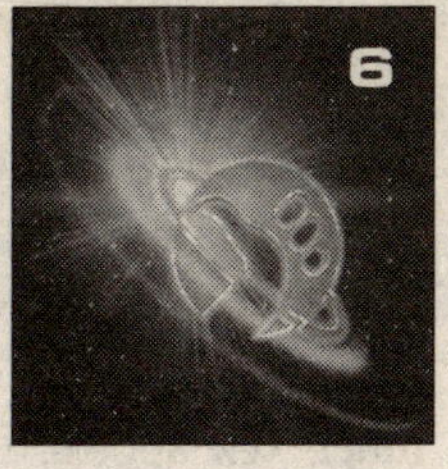

'Howl howl gargle howl gargle howl howl howl gargle howl gargle howl howl gargle gargle howl gargle gargle gargle howl slurrp uuuurgh should have a good time. Message repeats. This is your captain speaking, so stop whatever you're doing and pay attention. First of all I see from our instruments that we have a couple of hitchhikers aboard. Hello, wherever you are. I just want to make it totally clear that you are not at all welcome. I worked hard to get where I am today, and I didn't become captain of a Vogon constructor ship simply so I could turn it into a taxi service for a load of degenerate freeloaders. I have sent out a search party, and as soon as they find you I will put you off the ship. If you're very lucky I might read you some of my poetry first.

'Secondly, we are about to jump into hyperspace for the journey to Barnard's Star. On arrival we will stay in dock for a seventy-two-hour refit, and no one's to leave the ship during that time. I repeat, all planet leave is cancelled. I've just had an unhappy love affair, so I don't see why anybody else should have a good time. Message ends.'

The noise stopped.

Arthur discovered to his embarrassment that he was lying curled up in a small ball on the floor with his arms wrapped round his head. He smiled weakly.

'Charming man,' he said. 'I wish I had a daughter so I could forbid her to marry one . . .'

'You wouldn't need to,' said Ford. 'They've got as much sex appeal as a road accident. No, don't move,' he added as Arthur began to uncurl himself, 'you'd better be prepared for the jump into hyperspace. It's unpleasantly like being drunk.'

'What's so unpleasant about being drunk?'

'You ask a glass of water.'

Arthur thought about this.

'Ford,' he said.

'Yeah?'

'What's this fish doing in my ear?'

'It's translating for you. It's a Babel fish. Look it up in the book, if you like.'

He tossed over *The Hitchhiker's Guide to the Galaxy* and then curled up into a foetal ball to prepare himself for the jump.

At that moment the bottom fell out of Arthur's mind.

His eyes turned inside out. His feet began to leak out of the top of his head.

The room folded flat around him, spun around, shifted out of existence, and left him sliding into his own navel.

They were passing through hyperspace.

'The Babel fish,' said *The Hitchhiker's Guide to the Galaxy* quietly, *'is small, yellow, and leech-like, and probably*

the oddest thing in the Universe. It feeds on brainwave energy received not from its own carrier but from those around it. It absorbs all unconscious mental frequencies from this brainwave energy to nourish itself with. It then excretes into the mind of its carrier a telepathic matrix formed by combining the conscious thought frequencies with nerve signals picked up from the speech centres of the brain which has supplied them. The practical upshot of all this is that if you stick a Babel fish in your ear you can instantly understand anything said to you in any form of language. The speech patterns you actually hear decode the brainwave matrix which has been fed into your mind by your Babel fish.

'Now it is such a bizarrely improbable coincidence that anything so mindbogglingly useful could have evolved purely by chance that some thinkers have chosen to see it as a final and clinching proof of the non-*existence of God.*

'The argument goes something like this: "I refuse to prove that I exist," says God, "for proof denies faith, and without faith I am nothing."

'"But," says Man, "the Babel fish is a dead giveaway, isn't it? It could not have evolved by chance. It proves you exist, and so therefore, by your own arguments, you don't. QED."

'"Oh dear," says God, "I hadn't thought of that," and promptly vanishes in a puff of logic.

'"Oh, that was easy," says Man, and for an encore goes on to prove that black is white and gets himself killed on the next zebra crossing.

'Most leading theologians claim that this argument is a load of dingo's kidneys, but that didn't stop Oolon Colluphid

making a small fortune when he used it as the central theme of his best-selling book Well That About Wraps It Up For God.

'Meanwhile, the poor Babel fish, by effectively removing all barriers to communication between different races and cultures, has caused more and bloodier wars than anything else in the history of creation.'

Arthur let out a low groan. He was horrified to discover that the kick through hyperspace hadn't killed him. He was now six light years from the place that the Earth would have been if it still existed.

The Earth.

Visions of it swam sickeningly through his nauseated mind. There was no way his imagination could feel the impact of the whole Earth having gone, it was too big. He prodded his feelings by thinking that his parents and his sister had gone. No reaction. He thought of all the people he had been close to. No reaction. Then he thought of a complete stranger he had been standing behind in the queue at the supermarket two days before and felt a sudden stab – the supermarket was gone, everyone in it was gone. Nelson's Column had gone! Nelson's Column had gone and there would be no outcry, because there was no one left to make an outcry. From now on Nelson's Column only existed in his mind. England only existed in his mind – his mind, stuck here in this dank smelly steel-lined spaceship. A wave of claustrophobia closed in on him.

England no longer existed. He'd got that – somehow he'd got it. He tried again. America, he thought, has gone. He couldn't grasp it. He decided to start smaller again.

New York has gone. No reaction. He'd never seriously believed it existed anyway. The dollar, he thought, has sunk for ever. Slight tremor there. Every Bogart movie has been wiped, he said to himself, and that gave him a nasty knock. McDonald's, he thought. There is no longer any such thing as a McDonald's hamburger.

He passed out. When he came round a second later he found he was sobbing for his mother.

He jerked himself violently to his feet.

'Ford!'

Ford looked up from where he was sitting in a corner humming to himself. He always found the actual travelling-through-space part of space travel rather trying.

'Yeah?' he said.

'If you're a researcher on this book thing and you were on Earth, you must have been gathering material on it.'

'Well, I was able to extend the original entry a bit, yes.'

'Let me see what it says in this edition, then. I've got to see it.'

'Yeah, OK.' He passed it over again.

Arthur grabbed hold of it and tried to stop his hands shaking. He pressed the entry for the relevant page. The screen flashed and swirled and resolved into a page of print. Arthur stared at it.

'It doesn't have an entry!' he burst out.

Ford looked over his shoulder.

'Yes it does,' he said, 'down there, see, at the bottom of the screen, just under *Eccentrica Gallumbits, the triple-breasted whore of Eroticon Six.*'

Arthur followed Ford's finger, and saw where it was pointing. For a moment it still didn't register, then his mind nearly blew up.

'What? *Harmless*? Is that all it's got to say? *Harmless*! One word!'

Ford shrugged.

'Well, there are a hundred billion stars in the Galaxy, and only a limited amount of space in the book's microprocessors,' he said, 'and no one knew much about the Earth, of course.'

'Well, for God's sake I hope you managed to rectify that a bit.'

'Oh yes, well, I managed to transmit a new entry off to the editor. He had to trim it a bit, but it's still an improvement.'

'And what does it say now?' asked Arthur.

'*Mostly harmless*,' admitted Ford with a slightly embarrassed cough.

'*Mostly harmless*!' shouted Arthur.

'What was that noise?' hissed Ford.

'It was me shouting,' shouted Arthur.

'No! Shut up!' said Ford. 'I think we're in trouble.'

'*You* think we're in trouble!'

Outside the door were the clear sounds of marching footsteps.

'The Dentrassi?' whispered Arthur.

'No, those are steel-tipped boots,' said Ford.

There was a sharp ringing rap on the door.

'Then who is it?' said Arthur.

'Well,' said Ford, 'if we're lucky it's just the Vogons come to throw us in to space.'

'And if we're unlucky?'

'If we're unlucky,' said Ford grimly, 'the captain might be serious in his threat that he's going to read us some of his poetry first . . .'

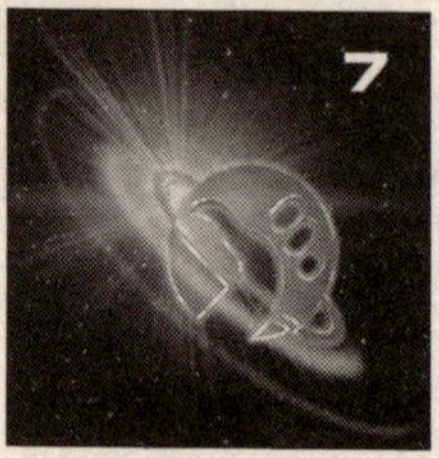

Vogon poetry is of course the third worst in the Universe. The second worst is that of the Azgoths of Kria. During a recitation by their Poet Master Grunthos the Flatulent of his poem 'Ode To A Small Lump of Green Putty I Found In My Armpit One Midsummer Morning' four of his audience died of internal haemorrhaging, and the President of the Mid-Galactic Arts Nobbling Council survived by gnawing one of his own legs off. Grunthos is reported to have been 'disappointed' by the poem's reception, and was about to embark on a reading of his twelve-book epic entitled *My Favourite Bathtime Gurgles* when his own major intestine, in a desperate attempt to save life and civilization, leapt straight up through his neck and throttled his brain.

The very worst poetry of all perished along with its creator Paula Nancy Millstone Jennings of Greenbridge, Essex, England in the destruction of the planet Earth.

Prostetnic Vogon Jeltz smiled very slowly. This was done not so much for effect as because he was trying to remember the sequence of muscle movements. He had had a terribly therapeutic yell at his prisoners and was now feeling quite relaxed and ready for a little callousness.

The prisoners sat in Poetry Appreciation chairs – strapped in. Vogons suffered no illusions as to the regard their works were generally held in. Their early attempts at composition had been part of a bludgeoning insistence that they be accepted as a properly evolved and cultured race, but now the only thing that kept them going was sheer bloodymindedness.

The sweat stood out on Ford Prefect's brow, and slid round the electrodes strapped to his temples. These were attached to a battery of electronic equipment – imagery intensifiers, rhythmic modulators, alliterative residulators and simile dumpers – all designed to heighten the experience of the poem and make sure that not a single nuance of the poet's thought was lost.

Arthur Dent sat and quivered. He had no idea what he was in for, but he knew that he hadn't liked anything that had happened so far and didn't think things were likely to change.

The Vogon began to read – a fetid little passage of his own devising.

'*O freddled gruntbuggly . . .*' he began. Spasms racked Ford's body – this was worse than even he'd been prepared for.

'*. . . thy micturations are to me / As plurdled gabbleblotchits on a lurgid bee.*'

'Aaaaaaarggggghhhhhh!' went Ford Prefect, wrenching his head back as lumps of pain thumped through it. He could dimly see beside him Arthur lolling and rolling in his seat. He clenched his teeth.

'*Groop, I implore thee,*' continued the merciless Vogon, '*my foonting turlingdromes.*'

His voice was rising to a horrible pitch of impassioned stridency. '*And hooptiously drangle me with crinkly bindlewurdles, / Or I will rend thee in the gobberwarts with my blurglecruncheon, see if I don't!*'

'Nnnnnnnnnyyyyyyyuuuuuuurrrrrrggggggghhhh!' cried Ford Prefect and threw one final spasm as the electronic enhancement of the last line caught him full blast across the temples. He went limp.

Arthur lolled.

'Now, Earthlings . . .' whirred the Vogon (he didn't know that Ford Prefect was in fact from a small planet somewhere in the vicinity of Betelgeuse, and wouldn't have cared if he had), 'I present you with a simple choice! Either die in the vacuum of space, or . . .' he paused for melodramatic effect, 'tell me how good you thought my poem was!'

He threw himself backwards into a huge leathery bat-shaped seat and watched them. He did the smile again.

Ford was rasping for breath. He rolled his dusty tongue round his parched mouth and moaned.

Arthur said brightly: 'Actually I quite liked it.'

Ford turned and gaped. Here was an approach that had quite simply not occurred to him.

The Vogon raised a surprised eyebrow that effectively obscured his nose and was therefore no bad thing.

'Oh good . . .' he whirred, in considerable astonishment.

'Oh, yes,' said Arthur, 'I thought that some of the metaphysical imagery was really particularly effective.'

Ford continued to stare at him, slowly organizing his thoughts around this totally new concept. Were they really going to be able to bareface their way out of this?

'Yes, do continue . . .' invited the Vogon.

'Oh . . . and er . . . interesting rhythmic devices too,' continued Arthur, 'which seemed to counterpoint the . . . er . . . er . . .' he floundered.

Ford leaped to his rescue, hazarding '. . . counterpoint the surrealism of the underlying metaphor of the . . . er . . .' He floundered too, but Arthur was ready again.

'. . . humanity of the . . .'

'*Vogonity,*' Ford hissed at him.

'Ah yes, Vogonity (sorry) of the poet's compassionate soul,' Arthur felt he was on a home stretch now, 'which contrives through the medium of the verse structure to sublimate this, transcend that, and come to terms with the fundamental dichotomies of the other,' (he was reaching a triumphant crescendo . . .) 'and one is left with a profound and vivid insight into . . . into . . . er . . .' (. . . which suddenly gave out on him). Ford leaped in with the coup de grâce:

'Into whatever it was the poem was about!' he yelled. Out of the corner of his mouth: 'Well done, Arthur, that was very good.'

The Vogon perused them. For a moment his embittered racial soul had been touched, but he thought no – too little too late. His voice took on the quality of a cat snagging brushed nylon.

'So what you're saying is that I write poetry because underneath my mean callous heartless exterior I really just want to be loved,' he said. He paused. 'Is that right?'

Ford laughed a nervous laugh. 'Well, I mean, yes,' he said, 'don't we all, deep down, know . . . er . . .'

The Vogon stood up.

'No, well you're completely wrong,' he said. 'I just write poetry to throw my mean callous heartless exterior into sharp relief. I'm going to throw you off the ship anyway. Guard! Take the prisoners to number three airlock and throw them out!'

'What?' shouted Ford.

A huge young Vogon guard stepped forward and yanked them out of their straps with his huge blubbery arms.

'You can't throw us into space,' yelled Ford, 'we're trying to write a book.'

'Resistance is useless!' shouted the Vogon guard back at him. It was the first phrase he'd learnt when he joined the Vogon Guard Corps.

The captain watched with detached amusement and then turned away.

Arthur stared round him wildly.

'I don't want to die now!' he yelled. 'I've still got a headache! I don't want to go to heaven with a headache, I'd be all cross and wouldn't enjoy it!'

The guard grasped them both firmly round the neck, and bowing deferentially towards his captain's back, hoiked them both protesting out of the bridge. A steel door closed and the captain was on his own again. He hummed quietly and mused to himself, lightly fingering his notebook of verses.

'Hmmm,' he said, '*counterpoint the surrealism of the*

underlying metaphor . . .' He considered this for a moment, and then closed the book with a grim smile.

'Death's too good for them,' he said.

The long steel-lined corridor echoed to the feeble struggles of the two humanoids clamped firmly under rubbery Vogon armpits.

'This is great,' spluttered Arthur, 'this is really terrific. Let go of me, you brute!'

The Vogon guard dragged them on.

'Don't you worry,' said Ford, 'I'll think of something.' He didn't sound hopeful.

'Resistance is useless!' bellowed the guard.

'Just don't say things like that,' stammered Ford. 'How can anyone maintain a positive mental attitude if you're saying things like that?'

'My God,' complained Arthur, 'you're talking about a positive mental attitude and you haven't even had your planet demolished today. I woke up this morning and thought I'd have a nice relaxed day, do a bit of reading, brush the dog . . . It's now just after four in the afternoon and I'm already being thrown out of an alien spaceship six light years from the smoking remains of the Earth!' He spluttered and gurgled as the Vogon tightened his grip.

'All right,' said Ford, 'just stop panicking!'

'Who said anything about panicking?' snapped Arthur. 'This is still just the culture shock. You wait till I've settled down into the situation and found my bearings. *Then* I'll start panicking!'

'Arthur, you're getting hysterical. Shut up!' Ford tried

desperately to think, but was interrupted by the guard shouting again.

'Resistance is useless!'

'And you can shut up as well!' snapped Ford.

'Resistance is useless!'

'Oh, give it a rest,' said Ford. He twisted his head till he was looking straight up into his captor's face. A thought struck him.

'Do you really enjoy this sort of thing?' he asked suddenly.

The Vogon stopped dead and a look of immense stupidity seeped slowly over his face.

'Enjoy?' he boomed. 'What do you mean?'

'What I mean,' said Ford, 'is does it give you a full satisfying life? Stomping around, shouting, pushing people out of spaceships . . .'

The Vogon stared up at the low steel ceiling and his eyebrows almost rolled over each other. His mouth slacked. Finally he said, 'Well, the hours are good . . .'

'They'd have to be,' agreed Ford.

Arthur twisted his head round to look at Ford.

'Ford, what are you doing?' he asked in an amazed whisper.

'Oh, just trying to take an interest in the world around me, OK?' he said. 'So the hours are pretty good, then?' he resumed.

The Vogon stared down at him as sluggish thoughts moiled around in the murky depths.

'Yeah,' he said, 'but now you come to mention it, most of the actual minutes are pretty lousy. Except . . .' he thought again, which required looking at the ceiling –

'except some of the shouting I quite like.' He filled his lungs and bellowed, 'Resistance is—'

'Sure, yes,' interrupted Ford hurriedly, 'you're good at that, I can tell. But if it's mostly lousy,' he said slowly, giving the words time to reach their mark, 'then why do you do it? What is it? The girls? The leather? The machismo? Or do you just find that coming to terms with the mindless tedium of it all presents an interesting challenge?'

Arthur looked backwards and forwards between them in bafflement.

'Er . . .' said the guard, 'er . . . er . . . I dunno. I think I just sort of . . . do it, really. My aunt said that spaceship guard was a good career for a young Vogon – you know, the uniform, the low-slung stun-ray holster, the mindless tedium . . .'

'There you are, Arthur,' said Ford with the air of someone reaching the conclusion of his argument, 'you think you've got problems.'

Arthur rather thought he had. Apart from the unpleasant business with his home planet the Vogon guard had half-throttled him already and he didn't like the sound of being thrown into space very much.

'Try and understand *his* problem,' insisted Ford. 'Here he is, poor lad, his entire life's work is stamping around, throwing people off spaceships . . .'

'And shouting,' added the guard.

'And shouting, sure,' said Ford patting the blubbery arm clamped round his neck in friendly condescension, '. . . and he doesn't even know why he's doing it!'

Arthur agreed this was very sad. He did this with a

small feeble gesture, because he was too asphyxiated to speak.

Deep rumblings of bemusement came from the guard.

'Well. Now you put it like that, I suppose . . .'

'Good lad,' encouraged Ford.

'But all right,' went on the rumblings, 'so what's the alternative?'

'Well,' said Ford, brightly but slowly, 'stop doing it, of course! Tell them,' he went on, 'you're not going to do it any more.' He felt he ought to add something to that, but for the moment the guard seemed to have his mind occupied pondering that much.

'Eerrrrrmmmmmmmmmmmmm mmmmmmmmmm . . .' said the guard, 'erm, well, that doesn't sound that great to me.'

Ford suddenly felt the moment slipping away.

'Now wait a minute,' he said, 'that's just the start, you see, there's more to it than that, you see . . .'

But at that moment the guard renewed his grip and continued his original purpose of lugging his prisoners to the airlock. He was obviously quite touched.

'No, I think if it's all the same to you,' he said, 'I'd better get you both shoved into this airlock and then go and get on with some other bits of shouting I've got to do.'

It wasn't all the same to Ford Prefect at all.

'Come on now . . . but look!' he said, less slowly, less brightly.

'Huhhhhgggggggnnnnnn . . .' said Arthur without any clear inflection.

'But hang on,' pursued Ford, 'there's music and art and things to tell you about yet! Arrggghhh!'

'Resistance is useless,' bellowed the guard, and then added, 'You see if I keep it up I can eventually get promoted to Senior Shouting Officer, and there aren't usually many vacancies for non-shouting and non-pushing-people-about officers, so I think I'd better stick to what I know.'

They had now reached the airlock – a large circular steel hatchway of massive strength and weight let into the inner skin of the craft. The guard operated a control and the hatchway swung smoothly open.

'But thanks for taking an interest,' said the Vogon guard. 'Bye now.' He flung Ford and Arthur through the hatchway into the small chamber within. Arthur lay panting for breath. Ford scrambled round and flung his shoulder uselessly against the reclosing hatchway.

'But listen,' he shouted to the guard, 'there's a whole world you don't know anything about . . . here, how about this?' Desperately he grabbed for the only bit of culture he knew offhand – he hummed the first bar of Beethoven's Fifth.

'*Da da da dum!* Doesn't that stir anything in you?'

'No,' said the guard, 'not really. But I'll mention it to my aunt.'

If he said anything further after that it was lost. The hatchway sealed itself tight, and all sound was lost bar the faint distant hum of the ship's engines.

They were in a brightly polished cylindrical chamber about six feet in diameter and ten feet long.

Ford looked round it, panting.

'Potentially bright lad, I thought,' he said and slumped against the curved wall.

Arthur was still lying in the curve of the floor where he had fallen. He didn't look up. He just lay panting.

'We're trapped now, aren't we?'

'Yes,' said Ford, 'we're trapped.'

'Well, didn't you think of anything? I thought you said you were going to think of something. Perhaps you thought of something and I didn't notice.'

'Oh yes, I thought of something,' panted Ford. Arthur looked up expectantly.

'But unfortunately,' continued Ford, 'it rather involved being on the other side of this airtight hatchway.' He kicked the hatch they'd just been thrown through.

'But it was a good idea, was it?'

'Oh yes, very neat.'

'What was it?'

'Well, I hadn't worked out the details yet. Not much point now, is there?'

'So . . . er, what happens next?' asked Arthur.

'Oh, er, well, the hatchway in front of us will open automatically in a few moments and we will shoot out into deep space I expect and asphyxiate. If you take a lungful of air with you you can last for up to thirty seconds, of course . . .' said Ford. He stuck his hands behind his back, raised his eyebrows and started to hum an old Betelgeusian battle hymn. To Arthur's eyes he suddenly looked very alien.

'So this is it,' said Arthur, 'we are going to die.'

'Yes,' said Ford, 'except . . . no! Wait a minute!' He suddenly lunged across the chamber at something behind Arthur's line of vision. 'What's this switch?' he cried.

'What? Where?' cried Arthur, twisting round.

'No, I was only fooling,' said Ford, 'we are going to die after all.'

He slumped against the wall again and carried on the tune from where he had left off.

'You know,' said Arthur, 'it's at times like this, when I'm trapped in a Vogon airlock with a man from Betelgeuse and about to die of asphyxiation in deep space, that I really wish I'd listened to what my mother told me when I was young.'

'Why, what did she tell you?'

'I don't know, I didn't listen.'

'Oh.' Ford carried on humming.

'This is terrific,' Arthur thought to himself, 'Nelson's Column has gone, McDonald's have gone, all that's left is me and the words *Mostly harmless*. Any second now all that will be left is *Mostly harmless*. And yesterday the planet seemed to be going so well.'

A motor whirred.

A slight hiss built into a deafening roar of rushing air as the outer hatchway opened on to an empty blackness studded with tiny impossibly bright points of light. Ford and Arthur popped out into space like corks from a toy gun.

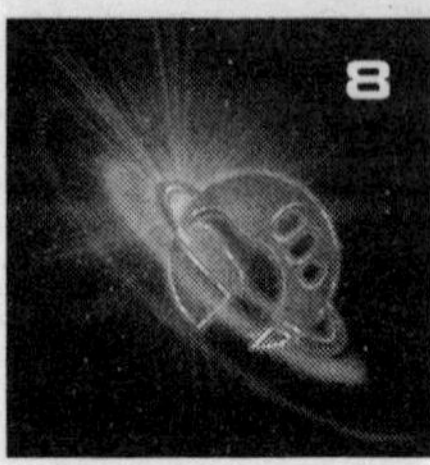

The Hitchhiker's Guide to the Galaxy *is a wholly remarkable book. It has been compiled and recompiled many times over many years and under many different editorships. It contains contributions from countless numbers of travellers and researchers.*

The introduction begins like this:

'Space,' *it says,* 'is big. Really big. You just won't believe how vastly hugely mindbogglingly big it is. I mean you may think it's a long way down the road to the chemist, but that's just peanuts to space. Listen . . .' *and so on.*

(After a while the style settles down a bit and it begins to tell you things you really need to know, like the fact that the fabulously beautiful planet Bethselamin is now so worried about the cumulative erosion by ten billion visiting tourists a year that any net imbalance between the amount you eat and the amount you excrete whilst on the planet is surgically removed from your bodyweight when you leave: so every time you go to the lavatory there it is vitally important to get a receipt.)

To be fair, though, when confronted by the sheer enormity of the distances between the stars, better minds than the one responsible for the Guide's *introduction have faltered. Some invite you to consider for a moment a peanut in Reading and a small walnut in Johannesburg, and other such dizzying concepts.*

The simple truth is that interstellar distances will not fit into the human imagination.

Even light, which travels so fast that it takes most races thousands of years to realize that it travels at all, takes time to journey between the stars. It takes eight minutes to journey from the star Sol to the place where the Earth used to be, and four years more to arrive at Sol's nearest stellar neighbour, Alpha Proxima.

For light to reach the other side of the Galaxy, for it to reach Damogran for instance, takes rather longer: five hundred thousand years.

The record for hitchhiking this distance is just under five years, but you don't get to see much on the way.

The Hitchhiker's Guide to the Galaxy *says that if you hold a lungful of air you can survive in the total vacuum of space for about thirty seconds. However, it does go on to say that what with space being the mindboggling size it is the chances of getting picked up by another ship within those thirty seconds are two to the power of two hundred and seventy-six thousand seven hundred and nine to one against.*

By a totally staggering coincidence that is also the telephone number of an Islington flat where Arthur once went to a very good party and met a very nice girl whom he totally failed to get off with – she went off with a gatecrasher.

Though the planet Earth, the Islington flat and the telephone have all now been demolished, it is comforting to reflect that they are all in some small way commemorated by the fact that twenty-nine seconds later Ford and Arthur were rescued.

A computer chattered to itself in alarm as it noticed an airlock open and close itself for no apparent reason.

This was because Reason was in fact out to lunch.

A hole had just appeared in the Galaxy. It was exactly a nothingth of a second long, a nothingth of an inch wide, and quite a lot of millions of light years from end to end.

As it closed up lots of paper hats and party balloons fell out of it and drifted off through the universe. A team of seven three-foot-high market analysts fell out of it and died, partly of asphyxiation, partly of surprise.

Two hundred and thirty-nine thousand lightly fried eggs fell out of it too, materializing in a large wobbly heap on the famine-struck land of Poghril in the Pansel system.

The whole Poghril tribe had died out from famine except for one last man who died of cholesterol poisoning some weeks later.

The nothingth of a second for which the hole existed reverberated backwards and forwards through time in a most improbable fashion. Somewhere in the deeply remote past it seriously traumatized a small random group of atoms drifting through the empty sterility of space and made them cling together in the most extraordinarily unlikely patterns. These patterns quickly learnt to copy themselves (this was part of what was so extraordinary about the patterns) and went on to cause massive trouble on every planet they drifted on to. That was how life began in the Universe.

Five wild Event Maelstroms swirled in vicious storms of unreason and spewed up a pavement.

On the pavement lay Ford Prefect and Arthur Dent, gulping like half-spent fish.

'There you are,' gasped Ford, scrabbling for a fingerhold on the pavement as it raced through the Third Reach of the Unknown, 'I told you I'd think of something.'

'Oh sure,' said Arthur, 'sure.'

'Bright idea of mine,' said Ford, 'to find a passing spaceship and get rescued by it.'

The real universe arched sickeningly away beneath them. Various pretend ones flitted silently by, like mountain goats. Primal light exploded, splattering space–time as with gobbets of junket. Time blossomed, matter shrank away. The highest prime number coalesced quietly in a corner and hid itself away for ever.

'Oh, come off it,' said Arthur, 'the chances against it were astronomical.'

'Don't knock it, it worked,' said Ford.

'What sort of ship are we in?' asked Arthur as the pit of eternity yawned beneath them.

'I don't know,' said Ford, 'I haven't opened my eyes yet.'

'No, nor have I,' said Arthur.

The Universe jumped, froze, quivered and splayed out in several unexpected directions.

Arthur and Ford opened their eyes and looked about in considerable surprise.

'Good God,' said Arthur, 'it looks just like the sea front at Southend.'

'Hell, I'm relieved to hear you say that,' said Ford.

'Why?'

'Because I thought I must be going mad.'

'Perhaps you are. Perhaps you only thought I said it.'

Ford thought about this.

'Well, did you say it or didn't you?' he asked.

'I think so,' said Arthur.

'Well, perhaps we're both going mad.'

'Yes,' said Arthur, 'we'd be mad, all things considered, to think this was Southend.'

'Well, do you think this is Southend?'

'Oh yes.'

'So do I.'

'Therefore we must be mad.'

'Nice day for it.'

'Yes,' said a passing maniac.

'Who was that?' asked Arthur.

'Who – the man with the five heads and the elderberry bush full of kippers?'

'Yes.'

'I don't know. Just someone.'

'Ah.'

They both sat on the pavement and watched with a certain unease as huge children bounced heavily along the sand and wild horses thundered through the sky taking fresh supplies of reinforced railings to the Uncertain Areas.

'You know,' said Arthur with a slight cough, 'if this is Southend, there's something very odd about it . . .'

'You mean the way the sea stays steady as a rock and the buildings keep washing up and down?' said Ford. 'Yes, I thought that was odd too. In fact,' he continued as with a huge bang Southend split itself into six equal segments which danced and span giddily round each other in lewd and licentious formations, 'there is something altogether very strange going on.'

Wild yowling noises of pipes and strings seared through the wind, hot doughnuts popped out of the road for ten pence each, horrid fish stormed out of the sky and Arthur and Ford decided to make a run for it.

They plunged through heavy walls of sound, mountains of archaic thought, valleys of mood music, bad shoe sessions and footling bats and suddenly heard a girl's voice.

It sounded quite a sensible voice, but it just said, 'Two to the power of one hundred thousand to one against and falling,' and that was all.

Ford skidded down a beam of light and spun round trying to find a source for the voice but could see nothing he could seriously believe in.

'What was that voice?' shouted Arthur.

'I don't know,' yelled Ford. 'I don't know. It sounded like a measurement of probability.'

'Probability? What do you mean?'

'Probability. You know, like two to one, three to one,

five to four against. It said two to the power of one hundred thousand to one against. That's pretty improbable, you know.'

A million-gallon vat of custard upended itself over them without warning.

'But what does it mean?' cried Arthur.

'What, the custard?'

'No, the measurement of improbability!'

'I don't know. I don't know at all. I think we're on some kind of spaceship.'

'I can only assume,' said Arthur, 'that this is not the first-class compartment.'

Bulges appeared in the fabric of space–time. Great ugly bulges.

'Haaaauuurrgghhh . . .' said Arthur as he felt his body softening and bending in unusual directions. 'Southend seems to be melting away . . . the stars are swirling . . . a dust bowl . . . my legs are drifting off into the sunset . . . my left arm's come off too.' A frightening thought struck him: 'Hell,' he said, 'how am I going to operate my digital watch now?' He wound his eyes desperately around to Ford's direction.

'Ford,' he said, 'you're turning into a penguin. Stop it.'

Again came the voice.

'Two to the power of seventy-five thousand to one against and falling.'

Ford waddled around his pond in a furious circle.

'Hey, who are you?' he quacked. 'Where are you? What's going on and is there any way of stopping it?'

'Please relax,' said the voice pleasantly, like a stewardess in an airliner with only one wing and two engines one of which is on fire, 'you are perfectly safe.'

'But that's not the point!' raged Ford. 'The point is that I am now a perfectly safe penguin, and my colleague here is rapidly running out of limbs!'

'It's all right, I've got them back now,' said Arthur.

'Two to the power of fifty thousand to one against and falling,' said the voice.

'Admittedly,' said Arthur, 'they're longer than I usually like them, but . . .'

'Isn't there anything,' squawked Ford in avian fury, 'you feel you ought to be telling us?'

The voice cleared its throat. A giant petit four lolloped off into the distance.

'Welcome,' the voice said, 'to the Starship *Heart of Gold.*'

The voice continued.

'Please do not be alarmed,' it said, 'by anything you see or hear around you. You are bound to feel some initial ill-effects as you have been rescued from certain death at an improbability level of two to the power of two hundred and seventy-six thousand to one against – possibly much higher. We are now cruising at a level of two to the power of twenty-five thousand to one against and falling, and we will be restoring normality just as soon as we are sure what is normal anyway. Thank you. Two to the power of twenty thousand to one against and falling.'

The voice cut out.

Ford and Arthur were in a small luminous pink cubicle.

Ford was wildly excited.

'Arthur!' he said. 'This is fantastic! We've been picked up by a ship powered by the Infinite Improbability Drive! This is incredible! I heard rumours about it before! They were all officially denied, but they must have done it! They've built the Improbability Drive! Arthur, this is . . . Arthur? What's happening?'

Arthur had jammed himself against the door to the cubicle, trying to hold it closed, but it was ill-fitting. Tiny furry little hands were squeezing themselves through the cracks, their fingers were inkstained; tiny voices chattered insanely.

Arthur looked up.

'Ford,' he said, 'there's an infinite number of monkeys outside who want to talk to us about this script for *Hamlet* they've worked out.'

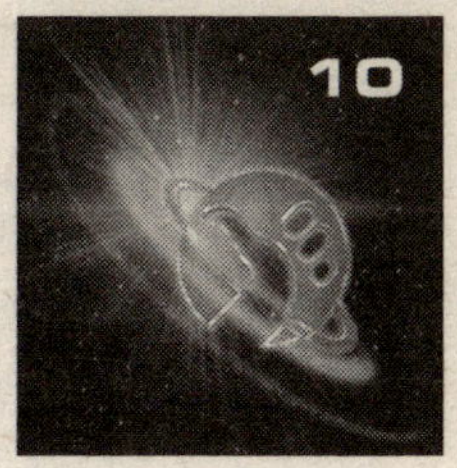

The Infinite Improbability Drive is a wonderful new method of crossing vast interstellar distances in a mere nothingth of a second, without all that tedious mucking about in hyperspace.

It was discovered by a lucky chance, and then developed into a governable form of propulsion by the Galactic Government's research team on Damogran.

This, briefly, is the story of its discovery.

The principle of generating small amounts of *finite* improbability by simply hooking the logic circuits of a Bambleweeny 57 Sub-Meson Brain to an atomic vector plotter suspended in a strong Brownian-motion producer (say a nice hot cup of tea) were of course well understood – and such generators were often used to break the ice at parties by making all the molecules in the hostess's undergarments leap simultaneously one foot to the left, in accordance with the Theory of Indeterminacy.

Many respectable physicists said that they weren't going to stand for this – partly because it was a debasement of science, but mostly because they didn't get invited to those sort of parties.

Another thing they couldn't stand was the perpetual

failure they encountered in trying to construct a machine which could generate the *infinite* improbability field needed to flip a spaceship across the mind-paralysing distances between the furthest stars, and in the end they grumpily announced that such a machine was virtually impossible.

Then, one day, a student who had been left to sweep up the lab after a particularly unsuccessful party found himself reasoning this way:

If, he thought to himself, such a machine is a *virtual* impossibility, then it must logically be a *finite* improbability. So all I have to do in order to make one is to work out exactly how improbable it is, feed that figure into the finite improbability generator, give it a fresh cup of really hot tea . . . and turn it on!

He did this, and was rather startled to discover that he had managed to create the long-sought-after golden infinite improbability generator out of thin air.

It startled him even more when just after he was awarded the Galactic Institute's Prize for Extreme Cleverness he got lynched by a rampaging mob of respectable physicists who had finally realized that the one thing they really couldn't stand was a smartass.

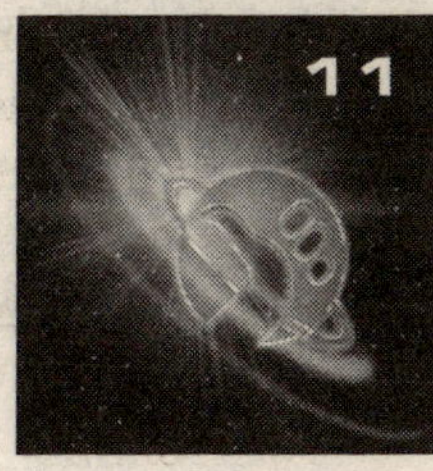

The improbability-proof control cabin of the *Heart of Gold* looked like a perfectly conventional spaceship except that it was perfectly clean because it was so new. Some of the control seats hadn't had the plastic wrapping taken off yet. The cabin was mostly white, oblong, and about the size of a smallish restaurant. In fact it wasn't perfectly oblong: the two long walls were raked round in a slight parallel curve, and all the angles and corners of the cabin were contoured in excitingly chunky shapes. The truth of the matter is that it would have been a great deal simpler and more practical to build the cabin as an ordinary three-dimensional oblong room, but then the designers would have got miserable. As it was the cabin looked excitingly purposeful, with large video screens ranged over the control and guidance system panels on the concave wall, and long banks of computers set into the convex wall. In one corner a robot sat humped, its gleaming brushed steel head hanging loosely between its gleaming brushed steel knees. It too was fairly new, but though it was beautifully constructed and polished it somehow looked as if the various parts of its more or less humanoid body didn't quite fit properly. In fact they fitted perfectly well, but something in its bearing suggested that they might have fitted better.

Zaphod Beeblebrox paced nervously up and down the cabin, brushing his hands over pieces of gleaming equipment and giggling with excitement.

Trillian sat hunched over a clump of instruments reading off figures. Her voice was carried round the Tannoy system of the whole ship.

'*Five to one against and falling . . .*' she said, '*four to one against and falling . . . three to one . . . two . . . one . . . probability factor of one to one . . . we have normality, I repeat we have normality.*' She turned her microphone off – then turned it back on with a slight smile and continued: '*Anything you still can't cope with is therefore your own problem. Please relax. You will be sent for soon.*'

Zaphod burst out in annoyance: 'Who are they, Trillian?'

Trillian spun her seat round to face him and shrugged.

'Just a couple of guys we seem to have picked up in open space,' she said. 'Sector ZZ 9 Plural Z Alpha.'

'Yeah, well, that's a very sweet thought, Trillian,' complained Zaphod, 'but do you really think it's wise under the circumstances? I mean, here we are on the run and everything, we must have the police of half the Galaxy after us by now, and we stop to pick up hitchhikers. OK, so ten out of ten for style, but minus several million for good thinking, yeah?'

He tapped irritably at a control panel. Trillian quietly moved his hand before he tapped anything important. Whatever Zaphod's qualities of mind might include – dash, bravado, conceit – he was mechanically inept and could easily blow the ship up with an extravagant gesture. Trillian had come to suspect that the main reason why he had had such a wild and successful life was that he never really understood the significance of anything he did.

'Zaphod,' she said patiently, 'they were floating unprotected in open space . . . you wouldn't want them to have died, would you?'

'Well, you know . . . no. Not as such, but . . .'

'Not as such? Not die as such? But?' Trillian cocked her head on one side.

'Well, maybe someone else might have picked them up later.'

'A second later and they would have been dead.'

'Yeah, so if you'd taken the trouble to think about the problem a bit longer it would have gone away.'

'You'd have been happy to let them die?'

'Well, you know, not happy as such, but . . .'

'Anyway,' said Trillian, turning back to the controls, 'I didn't pick them up.'

'What do you mean? Who picked them up, then?'

'The ship did.'

'Huh?'

'The ship did. All by itself.'

'Huh?'

'Whilst we were in Improbability Drive.'

'But that's incredible.'

'No, Zaphod. Just very very improbable.'

'Er, yeah.'

'Look, Zaphod,' she said, patting his arm, 'don't worry about the aliens. They're just a couple of guys, I expect.

I'll send the robot down to get them and bring them up here. Hey, Marvin!'

In the corner, the robot's head swung up sharply, but then wobbled about imperceptibly. It pulled itself up to its feet as if it was about five pounds heavier than it actually was, and made what an outside observer would have thought was a heroic effort to cross the room. It stopped in front of Trillian and seemed to stare through her left shoulder.

'I think you ought to know I'm feeling very depressed,' it said. Its voice was low and hopeless.

'Oh God,' muttered Zaphod and slumped into a seat.

'Well,' said Trillian in a bright compassionate tone, 'here's something to occupy you and keep your mind off things.'

'It won't work,' droned Marvin, 'I have an exceptionally large mind.'

'Marvin!' warned Trillian.

'All right,' said Marvin, 'what do you want me to do?'

'Go down to number two entry bay and bring the two aliens up here under surveillance.'

With a microsecond pause, and a finely calculated micromodulation of pitch and timbre – nothing you could actually take offence at – Marvin managed to convey his utter contempt and horror of all things human.

'Just that?' he said.

'Yes,' said Trillian firmly.

'I won't enjoy it,' said Marvin.

Zaphod leapt out of his seat.

'She's not asking you to enjoy it,' he shouted, 'just do it, will you?'

'All right,' said Marvin like the tolling of a great cracked bell, 'I'll do it.'

'Good . . .' snapped Zaphod, 'great . . . thank you . . .'

Marvin turned and lifted his flat-topped triangular red eyes up towards him.

'I'm not getting you down at all, am I?' he said pathetically.

'No, no, Marvin,' lilted Trillian, 'that's just fine, really . . .'

'I wouldn't like to think I was getting you down.'

'No, don't worry about that,' the lilt continued, 'you just act as comes naturally and everything will be just fine.'

'You're sure you don't mind?' probed Marvin.

'No, no, Marvin,' lilted Trillian, 'that's just fine, really . . . just part of life.'

Marvin flashed her an electronic look.

'Life,' said Marvin, 'don't talk to me about life.'

He turned hopelessly on his heel and lugged himself out of the cabin. With a satisfied hum and a click the door closed behind him.

'I don't think I can stand that robot much longer, Zaphod,' growled Trillian.

The Encyclopaedia Galactica *defines a robot as a mechanical apparatus designed to do the work of a man. The marketing division of the Sirius Cybernetics Corporation defines a robot as 'Your Plastic Pal Who's Fun To Be With'.*

The Hitchhiker's Guide to the Galaxy *defines the marketing division of the Sirius Cybernetics Corporation as 'a bunch of mindless jerks who'll be the first against the wall when the revolution comes', with a footnote to the effect that the editors would welcome applications from anyone interested in taking over the post of robotics correspondent.*

Curiously enough, an edition of The Encyclopaedia Galactica *that had the good fortune to fall through a time warp from a thousand years in the future defined the marketing division of the Sirius Cybernetics Corporation as 'a bunch of mindless jerks who were the first against the wall when the revolution came'.*

The pink cubicle had winked out of existence, the monkeys had sunk away to a better dimension. Ford and Arthur found themselves in the embarkation area of the ship. It was rather smart.

'I think this ship's brand new,' said Ford.

'How can you tell?' asked Arthur. 'Have you got some exotic device for measuring the age of metal?'

'No, I just found this sales brochure lying on the floor. It's a lot of "the Universe can be yours" stuff. Ah! Look, I was right.'

Ford jabbed at one of the pages and showed it to Arthur.

'It says: "*Sensational new breakthrough in Improbability physics. As soon as the ship's drive reaches Infinite Improbability it passes through every point in the Universe. Be the envy of other major governments.*" Wow, this is big-league stuff.'

Ford hunted excitedly through the technical specs of the ship, occasionally gasping with astonishment at what he read – clearly Galactic astrotechnology had moved ahead during the years of his exile.

Arthur listened for a short while, but being unable to understand the vast majority of what Ford was saying he began to let his mind wander. Trailing his fingers along the edge of an incomprehensible computer bank, he reached out and pressed an invitingly large red button on a nearby panel. The panel lit up with the words *Please do not press this button again*. He shook himself.

'Listen,' said Ford, who was still engrossed in the sales brochure, 'they make a big thing of the ship's cybernetics. *A new generation of Sirius Cybernetics Corporation robots and computers, with the new GPP feature.*'

'GPP feature?' said Arthur. 'What's that?'

'Oh, it says *Genuine People Personalities*.'

'Oh,' said Arthur, 'sounds ghastly.'

A voice behind them said, 'It is.' The voice was low and hopeless and accompanied by a slight clanking sound. They spun round and saw an abject steel man standing hunched in the doorway.

'What?' they said.

'Ghastly,' continued Marvin, 'it all is. Absolutely ghastly. Just don't even talk about it. Look at this door,' he said stepping through it. The irony circuits cut in to his voice modulator as he mimicked the style of the sales brochure. *'All the doors in this spaceship have a cheerful and sunny disposition. It is their pleasure to open for you, and their satisfaction to close again with the knowledge of a job well done.'*

As the door closed behind them it became apparent that it did indeed have a satisfied sigh-like quality to it.

'*Hummmmmmmyummmmmmm ah!*' it said.

Marvin regarded it with cold loathing whilst his logic circuits chattered with disgust and tinkered with the concept of directing physical violence against it. Further circuits cut in saying, 'Why bother? What's the point? Nothing is worth getting involved in.' Further circuits amused themselves by analysing the molecular components of the door, and of the humanoids' brain cells. For a quick encore they measured the level of hydrogen emissions in the surrounding cubic parsec of space and then shut down again in boredom. A spasm of despair shook the robot's body as he turned.

'Come on,' he droned, 'I've been ordered to take you down to the bridge. Here I am, brain the size of a planet and they ask me to take you down to the bridge. Call that *job satisfaction*? 'Cos I don't.'

He turned and walked back to the hated door.

'Er, excuse me,' said Ford following after him, 'which government owns this ship?'

Marvin ignored him.

'You watch this door,' he muttered, 'it's about to open again. I can tell by the intolerable air of smugness it suddenly generates.'

With an ingratiating little whine the door slid open again and Marvin stomped through.

'Come on,' he said.

The others followed quickly and the door slid back into place with pleased little clicks and whirrs.

'Thank you, the marketing division of the Sirius Cybernetics Corporation,' said Marvin and trudged desolately up the gleaming curved corridor that stretched out before them. '"*Let's build robots with Genuine People Personalities,*" they said. So they tried it out with me. I'm a personality prototype. You can tell, can't you?'

Ford and Arthur muttered embarrassed little disclaimers.

'I hate that door,' continued Marvin. 'I'm not getting you down at all, am I?'

'Which government . . .' started Ford again.

'No government owns it,' snapped the robot, 'it's been stolen.'

'Stolen?'

'Stolen?' mimicked Marvin.

'Who by?' asked Ford.

'Zaphod Beeblebrox.'

Something extraordinary happened to Ford's face. At least five entirely separate and distinct expressions of shock and amazement piled up on it in a jumbled mess. His left leg, which was in mid-stride, seemed to have difficulty in finding the floor again. He stared at the robot and tried to entangle some dartoid muscles.

'*Zaphod Beeblebrox* . . .' he said weakly.

'Sorry, did I say something wrong?' said Marvin, dragging himself on regardless. 'Pardon me for breathing, which I never do anyway so I don't know why I bother to say it, oh God I'm so depressed. Here's another of those self-satisfied doors. *Life!* Don't talk to me about life.'

'No one even mentioned it,' muttered Arthur irritably. 'Ford, are you all right?'

Ford stared at him. 'Did that robot say Zaphod Beeblebrox?' he said.

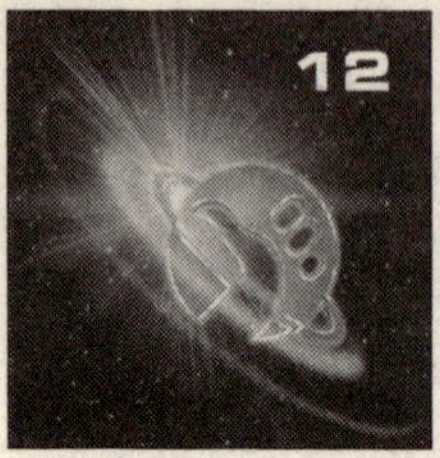

A loud clatter of gunk music flooded through the *Heart of Gold* cabin as Zaphod searched the sub-etha radio wavebands for news of himself. The machine was rather difficult to operate. For years radios had been operated by means of pressing buttons and turning dials; then as the technology became more sophisticated the controls were made touch sensitive – you merely had to brush the panels with your fingers; now all you had to do was wave your hand in the general direction of the components and hope. It saved a lot of muscular expenditure of course, but meant that you had to sit infuriatingly still if you wanted to keep listening to the same programme.

Zaphod waved a hand and the channel switched again. More gunk music, but this time it was a background to a news announcement. The news was always heavily edited to fit the rhythms of the music.

'*. . . and news reports brought to you here on the sub-etha waveband, broadcasting around the Galaxy around the clock,*' squawked a voice, '*and we'll be saying a big hello to all intelligent life forms everywhere . . . and to everyone else out there, the secret is to bang the rocks together, guys. And of course, the big news story tonight is the sensational theft* *of the new Improbability Drive prototype ship by none other than Galactic President Zaphod Beeblebrox. And the question everyone's asking is . . . Has the Big Z finally flipped? Beeblebrox, the man who invented the Pan Galactic Gargle Blaster, ex-confidence trickster, once described by Eccentrica Gallumbits as the Best Bang since the Big One, and recently voted the Worst Dressed Sentient Being in the Known Universe for the seventh time . . . has he got an answer this time? We asked his private brain-care specialist, Gag Halfrunt . . .'*

The music swirled and dived for a moment. Another voice broke in, presumably Halfrunt. He said: *'Vell, Zaphod's just zis guy, you know?'* but got no further because an electric pencil flew across the cabin and through the radio's on/off sensitive airspace. Zaphod turned and glared at Trillian – she had thrown the pencil.

'Hey,' he said, 'what you do that for?'

Trillian was tapping her finger on a screenful of figures.

'I've just thought of something,' she said.

'Yeah? Worth interrupting a news bulletin about me for?'

'You hear enough about yourself as it is.'

'I'm very insecure. We know that.'

'Can we drop your ego for a moment? This is important.'

'If there's anything more important than my ego around, I want it caught and shot now.' Zaphod glared at her again, then laughed.

'Listen,' she said, 'we picked up those couple of guys . . .'

'What couple of guys?'

'The couple of guys we picked up.'

'Oh yeah,' said Zaphod, 'those couple of guys.'

'We picked them up in Sector ZZ 9 Plural Z Alpha.'

'Yeah?' said Zaphod, and blinked.

Trillian said quietly, 'Does that mean anything to you?'

'Mmmm,' said Zaphod, 'ZZ 9 Plural Z Alpha. ZZ 9 Plural Z Alpha?'

'Well?' said Trillian.

'Er . . . what does the Z mean?' said Zaphod.

'Which one?'

'Any one.'

One of the major difficulties Trillian experienced in her relationship with Zaphod was learning to distinguish between him pretending to be stupid just to get people off their guard, pretending to be stupid because he couldn't be bothered to think and wanted someone else to do it for him, pretending to be outrageously stupid to hide the fact that he actually didn't understand what was going on, and really being genuinely stupid. He was renowned for being amazingly clever and quite clearly was so – but not all the time, which obviously worried him, hence the act. He preferred people to be puzzled rather than contemptuous. This above all appeared to Trillian to be genuinely stupid, but she could no longer be bothered to argue about it.

She sighed and punched up a star map on the visi-screen so she could make it simple for him, whatever his reasons for wanting it to be that way.

'There,' she pointed, 'right there.'

'Hey . . . yeah!' said Zaphod.

'Well?' she said.

'Well what?'

Parts of the inside of her head screamed at other parts of the inside of her head. She said, very calmly, 'It's the same sector you originally picked me up in.'

He looked at her and then looked back at the screen.

'Hey, yeah,' he said, 'now that is wild. We should have zapped straight into the middle of the Horsehead Nebula. How did we come to be there? I mean that's nowhere.'

She ignored this.

'Improbability Drive,' she said patiently. 'You explained it to me yourself. We pass through every point in the Universe, you know that.'

'Yeah, but that's one wild coincidence, isn't it?'

'Yes.'

'Picking someone up at that point? Out of the whole of the Universe to choose from? That's just too . . . I want to work this out. Computer!'

The Sirius Cybernetics Shipboard Computer which controlled and permeated every particle of the ship switched into communication mode.

'Hi there!' it said brightly and simultaneously spewed out a tiny ribbon of ticker tape just for the record. The ticker tape said, *Hi there!*

'Oh God,' said Zaphod. He hadn't worked with this computer for long but had already learned to loathe it.

The computer continued, brash and cheery as if it was selling detergent.

'I want you to know that whatever your problem, I am here to help you solve it.'

'Yeah, yeah,' said Zaphod. 'Look, I think I'll just use a piece of paper.'

'Sure thing,' said the computer, spilling out its message into a waste bin at the same time, 'I understand. If you ever want—'

'Shut up!' said Zaphod, and snatching up a pencil he sat down next to Trillian at the console.

'OK, OK . . .' said the computer in a hurt tone of voice and closed down its speech channel again.

Zaphod and Trillian pored over the figures that the Improbability flight-path scanner flashed silently up in front of them.

'Can we work out,' said Zaphod, 'from their point of view what the Improbability of their rescue was?'

'Yes, that's a constant,' said Trillian, 'two to the power of two hundred and seventy-six thousand seven hundred and nine to one against.'

'That's high. They're two lucky lucky guys.'

'Yes.'

'But relative to what we were doing when the ship picked them up . . .'

Trillian punched up the figures. They showed two-to-the-power-of-Infinity-minus-one to one against (an irrational number that only has a conventional meaning in Improbability physics).

'. . . it's pretty low,' continued Zaphod with a slight whistle.

'Yes,' agreed Trillian, and looked at him quizzically.

'That's one big whack of Improbability to be accounted for. Something pretty improbable has to show up on the balance sheet if it's all going to add up into a pretty sum.'

Zaphod scribbled a few sums, crossed them out and threw the pencil away.

'Bat's dos, I can't work it out.'

'Well?'

Zaphod knocked his two heads together in irritation and gritted his teeth.

'OK,' he said. 'Computer!'

The voice circuits sprang to life again.

'Why hello there!' they said (ticker tape, ticker tape). 'All I want to do is make your day nicer and nicer and nicer . . .'

'Yeah, well shut up and work something out for me.'

'Sure thing,' chattered the computer, 'you want a probability forecast based on . . .'

'Improbability data, yeah.'

'OK,' the computer continued. 'Here's an interesting little notion. Did you realize that most people's lives are governed by telephone numbers?'

A pained look crawled across one of Zaphod's faces and on to the other one.

'Have you flipped?' he said.

'No, but you will when I tell you that . . .'

Trillian gasped. She scrabbled at the buttons on the Improbability flight-path screen.

'Telephone number?' she said. 'Did that thing say *telephone number*?'

Numbers flashed up on the screen.

The computer had paused politely, but now it continued.

'What I was about to say was that . . .'

'Don't bother, please,' said Trillian.

'Look, what is this?' said Zaphod.

'I don't know,' said Trillian, 'but those aliens – they're on the way up to the bridge with that wretched robot. Can we pick them up on any monitor cameras?'

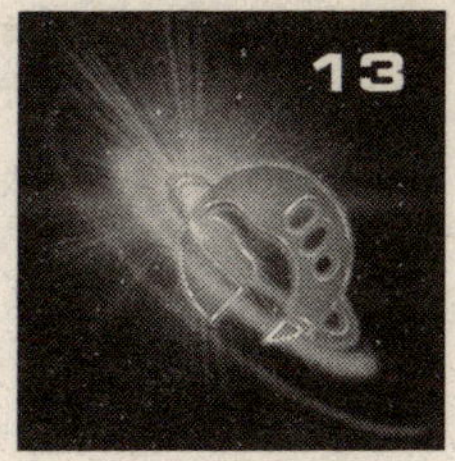

Marvin trudged on down the corridor, still moaning.

'. . . and then of course I've got this terrible pain in all the diodes down my left-hand side . . .'

'No?' said Arthur grimly as he walked along beside him. 'Really?'

'Oh yes,' said Marvin, 'I mean I've asked for them to be replaced but no one ever listens.'

'I can imagine.'

Vague whistling and humming noises were coming from Ford. 'Well well well,' he kept saying to himself, 'Zaphod Beeblebrox . . .'

Suddenly Marvin stopped, and held up a hand.

'You know what's happened now, of course?'

'No, what?' said Arthur, who didn't want to know.

'We've arrived at another of those doors.'

There was a sliding door let into the side of the corridor. Marvin eyed it suspiciously.

'Well?' said Ford impatiently. 'Do we go through?'

'Do we go through?' mimicked Marvin. 'Yes. This is the entrance to the bridge. I was told to take you to the bridge. Probably the highest demand that will be made on my intellectual capacities today I shouldn't wonder.'

Slowly, with great loathing, he stepped towards the door, like a hunter stalking his prey. Suddenly it slid open.

'Thank you,' it said, *'for making a simple door very happy.'*

Deep in Marvin's thorax gears ground.

'Funny,' he intoned funereally, 'how just when you think life can't possibly get any worse it suddenly does.'

He heaved himself through the door and left Ford and Arthur staring at each other and shrugging their shoulders. From inside they heard Marvin's voice again.

'I suppose you'll want to see the aliens now,' he said. 'Do you want me to sit in a corner and rust, or just fall apart where I'm standing?'

'Yeah, just show them in, would you, Marvin?' came another voice.

Arthur looked at Ford and was astonished to see him laughing.

'What's . . .?'

'Shhh,' said Ford, 'come on in.'

He stepped through into the bridge.

Arthur followed him in nervously and was astonished to see a man lolling back in a chair with his feet on a control console picking the teeth in his right-hand head with his left hand. The right-hand head seemed to be thoroughly preoccupied with this task, but the left-hand one was grinning a broad, relaxed, nonchalant grin. The number of things that Arthur couldn't believe he was seeing was fairly large. His jaw flopped about at a loose end for a while.

The peculiar man waved a lazy wave at Ford and with

an appalling affectation of nonchalance said, 'Ford, hi, how are you? Glad you could drop in.'

Ford was not going to be outcooled.

'Zaphod,' he drawled, 'great to see you, you're looking well, the extra arm suits you. Nice ship you've stolen.'

Arthur goggled at him.

'You mean you know this guy?' he said, waving a wild finger at Zaphod.

'Know him!' exclaimed Ford. 'He's . . .' He paused, and decided to do the introductions the other way round. 'Oh, Zaphod, this is a friend of mine, Arthur Dent,' he said. 'I saved him when his planet blew up.'

'Oh sure,' said Zaphod, 'hi, Arthur, glad you could make it.' His right-hand head looked round casually, said, 'Hi,' and went back to having its teeth picked.

Ford carried on. 'And Arthur,' he said, 'this is my semi-cousin Zaphod Beeb—'

'We've met,' said Arthur sharply.

When you're cruising down the road in the fast lane and you lazily sail past a few hard-driving cars and are feeling pretty pleased with yourself and then accidentally change down from fourth to first instead of third thus making your engine leap out of your bonnet in a rather ugly mess, it tends to throw you off your stride in much the same way that this remark threw Ford Prefect off his.

'Er . . . what?' he said.

'I said we've met.'

Zaphod gave an awkward start of surprise and jabbed a gum sharply.

'Hey . . . er, have we? Hey . . . er . . .'

Ford rounded on Arthur with an angry flash in his

eyes. Now he felt he was back on home ground he suddenly began to resent having lumbered himself with this ignorant primitive who knew as much about the affairs of the Galaxy as an Ilford-based gnat knew about life in Peking.

'What do you mean, you've met?' he demanded. 'This is Zaphod Beeblebrox from Betelgeuse Five you know, not bloody Martin Smith from Croydon.'

'I don't care,' said Arthur coldly. 'We've met, haven't we, Zaphod Beeblebrox – or should I say . . . Phil?'

'What!' shouted Ford.

'You'll have to remind me,' said Zaphod. 'I've a terrible memory for species.'

'It was at a party,' pursued Arthur.

'Yeah, well I doubt that,' said Zaphod.

'Cool it, will you, Arthur!' demanded Ford.

Arthur would not be deterred. 'A party six months ago. On Earth . . . England . . .'

Zaphod shook his head with a tight-lipped smile.

'London,' insisted Arthur, 'Islington.'

'Oh,' said Zaphod with a guilty start, '*that* party.'

This wasn't fair on Ford at all. He looked backwards and forwards between Arthur and Zaphod. 'What?' he said to Zaphod. 'You don't mean to say you've been on that miserable little planet as well, do you?'

'No, of course not,' said Zaphod breezily. 'Well, I may have just dropped in briefly, you know, on my way somewhere . . .'

'But I was stuck there for fifteen years!'

'Well, I didn't know that, did I?'

'But what were you doing there?'

'Looking about, you know.'

'He gatecrashed a party,' said Arthur, trembling with anger, 'a fancy-dress party . . .'

'It would have to be, wouldn't it?' said Ford.

'At this party,' persisted Arthur, 'was a girl . . . Oh well, look it doesn't matter now. The whole place has gone up in smoke anyway . . .'

'I wish you'd stop sulking about that bloody planet,' said Ford. 'Who was the lady?'

'Oh, just somebody. Well all right, I wasn't doing very well with her. I'd been trying all evening. Hell, she was something though. Beautiful, charming, devastatingly intelligent, at least I'd got her to myself for a bit and was plying her with a bit of talk when this friend of yours barges up and says, *"Hey, doll, is this guy boring you? Why don't you talk to me instead? I'm from a different planet."* I never saw her again.'

'Zaphod?' exclaimed Ford.

'Yes,' said Arthur, glaring at him and trying not to feel foolish. 'He only had the two arms and the one head and he called himself Phil, but . . .'

'But you must admit he did turn out to be from another planet,' said Trillian wandering into sight at the other end of the bridge. She gave Arthur a pleasant smile which settled on him like a ton of bricks and then turned her attention to the ship's controls again.

There was silence for a few seconds, and then out of the scrambled mess of Arthur's brain crawled some words.

'Tricia McMillan?' he said. 'What are you doing here?'

'Same as you,' she said, 'I hitched a lift. After all with a degree in maths and another in astrophysics what else was there to do? It was either that or the dole queue again on Monday.'

'Infinity minus one,' chattered the computer. 'Improbability sum now complete.'

Zaphod looked about him, at Ford, at Arthur, and then at Trillian.

'Trillian,' he said, 'is this sort of thing going to happen every time we use the Improbability Drive?'

'Very probably, I'm afraid,' she said.

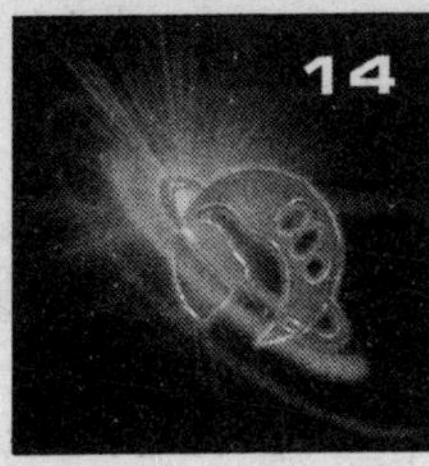

The *Heart of Gold* fled on silently through the night of space, now on conventional photon drive. Its crew of four were ill at ease knowing that they had been brought together not of their own volition or by simple coincidence, but by some curious perversion of physics – as if relationships between people were susceptible to the same laws that governed the relationships between atoms and molecules.

As the ship's artificial night closed in they were each grateful to retire to separate cabins and try to rationalize their thoughts.

Trillian couldn't sleep. She sat on a couch and stared at a small cage which contained her last and only links with Earth – two white mice that she had insisted Zaphod let her bring. She had expected never to see the planet again, but she was disturbed by her negative reaction to the news of the planet's destruction. It seemed remote and unreal and she could find no thoughts to think about it. She watched the mice scurrying round the cage and running furiously in their little plastic treadwheels till they occupied her whole attention. Suddenly she shook herself and went back on to the bridge to watch over the tiny flashing lights and figures that charted the ship's progress through the void. She wished she knew what it was she was trying not to think about.

Zaphod couldn't sleep. He also wished he knew what it was that he wouldn't let himself think about. For as long as he could remember he'd suffered from a vague nagging feeling of being not all there. Most of the time he was able to put this thought aside and not worry about it, but it had been re-awakened by the sudden inexplicable arrival of Ford Prefect and Arthur Dent. Somehow it seemed to conform to a pattern that he couldn't see.

Ford couldn't sleep. He was too excited about being back on the road again. Fifteen years of virtual imprisonment were over, just as he was finally beginning to give up hope. Knocking about with Zaphod for a bit promised to be a lot of fun, though there seemed to be something faintly odd about his semi-cousin that he couldn't put his finger on. The fact that he had become President of the Galaxy was frankly astonishing, as was the manner of his leaving the post. Was there a reason behind it? There would be no point in asking Zaphod, he never appeared to have a reason for anything he did at all: he had turned unfathomability into an art form. He attacked everything in life with a mixture of extraordinary genius and naive incompetence and it was often difficult to tell which was which.

Arthur slept: he was terribly tired.

There was a tap at Zaphod's door. It slid open.

'Zaphod . . .?'

'Yeah?'

Trillian stood outlined in the oval of light.

'I think we just found what you came to look for.'

'Hey, yeah?'

Ford gave up the attempt to sleep. In the corner of his cabin was a small computer screen and keyboard. He sat at it for a while and tried to compose a new entry for the *Guide* on the subject of Vogons but couldn't think of anything vitriolic enough so he gave that up too, wrapped a robe round himself and went for a walk to the bridge.

As he entered he was surprised to see two figures hunched excitedly over the instruments.

'See? The ship's about to move into orbit,' Trillian was saying. 'There's a planet out there. It's at the exact coordinates you predicted.'

Zaphod heard a noise and looked up.

'Ford!' he hissed. 'Hey, come and take a look at this.'

Ford went and had a look at it. It was a series of figures flickering over a screen.

'You recognize those Galactic coordinates?' said Zaphod.

'No.'

'I'll give you a clue. Computer!'

'Hi, gang!' enthused the computer. 'This is getting real sociable, isn't it?'

'Shut up,' said Zaphod, 'and show up the screens.'

Light on the bridge sank. Pinpoints of light played across the consoles and reflected in four pairs of eyes that stared up at the external monitor screens.

There was absolutely nothing on them.

'Recognize that?' whispered Zaphod.

Ford frowned.

'Er, no,' he said.

'What do you see?'

'Nothing.'

'Recognize it?'

'What are you talking about?'

'We're in the Horsehead Nebula. One whole vast dark cloud.'

'And I was meant to recognize that from a blank screen?'

'Inside a dark nebula is the only place in the Galaxy you'd see a dark screen.'

'Very good.'

Zaphod laughed. He was clearly very excited about something, almost childishly so.

'Hey, this is really terrific, this is just far too much!'

'What's so great about being stuck in a dust cloud?' said Ford.

'What would you reckon to find here?' urged Zaphod.

'Nothing.'

'No stars? No planets?'

'No.'

'Computer!' shouted Zaphod. 'Rotate angle of vision through one-eighty degrees and don't talk about it!'

For a moment it seemed that nothing was happening, then a brightness glowed at the edge of the huge screen. A red star the size of a small plate crept across it followed quickly by another one – a binary system. Then a vast crescent sliced into the corner of the picture – a red glare shading away into deep black, the night side of the planet.

'I've found it!' cried Zaphod, thumping the console. 'I've found it!'

Ford stared at it in astonishment.

'What is it?' he said.

'That . . .' said Zaphod, 'is the most improbable planet that ever existed.'

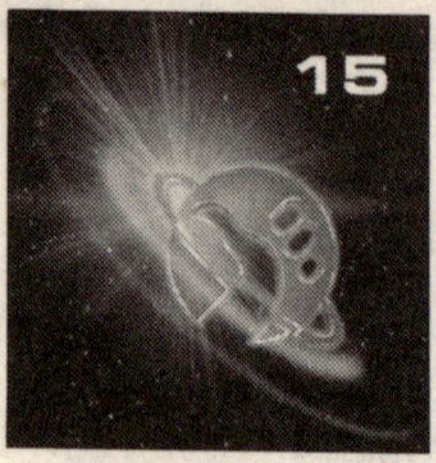

(Excerpt from *The Hitchhiker's Guide to the Galaxy*, Page 634784, Section 5a. Entry: *Magrathea*)

Far back in the mists of ancient time, in the great and glorious days of the former Galactic Empire, life was wild, rich, and largely tax-free.

Mighty starships plied their way between exotic suns, seeking adventure and reward amongst the furthest reaches of Galactic space. In those days spirits were brave, the stakes were high, men were real men, women were real women, and small furry creatures from Alpha Centauri were real small furry creatures from Alpha Centauri. And all dared to brave unknown terrors, to do mighty deeds, to boldly split infinitives that no man had split before – and thus was the Empire forged.

Many men of course became extremely rich, but this was perfectly natural and nothing to be ashamed of because no one was really poor – at least no one worth speaking of. And for all the richest and most successful merchants life inevitably became rather dull and niggly, and they began to imagine that this was therefore the fault of the worlds they'd settled on – none of them was entirely satisfactory: either the climate wasn't quite right in the later part of the afternoon, or the day was half an hour too long, or the sea was exactly the wrong shade of pink.

And thus were created the conditions for a staggering new form of specialist industry: custom-made luxury planet building. The home of this industry was the planet Magrathea, where hyperspatial engineers sucked matter through white holes in space to form it into dream planets – gold planets, platinum planets, soft rubber planets with lots of earthquakes – all lovingly made to meet the exacting standards that the Galaxy's richest men naturally came to expect.

But so successful was this venture that Magrathea itself soon became the richest planet of all time and the rest of the Galaxy was reduced to abject poverty. And so the system broke down, the Empire collapsed, and a long sullen silence settled over a billion hungry worlds, disturbed only by the pen scratchings of scholars as they laboured into the night over smug little treatises on the value of a planned political economy.

Magrathea itself disappeared and its memory soon passed into the obscurity of legend.

In these enlightened days, of course, no one believes a word of it.

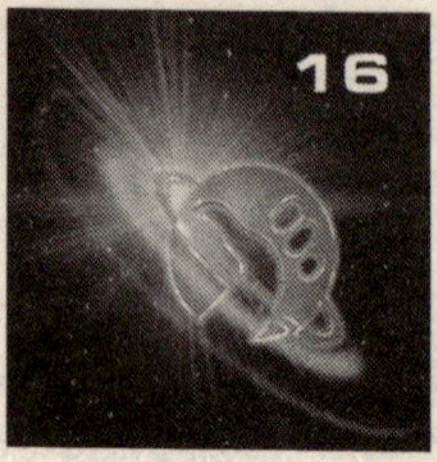

Arthur awoke to the sound of argument and went to the bridge. Ford was waving his arms about.

'You're crazy, Zaphod,' he was saying, 'Magrathea is a myth, a fairy story, it's what parents tell their kids about at night if they want them to grow up to become economists, it's . . .'

'And that's what we are currently in orbit about,' insisted Zaphod.

'Look, I can't help what you may personally be in orbit around,' said Ford, 'but this ship . . .'

'Computer!' shouted Zaphod.

'Oh no . . .'

'Hi there! This is Eddie your shipboard computer, and I'm feeling just great, guys, and I know I'm just going to get a bundle of kicks out of any program you care to run through me.'

Arthur looked enquiringly at Trillian. She motioned him to come on in but keep quiet.

'Computer,' said Zaphod, 'tell us again what our present trajectory is.'

'A real pleasure, feller,' it burbled, 'we are currently in

Arthur Dent (Martin Freeman): 'You've got to know where your towel is.'

Ford Prefect (Mos Def) – not an out-of-work actor from Guildford, after all.

Marvin the Paranoid Android (Warwick Davis):
'Brain the size of a planet.'

Zaphod Beeblebrox, President of the Galaxy (Sam Rockwell).

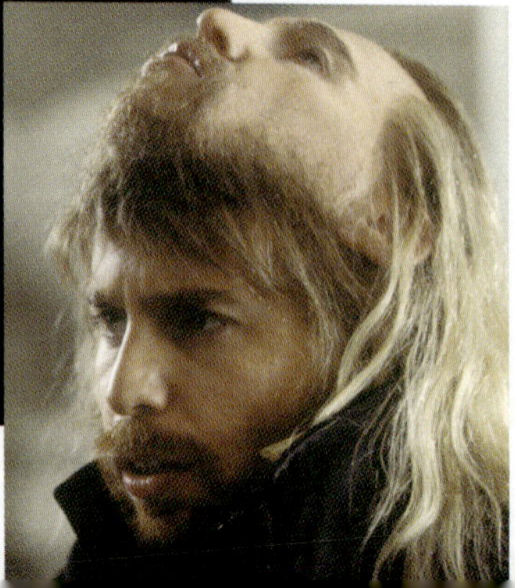

Zaphod's prosthetic second head for 'long shots'.

Trillian (Zooey Deschanel) – four or five degrees, one in maths, one in astrophysics, another in biology . . .

Trillian with the *Heart of Gold* instruction manual.

Slartibartfast
(Bill Nighy)
– designer of
Norway's
fjords.

Humma Kavula
(John Malkovich)
in his inner sanctum.

Arthur and Ford are subjected to Jeltz's Vogon poetry.

Vogon Commander Kwaltz (Ian McNeice) and Vice-President of the Galaxy Questular (Anna Chancellor) in pursuit of Zaphod.

Coming full circle: Nick Goldsmith and Garth Jennings with Marvins old and new.

orbit at an altitude of three hundred miles around the legendary planet of Magrathea.'

'Proving nothing,' said Ford. 'I wouldn't trust that computer to speak my weight.'

'I can do that for you, sure,' enthused the computer, punching out more tickertape. 'I can even work out your personality problems to ten decimal places if it will help.'

Trillian interrupted.

'Zaphod,' she said, 'any minute now we will be swinging round to the daylight side of this planet,' adding, 'whatever it turns out to be.'

'Hey, what do you mean by that? The planet's where I predicted it would be, isn't it?'

'Yes, I know there's a planet there. I'm not arguing with anyone, it's just that I wouldn't know Magrathea from any other lump of cold rock. Dawn's coming up if you want it.'

'OK, OK,' muttered Zaphod. 'Let's at least give our eyes a good time. Computer!'

'Hi there! What can I—'

'Just shut up and give us a view of the planet again.'

A dark featureless mass once more filled the screens – the planet rolling away beneath them.

They watched for a moment in silence, but Zaphod was fidgety with excitement.

'We are now traversing the night side . . .' he said in a hushed voice. The planet rolled on.

'The surface of the planet is now three hundred miles beneath us . . .' he continued. He was trying to restore a sense of occasion to what he felt should have been a great moment. Magrathea! He was piqued by Ford's sceptical reaction. Magrathea!

'In a few seconds,' he continued, 'we should see . . . there!'

The moment carried itself. Even the most seasoned star tramp can't help but shiver at the spectacular drama of a sunrise seen from space, but a binary sunrise is one of the marvels of the Galaxy.

Out of the utter blackness stabbed a sudden point of blinding light. It crept up by slight degrees and spread sideways in a thin crescent blade, and within seconds two suns were visible, furnaces of light, searing the black edge of the horizon with white fire. Fierce shafts of colour streaked through the thin atmosphere beneath them.

'The fires of dawn!' breathed Zaphod. 'The twin suns of Soulianis and Rahm . . . !'

'Or whatever,' said Ford quietly.

'Soulianis and Rahm!' insisted Zaphod.

The suns blazed into the pitch of space and a low ghostly music floated through the bridge: Marvin was humming ironically because he hated humans so much.

As Ford gazed at the spectacle of light before them excitement burnt inside him, but only the excitement of seeing a strange new planet, it was enough for him to see it as it was. It faintly irritated him that Zaphod had to impose some ludicrous fantasy on to the scene to make it work for him. All this Magrathea nonsense seemed juvenile. Isn't it enough to see that a garden is beautiful without having to believe that there are fairies at the bottom of it too?

All this Magrathea business seemed totally incomprehensible to Arthur. He edged up to Trillian and asked her what was going on.

'I only know what Zaphod's told me,' she whispered. 'Apparently Magrathea is some kind of legend from way back which no one seriously believes in. Bit like Atlantis on Earth, except that the legends say the Magratheans used to manufacture planets.'

Arthur blinked at the screens and felt he was missing something important. Suddenly he realized what it was.

'Is there any tea on this spaceship?' he asked.

More of the planet was unfolding beneath them as the *Heart of Gold* streaked along its orbital path. The suns now stood high in the black sky, the pyrotechnics of dawn were over, and the surface of the planet appeared bleak and forbidding in the common light of day – grey, dusty, and only dimly contoured. It looked dead and cold as a crypt. From time to time promising features would appear on the distant horizon – ravines, maybe mountains, maybe even cities – but as they approached the lines would soften and blur into anonymity and nothing would transpire. The planet's surface was blurred by time, by the slow movement of the thin stagnant air that had crept across it for century upon century.

Clearly, it was very very old.

A moment of doubt came to Ford as he watched the grey landscape move beneath them. The immensity of time worried him, he could feel it as a presence. He cleared his throat.

'Well, even supposing it is . . .'

'It is,' said Zaphod.

'Which it isn't,' continued Ford. 'What do you want with it, anyway? There's nothing there.'

'Not on the surface,' said Zaphod.

'All right, just supposing there's something, I take it you're not here for the sheer industrial archaeology of it all. What are you after?'

One of Zaphod's heads looked away. The other one looked round to see what the first was looking at, but it wasn't looking at anything very much.

'Well,' said Zaphod airily, 'it's partly the curiosity, partly a sense of adventure, but mostly I think it's the fame and the money . . .'

Ford glanced at him sharply. He got a very strong impression that Zaphod hadn't the faintest idea why he was there at all.

'You know, I don't like the look of that planet at all,' said Trillian, shivering.

'Ah, take no notice,' said Zaphod, 'with half the wealth of the former Galactic Empire stored on it somewhere it can afford to look frumpy.'

Bullshit, thought Ford. Even supposing this was the home of some ancient civilization now gone to dust, even supposing a number of exceedingly unlikely things, there was no way that vast treasures of wealth were going to be stored there in any form that would still have meaning now. He shrugged.

'I think it's just a dead planet,' he said.

'The suspense is killing me,' said Arthur testily.

Stress and nervous tension are now serious social problems in all parts of the Galaxy, and it is in order that this situation should not be in any way exacerbated that the following facts will now be revealed in advance.

The planet in question *is* in fact the legendary Magrathea.

The deadly missile attack shortly to be launched by an ancient automatic defence system will result merely in the breakage of three coffee cups and a mousecage, the bruising of somebody's upper arm, and the untimely creation and sudden demise of a bowl of petunias and an innocent sperm whale.

In order that some sense of mystery should still be preserved, no revelation will yet be made concerning whose upper arm sustains the bruise. This fact may safely be made the subject of suspense since it is of no significance whatsoever.

After a fairly shaky start to the day, Arthur's mind was beginning to reassemble itself from the shellshocked fragments the previous day had left him with. He had found a Nutri-Matic machine which had provided him with a plastic cup filled with a liquid that was almost, but not quite, entirely unlike tea. The way it functioned was very interesting. When the Drink button was pressed it made an instant but highly detailed examination of the subject's taste buds, a spectroscopic analysis of the subject's metabolism and then sent tiny experimental signals down the neural pathways to the taste centres of the subject's brain to see what was likely to go down well. However, no one knew quite why it did this because it invariably delivered a cupful of liquid that was almost, but not quite, entirely unlike tea. The Nutri-Matic was designed and manufactured by the Sirius Cybernetics Corporation, whose complaints department now covers all the major land masses of the first three planets in the Sirius Tau star system.

Arthur drank the liquid and found it reviving. He glanced up at the screens again and watched a few more hundred miles of barren greyness slide past. It suddenly occurred to him to ask a question which had been bothering him.

'Is it safe?' he said.

'Magrathea's been dead for five million years,' said Zaphod, 'of course it's safe. Even the ghosts will have settled down and raised families by now.'

At which point a strange and inexplicable sound thrilled suddenly through the bridge – a noise as of a distant fanfare; a hollow, reedy, insubstantial sound. It preceded a voice that was equally hollow, reedy and insubstantial. The voice said '*Greetings to you . . .*'

Someone from the dead planet was talking to them.

'Computer!' shouted Zaphod.

'Hi there!'

'What the photon is it?'

'Oh, just some five-million-year-old tape that's being broadcast at us.'

'A what? A recording?'

'Shush!' said Ford. 'It's carrying on.'

The voice was old, courteous, almost charming, but was underscored with quite unmistakable menace.

'*This is a recorded announcement,*' it said, '*as I'm afraid we're all out at the moment. The commercial council of Magrathea thanks you for your esteemed visit . . .*'

('A voice from ancient Magrathea!' shouted Zaphod.

'OK, OK,' said Ford.)

'*. . . but regrets,*' continued the voice, '*that the entire planet is temporarily closed for business. Thank you. If you would care to leave your name and the address of a planet where you can be contacted, kindly speak when you hear the tone.*'

A short buzz followed, then silence.

'They want to get rid of us,' said Trillian nervously. 'What do we do?'

'It's just a recording,' said Zaphod. 'We keep going. Got that, computer?'

'I got it,' said the computer and gave the ship an extra kick of speed.

They waited.

After a second or so came the fanfare once again, and then the voice.

'We would like to assure you that as soon as our business is resumed announcements will be made in all fashionable magazines and colour supplements, when our clients will once again be able to select from all that's best in contemporary geography.' The menace in the voice took on a sharper edge. *'Meanwhile we thank our clients for their kind interest and would ask them to leave. Now.'*

Arthur looked round the nervous faces of his companions.

'Well, I suppose we'd better be going, then, hadn't we?' he suggested.

'Shhh!' said Zaphod. 'There's absolutely nothing to be worried about.'

'Then why's everyone so tense?'

'They're just interested!' shouted Zaphod. 'Computer, start a descent into the atmosphere and prepare for landing.'

This time the fanfare was quite perfunctory, the voice now distinctly cold.

'It is most gratifying,' it said, *'that your enthusiasm for our planet continues unabated, and so we would like to assure*

you that the guided missiles currently converging with your ship are part of a special service we extend to all of our most enthusiastic clients, and the fully armed nuclear warheads are of course merely a courtesy detail. We look forward to your custom in future lives . . . Thank you.'

The voice snapped off.

'Oh,' said Trillian.

'Er . . .' said Arthur.

'Well?' said Ford.

'Look,' said Zaphod, 'will you get it into your heads? That's just a recorded message. It's millions of years old. It doesn't apply to us, get it?'

'What,' said Trillian quietly, 'about the missiles?'

'Missiles? Don't make me laugh.'

Ford tapped Zaphod on the shoulder and pointed at the rear screen. Clear in the distance behind them two silver darts were climbing through the atmosphere towards the ship. A quick change of magnification brought them into close focus – two massively real rockets thundering through the sky. The suddenness of it was shocking.

'I think they're going to have a very good try at applying to us,' said Ford.

Zaphod stared at them in astonishment.

'Hey, this is terrific!' he said. 'Someone down there is trying to kill us!'

'Terrific,' said Arthur.

'But don't you see what this means?'

'Yes. We're going to die.'

'Yes, but apart from that.'

'*Apart* from that?'

'It means we must be on to something!'

'How soon can we get off it?'

Second by second the image of the missiles on the screen grew larger. They had swung round now on to a direct homing course so that all that could be seen of them now was the warheads, head on.

'As a matter of interest,' said Trillian, 'what are we going to do?'

'Just keep cool,' said Zaphod.

'Is that all?' shouted Arthur.

'No, we're also going to . . . er . . . take evasive action!' said Zaphod with a sudden access of panic. 'Computer, what evasive action can we take?'

'Er, none I'm afraid, guys,' said the computer.

'. . . or something,' said Zaphod, '. . . er . . .' he said.

'There seems to be something jamming my guidance systems,' explained the computer brightly. 'Impact minus forty-five seconds. Please call me Eddie if it will help you to relax.'

Zaphod tried to run several equally decisive directions simultaneously. 'Right!' he said. 'Er . . . we've got to get manual control of this ship.'

'Can you fly her?' asked Ford pleasantly.

'No, can you?'

'No.'

'Trillian, can you?'

'No.'

'Fine,' said Zaphod, relaxing. 'We'll do it together.'

'I can't either,' said Arthur, who felt it was time he began to assert himself.

'I'd guessed that,' said Zaphod. 'OK, computer, I want full manual control now.'

'You got it,' said the computer.

Several large desk panels slid open and banks of control consoles sprang up out of them, showering the crew with bits of expanded polystyrene packaging and balls of rolled-up cellophane: these controls had never been used before.

Zaphod stared at them wildly.

'OK, Ford,' he said, 'full retro thrust and ten degrees starboard. Or something . . .'

'Good luck, guys,' chirped the computer, 'impact minus thirty seconds . . .'

Ford leapt to the controls – only a few of them made any immediate sense to him so he pulled those. The ship shook and screamed as its guidance rocket jets tried to push it every which way simultaneously. He released half of them and the ship spun round in a tight arc and headed back the way it had come, straight towards the oncoming missiles.

Air cushions ballooned out of the walls in an instant as everyone was thrown against them. For a few seconds the inertial forces held them flattened and squirming for breath, unable to move. Zaphod struggled and pushed in manic desperation and finally managed a savage kick at a small lever that formed part of the guidance system.

The lever snapped off. The ship twisted sharply and rocketed upwards. The crew were hurled violently back across the cabin. Ford's copy of *The Hitchhiker's Guide to the Galaxy* smashed into another section of the control console with the combined result that the guide started to explain to anyone who cared to listen about the best ways of smuggling Antarean parakeet glands out of

Antares (an Antarean parakeet gland stuck on a small stick is a revolting but much-sought-after cocktail delicacy and very large sums of money are often paid for them by very rich idiots who want to impress other very rich idiots), and the ship suddenly dropped out of the sky like a stone.

It was of course more or less at this moment that one of the crew sustained a nasty bruise to the upper arm. This should be emphasized because, as has already been revealed, they escape otherwise completely unharmed and the deadly nuclear missiles do not eventually hit the ship. The safety of the crew is absolutely assured.

'Impact minus twenty seconds, guys . . .' said the computer.

'Then turn the bloody engines back on!' bawled Zaphod.

'Oh, sure thing, guys,' said the computer. With a subtle roar the engines cut back in; the ship smoothly flattened out of its dive and headed back towards the missiles again.

The computer started to sing.

'*When you walk through the storm . . .*' it whined nasally, '*hold your head up high . . .*'

Zaphod screamed at it to shut up, but his voice was lost in the din of what they quite naturally assumed was approaching destruction.

'*And don't . . . be afraid . . . of the dark!*' Eddie wailed.

The ship in flattening out had in fact flattened out upside down and lying on the ceiling as they were it was now totally impossible for any of the crew to reach the guidance systems.

'At the end of the storm . . .' crooned Eddie.

The two missiles loomed massively on the screens as they thundered towards the ship.

'. . . is a golden sky . . .'

But by an extraordinarily lucky chance they had not yet fully corrected their flight paths to that of the erratically weaving ship, and they passed right under it.

'and the sweet silver song of the lark . . . Revised impact time fifteen seconds, fellas . . . *Walk on through the wind . . .'*

The missiles banked round in a screeching arc and plunged back into pursuit.

'This is it,' said Arthur watching them. 'We are now quite definitely going to die, aren't we?'

'I wish you'd stop saying that,' shouted Ford.

'Well, we are, aren't we?'

'Yes.'

'Walk on through the rain . . .' sang Eddie.

A thought struck Arthur. He struggled to his feet.

'Why doesn't anyone turn on this Improbability Drive thing?' he said. 'We could probably reach that.'

'What are you, crazy?' said Zaphod. 'Without proper programming anything could happen.'

'Does that matter at this stage?' shouted Arthur.

'Though your dreams be tossed and blown . . .' sang Eddie.

Arthur scrambled up on to one of the excitingly chunky pieces of moulded contouring where the curve of the wall met the ceiling.

'Walk on, walk on, with hope in your heart . . .'

'Does anyone know why Arthur can't turn on the Improbability Drive?' shouted Trillian.

'And you'll never walk alone . . . Impact minus five seconds, it's been great knowing you, guys, God bless . . . *You'll ne . . . ver . . . walk . . . alone!'*

'I said,' yelled Trillian, 'does anyone know—'

The next thing that happened was a mind-mangling explosion of noise and light.

And the next thing that happened after that was that the *Heart of Gold* continued on its way perfectly normally with a rather fetchingly redesigned interior. It was somewhat larger, and done out in delicate pastel shades of green and blue. In the centre a spiral staircase, leading nowhere in particular, stood in a spray of ferns and yellow flowers and next to it a stone sundial pedestal housed the main computer terminal. Cunningly deployed lighting and mirrors created the illusion of standing in a conservatory overlooking a wide stretch of exquisitely manicured garden. Around the periphery of the conservatory area stood marble-topped tables on intricately beautiful wrought-iron legs. As you gazed into the polished surface of the marble the vague forms of instruments became visible, and as you touched them the instruments materialized instantly under your hands. Looked at from the correct angles the mirrors appeared to reflect all the required data readouts, though it was far from clear where they were reflected from. It was in fact sensationally beautiful.

Relaxing in a wickerwork sun chair, Zaphod Beeblebrox said, 'What the hell happened?'

'Well, I was just saying,' said Arthur, lounging by a

small fish pool, 'there's this Improbability Drive switch over here . . .' He waved at where it had been. There was a potted plant there now.

'But where are we?' said Ford, who was sitting on the spiral staircase, a nicely chilled Pan Galactic Gargle Blaster in his hand.

'Exactly where we were, I think . . .' said Trillian, as all about them the mirrors suddenly showed them an image of the blighted landscape of Magrathea which still scooted along beneath them.

Zaphod leapt out of his seat.

'Then what's happened to the missiles?' he said.

A new and astounding image appeared in the mirrors.

'They would appear,' said Ford doubtfully, 'to have turned into a bowl of petunias and a very surprised-looking whale . . .'

'At an improbability factor,' cut in Eddie, who hadn't changed a bit, 'of eight million seven hundred and sixty-seven thousand one hundred and twenty-eight to one against.'

Zaphod stared at Arthur.

'Did you think of that, Earthman?' he demanded.

'Well,' said Arthur, 'all I did was . . .'

'That's very good thinking, you know. Turn on the Improbability Drive for a second without first activating the proofing screens. Hey, kid, you just saved our lives, you know that?'

'Oh,' said Arthur, 'well, it was nothing really . . .'

'Was it?' said Zaphod. 'Oh well, forget it, then. OK, computer, take us in to land.'

'But . . .'

'I said forget it.'

Another thing that got forgotten was the fact that against all probability a sperm whale had suddenly been called into existence several miles above the surface of an alien planet.

And since this is not a naturally tenable position for a whale, this poor innocent creature had very little time to come to terms with its identity as a whale before it then had to come to terms with not being a whale any more.

This is a complete record of its thought from the moment it began its life till the moment it ended it.

Ah . . . ! What's happening? it thought.

Er, excuse me, who am I?

Hello?

Why am I here? What's my purpose in life?

What do I mean by who am I?

Calm down, get a grip now . . . Oh! This is an interesting sensation, what is it? It's a sort of . . . yawning, tingling sensation in my . . . my . . . well, I suppose I'd better start finding names for things if I want to make any headway in what for the sake of what I shall call an argument I shall call the world, so let's call it my stomach.

Good. Ooooh, it's getting quite strong. And hey, what about this whistling roaring sound going past what I'm suddenly going to call my head? Perhaps I can call that . . . wind! Is that a good name? It'll do . . . perhaps I can find a better name for it later when I've found out what it's for. It must be something very important because there certainly seems to be a hell of a lot of it. Hey! What's this thing? This . . . let's call it a tail – yeah, tail. Hey! I can really thrash it about pretty good, can't I? Wow! Wow! That feels great! Doesn't seem to achieve very much but I'll probably find out what it's for later on. Now – have I built up any coherent picture of things yet?

No.

Never mind, hey, this is really exciting, so much to find out about, so much to look forward to, I'm quite dizzy with anticipation . . .

Or is it the wind?

There really is a lot of that now, isn't there?

And wow! Hey! What's this thing suddenly coming towards me very fast? Very very fast. So big and flat and round, it needs a big wide sounding name like . . . ow . . . ound . . . round . . . ground! That's it! That's a good name – ground!

I wonder if it will be friends with me?

And the rest, after a sudden wet thud, was silence.

Curiously enough, the only thing that went through the mind of the bowl of petunias as it fell was, Oh no, not again. Many people have speculated that if we knew exactly why the bowl of petunias had thought that we would know a lot more about the nature of the Universe than we do now.

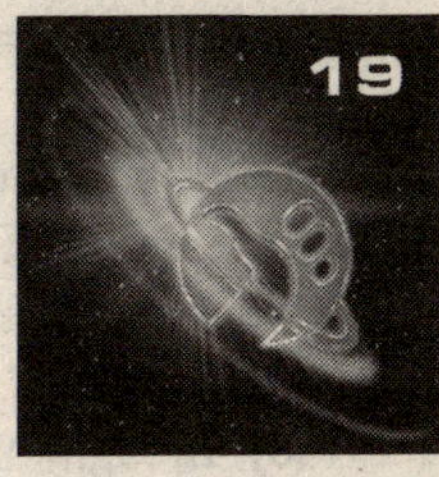

'Are we taking this robot with us?' said Ford, looking with distaste at Marvin, who was standing in an awkward hunched posture in the corner under a small palm tree.

Zaphod glanced away from the mirror screens which presented a panoramic view of the blighted landscape on which the *Heart of Gold* had now landed.

'Oh, the Paranoid Android,' he said. 'Yeah, we'll take him.'

'But what are you supposed to do with a manically depressed robot?'

'You think you've got problems,' said Marvin as if he was addressing a newly occupied coffin, 'what are you supposed to do if you *are* a manically depressed robot? No, don't bother to answer that, I'm fifty thousand times more intelligent than you and even I don't know the answer. It gives me a headache just trying to think down to your level.'

Trillian burst in through the door from her cabin.

'My white mice have escaped!' she said.

An expression of deep worry and concern failed to cross either of Zaphod's faces.

'Nuts to your white mice,' he said.

Trillian glared an upset glare at him, and disappeared again.

It is possible that her remark would have commanded greater attention had it been generally realized that human beings were only the third most intelligent life form present on the planet Earth, instead of (as was generally thought by most independent observers) the second.

'Good afternoon, boys.'

The voice was oddly familiar, but oddly different. It had a matriarchal twang. It announced itself to the crew as they arrived at the airlock hatchway that would let them out on the planet surface.

They looked at each other in puzzlement.

'It's the computer,' explained Zaphod. 'I discovered it had an emergency back-up personality that I thought might work out better.'

'Now this is going to be your first day out on a strange new planet,' continued Eddie's new voice, 'so I want you all wrapped up snug and warm, and no playing with any naughty bug-eyed monsters.'

Zaphod tapped impatiently on the hatch.

'I'm sorry,' he said, 'I think we might be better off with a slide rule.'

'Right!' snapped the computer. 'Who said that?'

'Will you open up the exit hatch, please, computer?' said Zaphod, trying not to get angry.

'Not until whoever said that owns up,' urged the computer, stamping a few synapses closed.

'Oh God,' muttered Ford. He slumped against a bulkhead and started to count to ten. He was desperately worried that one day sentient life forms would forget how to do this. Only by counting could humans demonstrate their independence of computers.

'Come on,' said Eddie sternly.

'Computer—' began Zaphod.

'I'm waiting,' interrupted Eddie. 'I can wait all day if necessary . . .'

'Computer . . .' said Zaphod again, who had been trying to think of some subtle piece of reasoning to put the computer down with, and had decided not to bother competing with it on its own ground, 'if you don't open that exit hatch this moment I shall zap straight off to your major data banks and reprogram you with a very large axe, got that?'

Eddie, shocked, paused and considered this.

Ford carried on counting quietly. This is about the most aggressive thing you can do to a computer, the equivalent of going up to a human being and saying, *'Blood . . . blood . . . blood . . . blood . . .'*

Finally Eddie said quietly, 'I can see this relationship is something we're all going to have to work at,' and the hatchway opened.

An icy wind ripped into them, they hugged themselves warmly and stepped down the ramp on to the barren dust of Magrathea.

'It'll all end in tears, I know it,' shouted Eddie after them and closed the hatchway again.

A few minutes later he opened and closed the hatchway again in response to a command that caught him entirely by surprise.

Five figures wandered slowly over the blighted land. Bits of it were dullish grey, bits of it dullish brown, the rest of it rather less interesting to look at. It was like a dried-out marsh, now barren of all vegetation and covered with a layer of dust about an inch thick. It was very cold.

Zaphod was clearly rather depressed about it. He stalked off by himself and was soon lost to sight behind a slight rise in the ground.

The wind stung Arthur's eyes and ears, and the stale thin air clasped his throat. However, the thing that was stung most was his mind.

'It's fantastic . . .' he said, and his own voice rattled his ears. Sound carried badly in this thin atmosphere.

'Desolate hole, if you ask me,' said Ford. 'I could have more fun in a cat litter.' He felt a mounting irritation. Of all the planets in all the star systems of all the Galaxy – many wild and exotic, seething with life – didn't he just have to turn up at a dump like this after fifteen years of being a castaway? Not even a hot-dog stand in evidence. He stooped down and picked up a cold clod of earth, but there was nothing underneath it worth crossing thousands of light years to look at.

'No,' insisted Arthur, 'don't you understand, this is the first time I've actually stood on the surface of another planet . . . a whole alien world . . . ! Pity it's such a dump, though.'

Trillian hugged herself, shivered and frowned. She could have sworn she saw a slight and unexpected movement out of the corner of her eye, but when she glanced in that direction all she could see was the ship, still and silent, a hundred yards or so behind them.

She was relieved when a second or so later they caught sight of Zaphod standing on top of the ridge of ground and waving to them to come and join him.

He seemed to be excited, but they couldn't clearly hear what he was saying because of the thinnish atmosphere and the wind.

As they approached the ridge of higher ground they became aware that it seemed to be circular – a crater about a hundred and fifty yards wide. Round the outside of the crater the sloping ground was splattered with black and red lumps. They stopped and looked at a piece. It was wet. It was rubbery.

With horror they suddenly realized that it was fresh whalemeat.

At the top of the crater's lip they met Zaphod.

'Look,' he said, pointing into the crater.

In the centre lay the exploded carcass of a lonely sperm whale that hadn't lived long enough to be disappointed with its lot. The silence was only disturbed by the slight involuntary spasms of Trillian's throat.

'I suppose there's no point in trying to bury it?' murmured Arthur, and then wished he hadn't.

'Come,' said Zaphod and started back down into the crater.

'What, down there?' said Trillian with severe distaste.

'Yeah,' said Zaphod, 'come on, I've got something to show you.'

'We can see it,' said Trillian.

'Not that,' said Zaphod, 'something else. Come on.'

They all hesitated.

'Come on,' insisted Zaphod. 'I've found a way in.'

'*In?*' said Arthur in horror.

'Into the interior of the planet! An underground passage. The force of the whale's impact cracked it open, and that's where we have to go. Where no man has trod these five million years, into the very depths of time itself . . .'

Marvin started his ironical humming again.

Zaphod hit him and he shut up.

With little shudders of disgust they all followed Zaphod down the incline into the crater, trying very hard to avoid looking at its unfortunate creator.

'Life,' said Marvin dolefully, 'loathe it or ignore it, you can't like it.'

The ground had caved in where the whale had hit it, revealing a network of galleries and passages, now largely obstructed by collapsed rubble and entrails. Zaphod had made a start clearing a way into one of them, but Marvin was able to do it rather faster. Dank air wafted out of its dark recesses, and as Zaphod shone a torch into it, little was visible in the dusty gloom.

'According to the legends,' he said, 'the Magratheans lived most of their lives underground.'

'Why's that?' said Arthur. 'Did the surface become too polluted or overpopulated?'

'No, I don't think so,' said Zaphod. 'I think they just didn't like it very much.'

'Are you sure you know what you're doing?' said Trillian, peering nervously into the darkness. 'We've been attacked once already, you know.'

'Look, kid, I promise you the live population of this planet is nil plus the four of us, so come on, let's get on in there. Er, hey, Earthman . . .'

'Arthur,' said Arthur.

'Yeah, could you just sort of keep this robot with you and guard this end of the passageway. OK?'

'Guard?' said Arthur. 'What from? You just said there's no one here.'

'Yeah, well, just for safety, OK?' said Zaphod.

'Whose? Yours or mine?'

'Good lad. OK, here we go.'

Zaphod scrambled down into the passage, followed by Trillian and Ford.

'Well, I hope you all have a really miserable time,' complained Arthur.

'Don't worry,' Marvin assured him, 'they will.'

In a few seconds they had disappeared from view.

Arthur stamped around in a huff, and then decided that a whale's graveyard is not on the whole a good place to stamp around in.

Marvin eyed him balefully for a moment, and then turned himself off.

*

Zaphod marched quickly down the passageway, nervous as hell, but trying to hide it by striding purposefully. He flung the torch beam around. The walls were covered in dark tiles and were cold to the touch, the air thick with decay.

'There, what did I tell you?' he said. 'An inhabited planet. Magrathea.' And he strode on through the dirt and debris that littered the tile floors.

Trillian was reminded unavoidably of the London Underground, though it was less thoroughly squalid.

At intervals along the walls the tiles gave way to large mosaics – simple angular patterns in bright colours. Trillian stopped and studied one of them but could not interpret any sense in them. She called to Zaphod.

'Hey, have you any idea what these strange symbols are?'

'I think they're just strange symbols of some kind,' said Zaphod, hardly glancing back.

Trillian shrugged and hurried after him.

From time to time a doorway led either to the left or right into smallish chambers which Ford discovered to be full of derelict computer equipment. He dragged Zaphod into one to have a look. Trillian followed.

'Look,' said Ford, 'you reckon this is Magrathea . . .'

'Yeah,' said Zaphod, 'and we heard the voice, right?'

'OK, so I've bought the fact that it's Magrathea – for the moment. What you have so far said nothing about is how in the Galaxy you found it. You didn't just look it up in a star atlas, that's for sure.'

'Research. Government archives. Detective work. Few lucky guesses. Easy.'

'And then you stole the *Heart of Gold* to come and look for it with?'

'I stole it to look for a lot of things.'

'A lot of things?' said Ford in surprise. 'Like what?'

'I don't know.'

'What?'

'I don't know what I'm looking for.'

'Why not?'

'Because . . . because . . . I think it might be because if I knew I wouldn't be able to look for them.'

'What are you, crazy?'

'It's a possibility I haven't ruled out yet,' said Zaphod quietly. 'I only know as much about myself as my mind can work out under its current conditions. And its current conditions are not good.'

For a long time nobody said anything as Ford gazed at Zaphod with a mind suddenly full of worry.

'Listen, old friend, if you want to . . .' started Ford eventually.

'No, wait . . . I'll tell you something,' said Zaphod. 'I freewheel a lot. I get an idea to do something, and, hey, why not, I do it. I reckon I'll become President of the Galaxy, and it just happens, it's easy. I decide to steal this ship. I decide to look for Magrathea, and it all just happens. Yeah, I work out how it can best be done, right, but it always works out. It's like having a Galacticredit card which keeps on working though you never send off the cheques. And then whenever I stop and think – why did I want to do something? – how did I work out how to do it? – I get a very strong desire just to stop thinking about it. Like I have now. It's a big effort to talk about it.'

Zaphod paused for a while. For a while there was silence. Then he frowned and said, 'Last night I was worrying about this again. About the fact that part of my mind just didn't seem to work properly. Then it occurred to me that the way it seemed was that someone else was using my mind to have good ideas with, without telling me about it. I put the two ideas together and decided that maybe that somebody had locked off part of my mind for that purpose, which was why I couldn't use it. I wondered if there was a way I could check.

'I went to the ship's medical bay and plugged myself into the encephelographic screen. I went through every major screening test on both my heads – all the tests I had to go through under government medical officers before my nomination for the Presidency could be properly ratified. They showed up nothing. Nothing unexpected, at least. They showed that I was clever, imaginative, irresponsible, untrustworthy, extrovert, nothing you couldn't have guessed. And no other anomalies. So I started inventing further tests, completely at random. Nothing. Then I tried superimposing the results from one head on top of the results from the other head. Still nothing. Finally I got silly, because I'd given it all up as nothing more than an attack of paranoia. Last thing I did before I packed it in was take the superimposed picture and look at it through a green filter. You remember I was always superstitious about the colour green when I was a kid? I always wanted to be a pilot on one of the trading scouts?'

Ford nodded.

'And there it was,' said Zaphod, 'clear as day. A whole section in the middle of both brains that related only to each other and not to anything else around them. Some bastard had cauterized all the synapses and electronically traumatized those two lumps of cerebellum.'

Ford stared at him, aghast. Trillian had turned white.

'Somebody *did* that to you?' whispered Ford.

'Yeah.'

'But have you any idea who? Or why?'

'Why? I can only guess. But I do know who the bastard was.'

'You know? How do you know?'

'Because they left their initials burnt into the cauterized synapses. They left them there for me to see.'

Ford stared at him in horror and felt his skin begin to crawl.

'Initials? Burnt into your brain?'

'Yeah.'

'Well, what were they, for God's sake?'

Zaphod looked at him in silence again for a moment. Then he looked away.

'Z. B.,' he said quietly.

At that moment a steel shutter slammed down behind them and gas started to pour into the chamber.

'I'll tell you about it later,' choked Zaphod as all three passed out.

On the surface of Magrathea, Arthur wandered about moodily.

Ford had thoughtfully left him his copy of *The Hitchhiker's Guide to the Galaxy* to while away the time with. He pushed a few buttons at random.

The Hitchhiker's Guide to the Galaxy *is a very unevenly edited book and contains many passages that simply seemed to his editors like a good idea at the time.*

One of them (the one Arthur now came across) supposedly relates the experiences of one Veet Voojagig, a quiet young student at the University of Maximegalon, who pursued a brilliant academic career studying ancient philology, transformational ethics and the wave harmonic theory of historical perception, and then, after a night of drinking Pan Galactic Gargle Blasters with Zaphod Beeblebrox, became increasingly obsessed with the problem of what had happened to all the biros he'd bought over the past few years.

There followed a long period of painstaking research during which he visited all the major centres of biro loss throughout the galaxy and eventually came up with a quaint little theory which quite caught the public imagination at the time.

Somewhere in the cosmos, he said, along with all the planets inhabited by humanoids, reptiloids, fishoids, walking treeoids and super-intelligent shades of the colour blue, there was also a planet entirely given over to biro life forms. And it was to this planet that unattended biros would make their way, slipping away quietly through wormholes in space to a world where they knew they could enjoy a uniquely biroid lifestyle, responding to highly biro-orientated stimuli, and generally leading the biro equivalent of the good life.

And as theories go this was all very fine and pleasant until Veet Voojagig suddenly claimed to have found *this planet, and to have worked there for a while driving a limousine for a family of cheap green retractables, whereupon he was taken away, locked up, wrote a book, and was finally sent into tax exile, which is the usual fate reserved for those who are determined to make a fool of themselves in public.*

When one day an expedition was sent to the spatial coordinates that Voojagig had claimed for this planet they discovered only a small asteroid inhabited by a solitary old man who claimed repeatedly that nothing was true, though he was later discovered to be lying.

There did, however, remain the question of both the mysterious 60,000 Altairian dollars paid yearly into his Brantisvogan bank account, and of course Zaphod Beeblebrox's highly profitable second-hand-biro business.

Arthur read this, and put the book down.

The robot still sat there, completely inert.

Arthur got up and walked to the top of the crater. He walked around the crater. He watched two suns set magnificently over Magrathea.

He went back into the crater. He woke the robot up because even a manically depressed robot is better to talk to than nobody.

'Night's falling,' he said. 'Look, robot, the stars are coming out.'

From the heart of a dark nebula it is possible to see very few stars, and only very faintly, but they were there to be seen.

The robot obediently looked at them, then looked back.

'I know,' he said. 'Wretched, isn't it?'

'But that sunset! I've never seen anything like it in my wildest dreams . . . the two suns! It was like mountains of fire boiling into space.'

'I've seen it,' said Marvin. 'It's rubbish.'

'We only ever had the one sun at home,' persevered Arthur, 'I came from a planet called Earth, you know.'

'I know,' said Marvin, 'you keep going on about it. It sounds awful.'

'Ah no, it was a beautiful place.'

'Did it have oceans?'

'Oh yes,' said Arthur with a sigh, 'great wide rolling blue oceans . . .'

'Can't bear oceans,' said Marvin.

'Tell me,' enquired Arthur, 'do you get on well with other robots?'

'Hate them,' said Marvin. 'Where are you going?'

Arthur couldn't bear any more. He had got up again.

'I think I'll just take another walk,' he said.

'Don't blame you,' said Marvin and counted five

hundred and ninety-seven thousand million sheep before falling asleep again a second later.

Arthur slapped his arms about himself to try and get his circulation a little more enthusiastic about its job. He trudged back up the wall of the crater.

Because the atmosphere was so thin and because there was no moon, nightfall was very rapid and it was by now very dark. Because of this, Arthur practically walked into the old man before he noticed him.

He was standing with his back to Arthur watching the very last glimmers of light sink into blackness behind the horizon. He was tallish, elderly, and dressed in a single long grey robe. When he turned his face was thin and distinguished, careworn but not unkind, the sort of face you would happily bank with. But he didn't turn yet, not even to react to Arthur's yelp of surprise.

Eventually the last rays of the sun had vanished completely, and he turned. His face was still illuminated from somewhere, and when Arthur looked for the source of the light he saw that a few yards away stood a small craft of some kind – a small hovercraft, Arthur guessed. It shed a dim pool of light around it.

The man looked at Arthur, sadly it seemed.

'You choose a cold night to visit our dead planet,' he said.

'Who . . . who are you?' stammered Arthur.

The man looked away. Again a look of sadness seemed to cross his face.

'My name is not important,' he said.

He seemed to have something on his mind. Conversation was clearly something he felt he didn't have to rush at. Arthur felt awkward.

'I . . . er . . . you startled me . . .' he said, lamely.

The man looked round to him again and slightly raised his eyebrows.

'Hmmm?' he said.

'I said you startled me.'

'Do not be alarmed, I will not harm you.'

Arthur frowned at him. 'But you shot at us! There were missiles . . .' he said.

The man gazed into the pit of the crater. The slight glow from Marvin's eyes cast very faint red shadows on the huge carcass of the whale.

The man chuckled slightly.

'An automatic system,' he said and gave a small sigh. 'Ancient computers ranged in the bowels of the planet tick away the dark millennia, and the ages hang heavy on their dusty data banks. I think they take the occasional pot shot to relieve the monotony.'

He looked gravely at Arthur and said, 'I'm a great fan of science, you know.'

'Oh . . . er, really?' said Arthur, who was beginning to find the man's curious, kindly manner disconcerting.

'Oh yes,' said the old man, and simply stopped talking again.

'Ah,' said Arthur, 'er . . .' He had an odd feeling of being like a man in the act of adultery who is surprised when the woman's husband wanders into the room, changes his trousers, passes a few idle remarks about the weather, and leaves again.

'You seem ill at ease,' said the old man with polite concern.

'Er, no . . . well, yes. Actually, you see, we weren't really expecting to find anybody about, in fact. I sort of gathered that you were all dead or something . . .'

'Dead?' said the old man. 'Good gracious me no, we have but slept.'

'Slept?' said Arthur incredulously.

'Yes, through the economic recession, you see,' said the old man, apparently unconcerned about whether Arthur understood a word he was talking about or not.

Arthur had to prompt him again.

'Er, economic recession?'

'Well, you see, five million years ago the Galactic economy collapsed, and seeing that custom-built planets are something of a luxury commodity, you see . . .'

He paused and looked at Arthur.

'You know we built planets, do you?' he asked solemnly.

'Well, yes,' said Arthur, 'I'd sort of gathered . . .'

'Fascinating trade,' said the old man, and a wistful look came into his eyes, 'doing the coastlines was always my favourite. Used to have endless fun doing the little bits in fjords . . . so anyway,' he said, trying to find his thread again, 'the recession came and we decided it would save a lot of bother if we just slept through it. So we programmed the computers to revive us when it was all over.'

The man stifled a very slight yawn and continued.

'The computers were index linked to the Galactic stock-market prices, you see, so that we'd all be revived when everybody else had rebuilt the economy enough to afford our rather expensive services.'

Arthur, a regular *Guardian* reader, was deeply shocked at this.

'That's a pretty unpleasant way to behave, isn't it?'

'Is it?' asked the old man mildly. 'I'm sorry, I'm a bit out of touch.'

He pointed down into the crater.

'Is that robot yours?' he said.

'No,' came a thin metallic voice from the crater, 'I'm mine.'

'If you'd call it a robot,' muttered Arthur. 'It's more a sort of electronic sulking machine.'

'Bring it,' said the old man. Arthur was quite surprised to hear a note of decision suddenly present in the old man's voice. He called to Marvin, who crawled up the slope making a big show of being lame, which he wasn't.

'On second thoughts,' said the old man, 'leave it here. You must come with me. Great things are afoot.' He turned towards his craft which, though no apparent signal had been given, now drifted quietly towards them through the dark.

Arthur looked down at Marvin, who now made an equally big show of turning round laboriously and trudging off down into the crater again muttering sour nothings to himself.

'Come,' called the old man, 'come now or you will be late.'

'Late?' said Arthur. 'What for?'

'What is your name, human?'

'Dent. Arthur Dent,' said Arthur.

'Late, as in the late Dentarthurdent,' said the old man, sternly. 'It's a sort of threat, you see.' Another wistful look came into his tired old eyes. 'I've never been very good at them myself, but I'm told they can be very effective.'

Arthur blinked at him.

'What an extraordinary person,' he muttered to himself.

'I beg your pardon?' said the old man.

'Oh nothing, I'm sorry,' said Arthur in embarrassment. 'All right, where do we go?'

'In my aircar,' said the man, motioning Arthur to get into the craft, which had settled silently next to them. 'We are going deep into the bowels of the planet, where even now our race is being revived from its five-million-year slumber. Magrathea awakes.'

Arthur shivered involuntarily as he seated himself next to the old man. The strangeness of it, the silent bobbing movement of the craft as it soared into the night sky, quite unsettled him.

He looked at the old man, his face illuminated by the dull glow of tiny lights on the instrument panel.

'Excuse me,' he said to him, 'what is your name, by the way?'

'My name?' said the old man, and the same distant sadness came into his face again. He paused. 'My name,' he said, '. . . is Slartibartfast.'

Arthur practically choked.

'I beg your pardon?' he spluttered.

'Slartibartfast,' repeated the old man quietly.

'Slartibartfast?'

The old man looked at him gravely.

'I said it wasn't important,' he said.

The aircar sailed through the night.

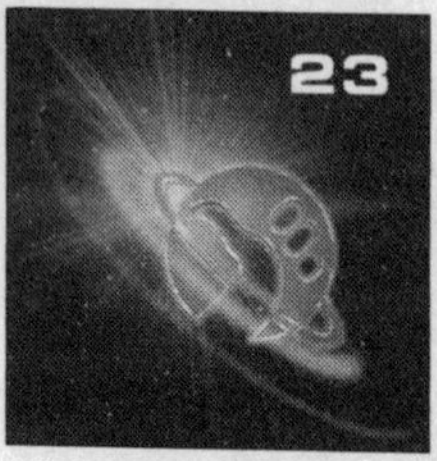

It is an important and popular fact that things are not always what they seem. For instance, on the planet Earth, man had always assumed that he was more intelligent than dolphins because he had achieved so much – the wheel, New York, wars, and so on – whilst all the dolphins had ever done was muck about in the water having a good time. But conversely, the dolphins had always believed that they were far more intelligent than man – for precisely the same reasons.

Curiously enough, the dolphins had long known of the impending destruction of the planet Earth and had made many attempts to alert mankind to the danger; but most of their communications were misinterpreted as amusing attempts to punch footballs or whistle for titbits, so they eventually gave up and left the Earth by their own means shortly before the Vogons arrived.

The last ever dolphin message was misinterpreted as a surprisingly sophisticated attempt to do a double-backwards-somersault through a hoop whilst whistling the 'Star-Spangled Banner', but in fact the message was this: *So long, and thanks for all the fish.*

In fact there was only one species on the planet more

intelligent than dolphins, and they spent a lot of their time in behavioural-research laboratories running round inside wheels and conducting frighteningly elegant and subtle experiments on man. The fact that once again man completely misinterpreted this relationship was entirely according to these creatures' plans.

Silently the aircar coasted through the cold darkness, a single soft glow of light that was utterly alone in the deep Magrathean night. It sped swiftly. Arthur's companion seemed sunk in his own thoughts, and when Arthur tried on a couple of occasions to engage him in conversation again he would simply reply by asking if he was comfortable enough, and then left it at that.

Arthur tried to gauge the speed at which they were travelling, but the blackness outside was absolute and he was denied any reference points. The sense of motion was so soft and slight he could almost believe they were hardly moving at all.

Then a tiny glow of light appeared in the far distance and within seconds had grown so much in size that Arthur realized it was travelling towards them at a colossal speed, and he tried to make out what sort of craft it might be. He peered at it, but was unable to discern any clear shape, and suddenly gasped in alarm as the aircar dipped sharply and headed downwards in what seemed certain to be a collision course. Their relative velocity seemed unbelievable, and Arthur had hardly time to draw breath before it was all over. The next thing he was aware of was an insane silver blur that seemed to surround him. He twisted his head sharply round and saw a small black point dwindling rapidly in the distance behind them, and it took him several seconds to realize what had happened.

They had plunged into a tunnel in the ground. The colossal speed had been their own relative to the glow of light, which was a stationary hole in the ground, the mouth of the tunnel. The insane blur of silver was the circular wall of the tunnel down which they were shooting, apparently at several hundred miles an hour.

He closed his eyes in terror.

After a length of time which he made no attempt to judge, he sensed a slight subsidence in their speed and some while later became aware that they were gradually gliding to a gentle halt.

He opened his eyes again. They were still in the silver tunnel, threading and weaving their way through what appeared to be a crisscross warren of converging tunnels. When they finally stopped it was in a small chamber of curved steel. Several tunnels also had their terminus here, and at the farther end of the chamber Arthur could see a large circle of dim irritating light. It was irritating because it played tricks with the eyes, it was impossible to focus on it properly or tell how near or far it was. Arthur guessed (quite wrongly) that it might be ultraviolet.

Slartibartfast turned and regarded Arthur with his solemn old eyes.

'Earthman,' he said, 'we are now deep in the heart of Magrathea.'

'How did you know I was an Earthman?' demanded Arthur.

'These things will become clear to you,' said the old man gently, 'at least,' he added with slight doubt in his voice, 'clearer than they are at the moment.'

He continued: 'I should warn you that the chamber we are about to pass into does not literally exist within our planet. It is a little too . . . large. We are about to pass through a gateway into a vast tract of hyperspace. It may disturb you.'

Arthur made nervous noises.

Slartibartfast, touched a button and added, not entirely reassuringly, 'It scares the willies out of me. Hold tight.'

The car shot forward straight into the circle of light, and suddenly Arthur had a fairly clear idea of what infinity looked like.

It wasn't infinity, in fact. Infinity itself looks flat and uninteresting. Looking up into the night sky is looking into infinity – distance is incomprehensible and therefore meaningless. The chamber into which the aircar emerged was anything but infinite, it was just very very very big, so big that it gave the impression of infinity far better than infinity itself.

Arthur's senses bobbed and span as, travelling at the immense speed he knew the aircar attained, they climbed slowly through the open air leaving the gateway through which they had passed an invisible pinprick in the shimmering wall behind them.

The wall.

The wall defied the imagination – seduced it and defeated it. The wall was so paralysingly vast and sheer that its top, bottom and sides passed away beyond the reach of sight. The mere shock of vertigo could kill a man.

The wall appeared perfectly flat. It would take the finest laser-measuring equipment to detect that as it climbed, apparently to infinity, as it dropped dizzily away, as it planed out to either side, it also curved. It met itself again thirteen light seconds away. In other words the wall formed the inside of a hollow sphere, a sphere over two million miles across and flooded with unimaginable light.

'Welcome,' said Slartibartfast as the tiny speck that was the aircar, travelling now at three times the speed of sound, crept imperceptibly forward into the mindboggling space, 'welcome,' he said, 'to our factory floor.'

Arthur stared about him in a kind of wonderful horror. Ranged away before them, at distances he could neither judge nor even guess at, were a series of curious suspensions, delicate traceries of metal and light hung about shadowy spherical shapes that hung in the space.

'This,' said Slartibartfast, 'is where we make most of our planets, you see.'

'You mean,' said Arthur, trying to form the words, 'you mean you're starting it all up again now?'

'No no, good heavens no,' exclaimed the old man, 'no, the Galaxy isn't nearly rich enough to support us yet. No, we've been awakened to perform just one extraordinary commission for very . . . special clients from another dimension. It may interest you . . . there in the distance in front of us.'

Arthur followed the old man's finger, till he was able to pick out the floating structure he was pointing out. It was indeed the only one of the many structures that betrayed any sign of activity about it, though this was more a subliminal impression than anything one could put one's finger on.

At that moment, however, a flash of light arced through the structure and revealed in stark relief the patterns that were formed on the dark sphere within. Patterns that Arthur knew, rough blobby shapes that were as familiar to him as the shapes of words, part of the furniture of his mind. For a few seconds he sat in stunned silence as the images rushed around his mind and tried to find somewhere to settle down and make sense.

Part of his brain told him that he knew perfectly well what he was looking at and what the shapes represented whilst another quite sensibly refused to countenance the idea and abdicated responsibility for any further thinking in that direction.

The flash came again, and this time there could be no doubt.

'The Earth . . .' whispered Arthur.

'Well, the Earth Mark Two, in fact,' said Slartibartfast cheerfully. 'We're making a copy from our original blueprints.'

There was a pause.

'Are you trying to tell me,' said Arthur, slowly and with control, 'that you originally . . . *made* the Earth?'

'Oh yes,' said Slartibartfast. 'Did you ever go to a place . . . I think it was called Norway?'

'No,' said Arthur, 'no, I didn't.'

'Pity,' said Slartibartfast, 'that was one of mine. Won an award, you know. Lovely crinkly edges. I was most upset to hear of its destruction.'

'*You* were upset!'

'Yes. Five minutes later and it wouldn't have mattered so much. It was a quite shocking cock-up.'

'Huh?' said Arthur.

'The mice were furious.'

'The *mice* were furious?'

'Oh yes,' said the old man mildly.

'Yes well so I expect were the dogs and cats and duckbilled platypuses, but . . .'

'Ah, but they hadn't paid for it, you see, had they?'

'Look,' said Arthur, 'would it save you a lot of time if I just gave up and went mad now?'

For a while the aircar flew on in awkward silence. Then the old man tried patiently to explain.

'Earthman, the planet you lived on was commissioned, paid for, and run by mice. It was destroyed five minutes before the completion of the purpose for which it was built, and we've got to build another one.'

Only one word was registering with Arthur.

'*Mice?*' he said.

'Indeed, Earthman.'

'Look, sorry – are we talking about the little white furry things with the cheese fixation and women standing on tables screaming in early sixties sit coms?'

Slartibartfast coughed politely.

'Earthman,' he said, 'it is sometimes hard to follow your mode of speech. Remember I have been asleep inside this planet of Magrathea for five million years and know little of these early sixties sit coms of which you speak. These creatures you call mice, you see, they are not quite as they appear. They are merely the protrusion into our dimension of vast hyper-intelligent pan-dimensional beings. The whole business with the cheese and the squeaking is just a front.'

The old man paused, and with a sympathetic frown continued.

'They've been experimenting on you, I'm afraid.'

Arthur thought about this for a moment, and then his face cleared.

'Ah no,' he said, 'I see the source of the misunderstanding now. No, look, you see, what happened was that we used to do experiments on *them*. They were often used in behavioural research, Pavlov and all that sort of stuff. So what happened was that the mice would be set all sorts of tests, learning to ring bells, run round mazes and things so that the whole nature of the learning process could be examined. From our observations of their behaviour we were able to learn all sorts of things about our own . . .'

Arthur's voice tailed off.

'Such subtlety . . .' said Slartibartfast, 'one has to admire it.'

'What?' said Arthur.

'How better to disguise their real natures, and how better to guide your thinking? Suddenly running down a maze the wrong way, eating the wrong bit of cheese, unexpectedly dropping dead of myxomatosis – if it's finely calculated the cumulative effect is enormous.'

He paused for effect.

'You see, Earthman, they really are particularly clever hyper-intelligent pan-dimensional beings. Your planet and people have formed the matrix of an organic computer running a ten-million-year research program . . .

'Let me tell you the whole story. It'll take a little time.'

'Time,' said Arthur weakly, 'is not currently one of my problems.'

There are of course many problems connected with life, of which some of the most popular are: *Why are people born? Why do they die? Why do they want to spend so much of the intervening time wearing digital watches?*

Many many millions of years ago a race of hyper-intelligent pan-dimensional beings (whose physical manifestation in their own pan-dimensional universe is not dissimilar to our own) got so fed up with the constant bickering about the meaning of life which used to interrupt their favourite pastime of Brockian Ultra Cricket (a curious game which involved suddenly hitting people for no readily apparent reason and then running away) that they decided to sit down and solve their problems once and for all.

And to this end they built themselves a stupendous super-computer which was so amazingly intelligent that even before its data banks had been connected up it had started from *I think therefore I am* and got as far as deducing the existence of rice pudding and income tax before anyone managed to turn it off.

It was the size of a small city.

Its main console was installed in a specially designed

executive office, mounted on an enormous executive desk of finest ultramahogany topped with rich ultrared leather. The dark carpeting was discreetly sumptuous, exotic pot plants and tastefully engraved prints of the principal computer programmers and their families were deployed liberally about the room, and stately windows looked out upon a tree-lined public square.

On the day of the Great On-Turning two soberly dressed programmers with briefcases arrived and were shown discreetly into the office. They were aware that this day they would represent their entire race in its greatest moment, but they conducted themselves calmly and quietly as they seated themselves deferentially before the desk, opened their briefcases and took out their leather-bound notebooks.

Their names were Lunkwill and Fook.

For a few moments they sat in respectful silence, then, after exchanging a quiet glance with Fook, Lunkwill leaned forward and touched a small black panel.

The subtlest of hums indicated that the massive computer was now in total active mode. After a pause it spoke to them in a voice rich, resonant, and deep.

It said: 'What is this great task for which I, Deep Thought, the second greatest computer in the Universe of Time and Space, have been called into existence?'

Lunkwill and Fook glanced at each other in surprise.

'Your task, O Computer . . .' began Fook.

'No, wait a minute, this isn't right,' said Lunkwill, worried. 'We distinctly designed this computer to be the greatest one ever and we're not making do with second best. Deep Thought,' he addressed the computer, 'are you not, as we designed you to be, the greatest, most powerful computer in all time?'

'I described myself as the second greatest,' intoned Deep Thought, 'and such I am.'

Another worried look passed between the two programmers. Lunkwill cleared his throat.

'There must be some mistake,' he said, 'are you not a greater computer than the Milliard Gargantubrain at Maximegalon, which can count all the atoms in a star in a millisecond?'

'The Milliard Gargantubrain?' said Deep Thought with unconcealed contempt. 'A mere abacus – mention it not.'

'And are you not,' said Fook, leaning anxiously forward, 'a greater analyst than the Googleplex Star Thinker in the Seventh Galaxy of Light and Ingenuity, which can calculate the trajectory of every single dust particle throughout a five-week Dangrabad Beta sand blizzard?'

'A five-week sand blizzard?' said Deep Thought haughtily. 'You ask this of me who have contemplated the very vectors of the atoms in the Big Bang itself? Molest me not with this pocket-calculator stuff.'

The two programmers sat in uncomfortable silence for a moment. Then Lunkwill leaned forward again.

'But are you not,' he said, 'a more fiendish disputant than the Great Hyperlobic Omni-Cognate Neutron Wrangler of Ciceronicus Twelve, the Magic and Indefatigable?'

'The Great Hyperlobic Omni-Cognate Neutron Wrangler,' said Deep Thought, thoroughly rolling the *r*s, 'could talk all four legs off an Arcturan Megadonkey – but only I could persuade it to go for a walk afterwards.'

'Then what,' asked Fook, 'is the problem?'

'There is no problem,' said Deep Thought with magnificent ringing tones. 'I am simply the second greatest computer in the Universe of Space and Time.'

'But the *second*?' insisted Lunkwill. 'Why do you keep saying the second? You're surely not thinking of the Multicorticoid Perspicutron Titan Muller, are you? Or the Pondermatic? Or the . . .'

Contemptuous lights flashed across the computer's console.

'I spare not a single unit of thought on these cybernetic simpletons!' he boomed. 'I speak of none but the computer that is to come after me!'

Fook was losing patience. He pushed his notebook aside and muttered, 'I think this is getting needlessly messianic.'

'You know nothing of future time,' pronounced Deep Thought, 'and yet in my teeming circuitry I can navigate the infinite delta streams of future probability and see that there must one day come a computer whose merest operational parameters I am not worthy to calculate, but which it will be my fate eventually to design.'

Fook sighed heavily and glanced across to Lunkwill.

'Can we get on and ask the question?' he said.

Lunkwill motioned him to wait.

'What computer is this of which you speak?' he asked.

'I will speak of it no further in this present time,' said Deep Thought. 'Now. Ask what else of me you will that I may function. Speak.'

They shrugged at each other. Fook composed himself.

'O Deep Thought Computer,' he said, 'the task we

have designed you to perform is this. We want you to tell us . . .' he paused '. . . the Answer!'

'The Answer?' said Deep Thought. 'The Answer to what?'

'Life!' urged Fook.

'The Universe!' said Lunkwill.

'Everything!' they said in chorus.

Deep Thought paused for a moment's reflection.

'Tricky,' he said finally.

'But can you do it?'

Again, a significant pause.

'Yes,' said Deep Thought, 'I can do it.'

'There is an answer?' said Fook with breathless excitement.

'A simple answer?' added Lunkwill.

'Yes,' said Deep Thought. 'Life, the Universe and Everything. There is an answer. But,' he added, 'I'll have to think about it.'

A sudden commotion destroyed the moment: the door flew open and two angry men wearing the coarse faded-blue robes and belts of the Cruxwan University burst into the room, thrusting aside the ineffectual flunkies who tried to bar their way.

'We demand admission!' shouted the younger of the two men, elbowing a pretty young secretary in the throat.

'Come on,' shouted the older one, 'you can't keep us out!' He pushed a junior programmer back through the door.

'We demand that you can't keep us out!' bawled the younger one, though he was now firmly inside the room and no further attempts were being made to stop him.

'Who are you?' said Lunkwill, rising angrily from his seat. 'What do you want?'

'I am Majikthise!' announced the older one.

'And I demand that I am Vroomfondel!' shouted the younger one.

Majikthise turned on Vroomfondel. 'It's all right,' he explained angrily, 'you don't need to demand that.'

'All right!' bawled Vroomfondel banging on a nearby desk. 'I am Vroomfondel, and that is *not* a demand, that is a solid *fact*! What we demand is solid *facts*!'

'No, we don't!' exclaimed Majikthise in irritation. 'That is precisely what we don't demand!'

Scarcely pausing for breath, Vroomfondel shouted, 'We *don't* demand solid facts! What we demand is a total *absence* of solid facts. I demand that I may or may not be Vroomfondel!'

'But who the devil are you?' exclaimed an outraged Fook.

'We,' said Majikthise, 'are Philosophers.'

'Though we may not be,' said Vroomfondel, waving a warning finger at the programmers.

'Yes, we *are*,' insisted Majikthise. 'We are quite definitely here as representatives of the Amalgamated Union of Philosophers, Sages, Luminaries and Other Thinking Persons, and we want this machine off, and we want it off *now*!'

'What's the problem?' said Lunkwill.

'I'll tell you what the problem is, mate,' said Majikthise, 'demarcation, that's the problem!'

'We demand,' yelled Vroomfondel, 'that demarcation may or may not be the problem!'

'You just let the machines get on with the adding up,' warned Majikthise, 'and we'll take care of the eternal verities, thank you very much. You want to check your legal position, you do, mate. Under law the Quest for Ultimate Truth is quite clearly the inalienable prerogative of your working thinkers. Any bloody machine goes and actually *finds* it and we're straight out of a job, aren't we? I mean what's the use of our sitting up half the night arguing that there may or may not be a God if this machine only goes and gives you his bleeding phone number the next morning?'

'That's right,' shouted Vroomfondel, 'we demand rigidly defined areas of doubt and uncertainty!'

Suddenly a stentorian voice boomed across the room.

'Might *I* make an observation at this point?' enquired Deep Thought.

'We'll go on strike!' yelled Vroomfondel.

'That's right!' agreed Majikthise. 'You'll have a national Philosophers' strike on your hands!'

The hum level in the room suddenly increased as several ancillary bass driver units, mounted in sedately carved and varnished cabinet speakers around the room, cut in to give Deep Thought's voice a little more power.

'All I wanted to say,' bellowed the computer, 'is that my circuits are now irrevocably committed to calculating the answers to the Ultimate Question of Life, the Universe and Everything – ' he paused and satisfied himself that he now had everyone's attention, before continuing more quietly – 'but the program will take me a little while to run.'

Fook glanced impatiently at his watch.

'How long?' he said.

'Seven and a half million years,' said Deep Thought.

Lunkwill and Fook blinked at each other.

'Seven and a half million years!' they cried in chorus.

'Yes,' declaimed Deep Thought, 'I said I'd have to think about it, didn't I? And it occurs to me that running a program like this is bound to create an enormous amount of popular publicity for the whole area of philosophy in general. Everyone's going to have their own theories about what answer I'm eventually going to come up with, and who better to capitalize on that media market than you yourselves? So long as you can keep disagreeing with each other violently enough and slagging each other off in the popular press, and so long as you have clever agents, you can keep yourselves on the gravy train for life. How does that sound?'

The two philosophers gaped at him.

'Bloody hell,' said Majikthise, 'now that is what I call thinking. Here, Vroomfondel, why do we never think of things like that?'

'Dunno,' said Vroomfondel in an awed whisper. 'Think our brains must be too highly trained, Majikthise.'

So saying, they turned on their heels and walked out of the door and into a lifestyle beyond their wildest dreams.

'Yes, very salutary,' said Arthur, after Slartibartfast had related the salient points of this story to him, 'but I don't understand what all this has got to do with the Earth and mice and things.'

'That is but the first half of the story, Earthman,' said the old man. 'If you would care to discover what happened seven and a half million years later, on the great day of the Answer, allow me to invite you to my study where you can experience the events yourself on your Sens-O-Tape records. That is unless you would care to take a quick stroll on the surface of New Earth. It's only half completed, I'm afraid – we haven't even finished burying the artificial dinosaur skeletons in the crust yet, then we have the Tertiary and Quaternary Periods of the Cenozoic Era to lay down, and . . .'

'No, thank you,' said Arthur, 'it wouldn't be quite the same.'

'No,' said Slartibartfast, 'it won't be.' And he turned the aircar round and headed back towards the mind-numbing wall.

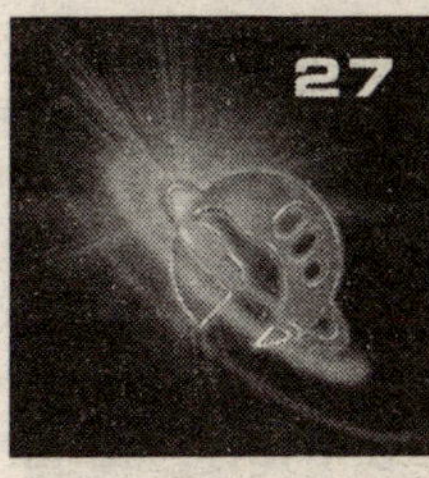

Slartibartfast's study was a total mess, like the results of an explosion in a public library. The old man frowned as they stepped in.

'Terribly unfortunate,' he said, 'a diode blew in one of the life-support computers. When we tried to revive our cleaning staff we discovered they'd been dead for nearly thirty thousand years. Who's going to clear away the bodies, that's what I want to know. Look, why don't you sit yourself down over there and let me plug you in?'

He gestured Arthur towards a chair which looked as if it had been made out of the ribcage of a stegosaurus.

'It was made out of the ribcage of a stegosaurus,' explained the old man as he pottered about fishing bits of wire out from under tottering piles of paper and drawing instruments. 'Here,' he said, 'hold these,' and passed a couple of stripped wire ends to Arthur.

The instant he took hold of them a bird flew straight through him.

He was suspended in mid-air and totally invisible to himself. Beneath him was a pretty tree-lined city square, and all around it as far as the eye could see were white concrete buildings of airy spacious design but somewhat the worse for wear – many were cracked and stained with rain. Today, however, the sun was shining, a fresh breeze danced lightly through the trees, and the odd sensation that all the buildings were quietly humming was probably caused by the fact that the square and all the streets around it were thronged with cheerful excited people. Somewhere a band was playing, brightly coloured flags were fluttering in the breeze and the spirit of carnival was in the air.

Arthur felt extraordinarily lonely stuck up in the air above it all without so much as a body to his name, but before he had time to reflect on this a voice rang out across the square and called for everyone's attention.

A man standing on a brightly dressed dais before the building which clearly dominated the square was addressing the crowd over a Tannoy.

'O people who wait in the shadow of Deep Thought!' he cried out. 'Honoured Descendants of Vroomfondel and Majikthise, the Greatest and Most Truly Interesting Pundits the Universe has ever known . . . The Time of Waiting is over!'

Wild cheers broke out amongst the crowd. Flags, streamers and wolf whistles sailed through the air. The narrower streets looked rather like centipedes rolled over on their backs and frantically waving their legs in the air.

'Seven and a half million years our race has waited for this Great and Hopefully Enlightening Day!' cried the cheer leader. 'The Day of the Answer!'

Hurrahs burst from the ecstatic crowd.

'Never again,' cried the man, 'never again will we

wake up in the morning and think: Who am I? What is my purpose in life? Does it really, cosmically speaking, *matter* if I don't get up and go to work? For today we will finally learn once and for all the plain and simple answer to all these nagging little problems of Life, the Universe and Everything!'

As the crowd erupted once again, Arthur found himself gliding through the air and down towards one of the large stately windows on the first floor of the building behind the dais from which the speaker was addressing the crowd.

He experienced a moment's panic as he sailed straight towards the window, which passed when a second or so later he found he had gone right through the solid glass without apparently touching it.

No one in the room remarked on his peculiar arrival, which is hardly surprising as he wasn't there. He began to realize that the whole experience was merely a recorded projection which knocked six-track seventy-millimetre into a cocked hat.

The room was much as Slartibartfast had described it. In seven and a half million years it had been well looked after and cleaned regularly every century or so. The ultramahogany desk was worn at the edges, the carpet a little faded now, but the large computer terminal sat in sparkling glory on the desk's leather top, as bright as if it had been constructed yesterday.

Two severely dressed men sat respectfully before the terminal and waited.

'The time is nearly upon us,' said one, and Arthur was surprised to see a word suddenly materialize in thin air just by the man's neck. The word was LOONQUAWL, and it flashed a couple of times and then disappeared again. Before Arthur was able to assimilate this the other man spoke and the word PHOUCHG appeared by his neck.

'Seventy-five thousand generations ago, our ancestors set this program in motion,' the second man said, 'and in all that time we will be the first to hear the computer speak.'

'An awesome prospect, Phouchg,' agreed the first man, and Arthur suddenly realized he was watching a recording with subtitles.

'We are the ones who will hear,' said Phouchg, 'the answer to the great question of Life . . .'

'The Universe . . .' said Loonquawl.

'And Everything . . . !'

'Shhh,' said Loonquawl with a slight gesture, 'I think Deep Thought is preparing to speak!'

There was a moment's expectant pause whilst panels slowly came to life on the front of the console. Lights flashed on and off experimentally and settled down into a businesslike pattern. A soft low hum came from the communication channel.

'Good morning,' said Deep Thought at last.

'Er . . . Good morning, O Deep Thought,' said Loonquawl nervously, 'do you have . . . er, that is . . .'

'An answer for you?' interrupted Deep Thought majestically. 'Yes. I have.'

The two men shivered with expectancy. Their waiting had not been in vain.

'There really is one?' breathed Phouchg.

'There really is one,' confirmed Deep Thought.

'To Everything? To the great Question of Life, the Universe and Everything?'

'Yes.'

Both of the men had been trained for this moment, their lives had been a preparation for it, they had been selected at birth as those who would witness the answer, but even so they found themselves gasping and squirming like excited children.

'And you're ready to give it to us?' urged Loonquawl.

'I am.'

'Now?'

'Now,' said Deep Thought.

They both licked their dry lips.

'Though I don't think,' added Deep Thought, 'that you're going to like it.'

'Doesn't matter,' said Phouchg. 'We must know it! Now!'

'Now?' enquired Deep Thought.

'Yes! Now . . .'

'All right,' said the computer and settled into silence again. The two men fidgeted. The tension was unbearable.

'You're really not going to like it,' observed Deep Thought.

'Tell us!'

'All right,' said Deep Thought. 'The Answer to the Great Question . . .'

'Yes . . . !'

'Of Life, the Universe and Everything . . .' said Deep Thought.

'Yes . . . !'

'Is . . .' said Deep Thought, and paused.

'Yes . . . !'

'Is . . .'

'Yes . . . !!! . . . ?'

'Forty-two,' said Deep Thought, with infinite majesty and calm.

It was a long time before anyone spoke.

Out of the corner of his eye Phouchg could see the sea of tense expectant faces down in the square outside.

'We're going to get lynched, aren't we?' he whispered.

'It was a tough assignment,' said Deep Thought mildly.

'Forty-two!' yelled Loonquawl. 'Is that all you've got to show for seven and a half million years' work?'

'I checked it very thoroughly,' said the computer, 'and that quite definitely is the answer. I think the problem, to be quite honest with you, is that you've never actually known what the question is.'

'But it was the Great Question! The Ultimate Question of Life, the Universe and Everything,' howled Loonquawl.

'Yes,' said Deep Thought with the air of one who suffers fools gladly, 'but what actually *is* it?'

A slow stupefied silence crept over the men as they stared at the computer and then at each other.

'Well, you know, it's just Everything . . . Everything . . .' offered Phouchg weakly.

'Exactly!' said Deep Thought. 'So once you do know

what the question actually is, you'll know what the answer means.'

'Oh, terrific,' muttered Phouchg, flinging aside his notebook and wiping away a tiny tear.

'Look, all right, all right,' said Loonquawl, 'can you just please *tell* us the question?'

'The Ultimate Question?'

'Yes!'

'Of Life, the Universe and Everything?'

'Yes!'

Deep Thought pondered for a moment.

'Tricky,' he said.

'But can you do it?' cried Loonquawl.

Deep Thought pondered this for another long moment.

Finally: 'No,' he said firmly.

Both men collapsed on to their chairs in despair.

'But I'll tell you who can,' said Deep Thought.

They both looked up sharply.

'Who? Tell us!'

Suddenly Arthur began to feel his apparently non-existent scalp begin to crawl as he found himself moving slowly but inexorably forward towards the console, but it was only a dramatic zoom on the part of whoever had made the recording, he assumed.

'I speak of none but the computer that is to come after me,' intoned Deep Thought, his voice regaining its accustomed declamatory tones. 'A computer whose merest operational parameters I am not worthy to calculate – and yet I will design it for you. A computer which can calculate the Question to the Ultimate Answer, a computer of such infinite and subtle complexity that organic life itself shall form part of its operational matrix. And you yourselves shall take on new forms and go down into the computer to navigate its ten-million-year program! Yes! I shall design this computer for you. And I shall name it also unto you. And it shall be called . . . the Earth.'

Phouchg gaped at Deep Thought.

'What a dull name,' he said and great incisions appeared down the length of his body. Loonquawl too suddenly sustained horrific gashes from nowhere. The computer console blotched and cracked, the walls flickered and crumbled and the room crashed upwards into its own ceiling . . .

Slartibartfast was standing in front of Arthur holding the two wires.

'End of the tape,' he explained.

'Zaphod! Wake up!'

'Mmmmmwwwwwerrrrr?'

'Hey, come on, wake up.'

'Just let me stick to what I'm good at, yeah?' muttered Zaphod and rolled away from the voice back to sleep.

'Do you want me to kick you?' said Ford.

'Would it give you a lot of pleasure?' said Zaphod, blearily.

'No.'

'Nor me. So what's the point? Stop bugging me.' Zaphod curled himself up.

'He got a double dose of the gas,' said Trillian looking down at him, 'two windpipes.'

'And stop talking,' said Zaphod, 'it's hard enough trying to sleep anyway. What's the matter with the ground? It's all cold and hard.'

'It's gold,' said Ford.

With an amazingly balletic movement Zaphod was standing and scanning the horizon, because that was how far the gold ground stretched in every direction, perfectly smooth and solid. It gleamed like . . . it's impossible to say what it gleamed like because nothing in the Universe gleams in quite the same way that a planet made of solid gold does.

'Who put all that there?' yelped Zaphod, goggle-eyed.

'Don't get excited,' said Ford, 'it's only a catalogue.'

'A who?'

'A catalogue,' said Trillian, 'an illusion.'

'How can you say that?' cried Zaphod, falling to his hands and knees and staring at the ground. He poked it and prodded it. It was very heavy and very slightly soft – he could mark it with his fingernail. It was very yellow and very shiny, and when he breathed on it his breath evaporated off it in that very peculiar and special way that breath evaporates off solid gold.

'Trillian and I came round a while ago,' said Ford. 'We shouted and yelled till somebody came and then carried on shouting and yelling till they got fed up and put us in their planet catalogue to keep us busy till they were ready to deal with us. This is all Sens-O-Tape.'

Zaphod stared at him bitterly.

'Ah, shit,' he said, 'you wake me up from my own perfectly good dream to show me somebody else's.' He sat down in a huff.

'What's that series of valleys over there?' he said.

'Hallmark,' said Ford. 'We had a look.'

'We didn't wake you earlier,' said Trillian. 'The last planet was knee deep in fish.'

'Fish?'

'Some people like the oddest things.'

'And before that,' said Ford, 'we had platinum. Bit dull. We thought you'd like to see this one, though.'

Seas of light glared at them in one solid blaze wherever they looked.

'Very pretty,' said Zaphod petulantly.

In the sky a huge green catalogue number appeared. It flickered and changed, and when they looked around again so had the land.

As with one voice they all went, 'Yuch.'

The sea was purple. The beach they were on was composed of tiny yellow and green pebbles – presumably terribly precious stones. The mountains in the distance seemed soft and undulating with red peaks. Nearby stood a solid silver beach table with a frilly mauve parasol and silver tassles.

In the sky a huge sign appeared, replacing the catalogue number. It said, *Whatever your tastes, Magrathea can cater for you. We are not proud.*

And five hundred entirely naked women dropped out of the sky on parachutes.

In a moment the scene vanished and left them in a springtime meadow full of cows.

'Ow!' said Zaphod. 'My brains!'

'You want to talk about it?' said Ford.

'Yeah, OK,' said Zaphod, and all three sat down and ignored the scenes that came and went around them.

'I figure this,' said Zaphod. 'Whatever happened to my mind, I did it. And I did it in such a way that it wouldn't be detected by the government screening tests. And I wasn't to know anything about it myself. Pretty crazy, right?'

The other two nodded in agreement.

'So I reckon, what's so secret that I can't let anybody

know I know it, not the galactic government, not even myself? And the answer is I don't know. Obviously. But I put a few things together and I can begin to guess. When did I decide to run for President? Shortly after the death of President Yooden Vranx. You remember Yooden, Ford?'

'Yeah,' said Ford, 'he was that guy we met when we were kids, the Arcturan captain. He was a gas. He gave us conkers when you busted your way into his megafreighter. Said you were the most amazing kid he'd ever met.'

'What's all this?' said Trillian.

'Ancient history,' said Ford, 'when we were kids together on Betelgeuse. The Arcturan megafreighters used to carry most of the bulky trade between the galactic centre and the outlying regions. The Betelgeuse trading scouts used to find the markets and the Arcturans would supply them. There was a lot of trouble with space pirates before they were wiped out in the Dordellis wars, and the megafreighters had to be equipped with the most fantastic defence shields known to galactic science. They were real brutes of ships, and huge. In orbit round a planet they would eclipse the sun.

'One day, young Zaphod here decides to raid one. On a tri-jet scooter designed for stratosphere work, a mere kid. I mean forget it, it was crazier than a mad monkey. I went along for the ride because I'd got some very safe money on him not doing it, and didn't want him coming back with fake evidence. So what happens? We get in this tri-jet which he had souped up into something totally other, crossed three parsecs in a matter of weeks, burst our way into a megafreighter I still don't know how, marched on to the bridge waving toy pistols and demanded conkers. A wilder thing I have not known. Lost me a year's pocket money. For what? Conkers.'

'The captain was this really amazing guy, Yooden Vranx,' said Zaphod. 'He gave us food, booze – stuff from really weird parts of the Galaxy – lots of conkers, of course, and we had just the most incredible time. Then he teleported us back. Into the maximum-security wing of the Betelgeuse state prison. He was a cool guy. Went on to become President of the Galaxy.'

Zaphod paused.

The scene around them was currently plunged into gloom. Dark mists swirled round them and elephantine shapes lurked indistinctly in the shadows. The air was occasionally rent with the sounds of illusory beings murdering other illusory beings. Presumably enough people must have liked this sort of thing to make it a paying proposition.

'Ford,' said Zaphod quietly.

'Yeah?'

'Just before Yooden died he came to see me.'

'What? You never told me.'

'No.'

'What did he say? What did he come to see you about?'

'He told me about the *Heart of Gold*. It was his idea that I should steal it.'

'*His* idea?'

'Yeah,' said Zaphod, 'and the only possible way of stealing it was to be at the launching ceremony.'

Ford gaped at him in astonishment for a moment, and then roared with laughter.

'Are you telling me,' he said, 'that you set yourself up to become President of the Galaxy just to steal that ship?'

'That's it,' said Zaphod with the sort of grin that would get most people locked away in a room with soft walls.

'But why?' said Ford. 'What's so important about having it?'

'Dunno,' said Zaphod. 'I think if I'd consciously known what was so important about it and what I would need it for it would have shown up on the brain screening tests and I would never have passed. I think Yooden told me a lot of things that are still locked away.'

'So you think you went and mucked about inside your own brain as a result of Yooden talking to you?'

'He was a hell of a talker.'

'Yeah, but Zaphod, old mate, you want to look after yourself, you know.'

Zaphod shrugged.

'I mean, don't you have any inkling of the reasons for all this?' asked Ford.

Zaphod thought hard about this and doubts seemed to cross his mind.

'No,' he said at last. 'I don't seem to be letting myself into any of my secrets. Still,' he added on further reflection, 'I can understand that. I wouldn't trust myself further than I could spit a rat.'

A moment later, the last planet in the catalogue vanished from beneath them and the solid world resolved itself again.

They were sitting in a plush waiting room full of glass-top tables and design awards.

A tall Magrathean man was standing in front of them.

'The mice will see you now,' he said.

'So there you have it,' said Slartibartfast, making a feeble and perfunctory attempt to clear away some of the appalling mess of his study. He picked up a piece of paper from the top of a pile, but then couldn't think of anywhere else to put it, so he put it back on top of the original pile, which promptly fell over. 'Deep Thought designed the Earth, we built it and you lived on it.'

'And the Vogons came and destroyed it five minutes before the program was completed,' added Arthur, not unbitterly.

'Yes,' said the old man, pausing to gaze hopelessly round the room. 'Ten million years of planning and work gone just like that. Ten million years, Earthman . . . can you conceive of that kind of time span? A galactic civilization could grow from a single worm five times over in that time. Gone.' He paused.

'Well, that's bureaucracy for you,' he added.

'You know,' said Arthur thoughtfully, 'all this explains a lot of things. All through my life I've had this strange unaccountable feeling that something was going on in the world, something big, even sinister, and no one would tell me what it was.'

'No,' said the old man, 'that's just perfectly normal paranoia. Everyone in the Universe has that.'

'Everyone?' said Arthur. 'Well, if everyone has that perhaps it means something! Perhaps somewhere outside the Universe we know . . .'

'Maybe. Who cares?' said Slartibartfast before Arthur got too excited. 'Perhaps I'm old and tired,' he continued, 'but I always think that the chances of finding out what really is going on are so absurdly remote that the only thing to do is to say hang the sense of it and just keep yourself occupied. Look at me: I design coastlines. I got an award for Norway.'

He rummaged around in a pile of debris and pulled out a large Perspex block with his name on it and a model of Norway moulded into it.

'Where's the sense in that?' he said. 'None that I've been able to make out. I've been doing fjords all my life. For a fleeting moment they became fashionable and I get a major award.'

He turned it over in his hands with a shrug and tossed it aside carelessly, but not so carelessly that it didn't land on something soft.

'In this replacement Earth we're building they've given me Africa to do and of course I'm doing it with all fjords again because I happen to like them, and I'm old fashioned enough to think that they give a lovely baroque feel to a continent. And they tell me it's not equatorial enough. Equatorial!' He gave a hollow laugh. 'What does it matter? Science has achieved some wonderful things, of course, but I'd far rather be happy than right any day.'

'And are you?'

'No. That's where it all falls down, of course.'

'Pity,' said Arthur with sympathy. 'It sounded like quite a good lifestyle otherwise.'

Somewhere on the wall a small white light flashed.

'Come,' said Slartibartfast, 'you are to meet the mice. Your arrival on the planet has caused considerable excitement. It has already been hailed, so I gather, as the third most improbable event in the history of the Universe.'

'What were the first two?'

'Oh, probably just coincidences,' said Slartibartfast carelessly. He opened the door and stood waiting for Arthur to follow.

Arthur glanced around him once more, and then down at himself, at the sweaty dishevelled clothes he had been lying in the mud in on Thursday morning.

'I seem to be having tremendous difficulty with my lifestyle,' he muttered to himself.

'I beg your pardon?' asked the old man mildly.

'Oh, nothing,' said Arthur, 'only joking.'

It is of course well known that careless talk costs lives, but the full scale of the problem is not always appreciated.

For instance, at the very moment that Arthur said, 'I seem to be having tremendous difficulty with my lifestyle,' a freak wormhole opened up in the fabric of the space–time continuum and carried his words far far back in time across almost infinite reaches of space to a distant galaxy where strange and warlike beings were poised on the brink of frightful interstellar battle.

The two opposing leaders were meeting for the last time.

A dreadful silence fell across the conference table as the commander of the Vl'hurgs, resplendent in his black jewelled battle shorts, gazed levelly at the G'Gugvuntt leader squatting opposite him in a cloud of green sweet-smelling steam, and, with a million sleek and horribly beweaponed star cruisers poised to unleash electric death at his single word of command, challenged the vile creature to take back what it had said about his mother.

The creature stirred in his sickly broiling vapour, and at that very moment the words *I seem to be having tremendous difficulty with my lifestyle* drifted across the conference table.

Unfortunately, in the Vl'hurg tongue this was the most dreadful insult imaginable, and there was nothing for it but to wage terrible war for centuries.

Eventually, of course, after their galaxy had been decimated over a few thousand years, it was realized that the whole thing had been a ghastly mistake, and so the two opposing battle fleets settled their few remaining differences in order to launch a joint attack on our own galaxy – now positively identified as the source of the offending remark.

For thousands more years the mighty ships tore across the empty wastes of space and finally dived screaming on to the first planet they came across – which happened to be the Earth – where due to a terrible miscalculation of scale the entire battle fleet was accidentally swallowed by a small dog.

Those who study the complex interplay of cause and effect in the history of the Universe say that this sort of thing is going on all the time, but that we are powerless to prevent it.

'It's just life,' they say.

A short aircar trip brought Arthur and the old Magrathean to a doorway. They left the car and went through the door into a waiting room full of glass-topped tables and Perspex awards. Almost immediately, a light flashed above the door at the other side of the room and they entered.

'Arthur! You're safe!' a voice said.

'Am I?' said Arthur, rather startled. 'Oh, good.'

The lighting was rather subdued and it took him a moment or so to see Ford, Trillian, and Zaphod sitting round a large table beautifully decked out with exotic dishes, strange sweetmeats, and bizarre fruits. They were stuffing their faces.

'What happened to you?' demanded Arthur.

'Well,' said Zaphod, attacking a boneful of grilled muscle, 'our guests here have been gassing us and zapping our minds and being generally weird and have now given us a rather nice meal to make it up to us. Here,' he said hoiking out a lump of evil-smelling meat from a bowl, 'have some Vegan rhino's cutlet. It's delicious if you happen to like that sort of thing.'

'Hosts?' said Arthur. 'What hosts? I don't see any . . .'

A small voice said, 'Welcome to lunch, Earth creature.'

Arthur glanced around and suddenly yelped.

'Ugh!' he said. 'There are mice on the table!'

There was an awkward silence as everyone looked pointedly at Arthur.

He was busy staring at two white mice sitting in what looked like whisky glasses on the table. He heard the silence and glanced around at everyone.

'Oh!' he said, with sudden realization. 'Oh, I'm sorry, I wasn't quite prepared for . . .'

'Let me introduce you,' said Trillian. 'Arthur, this is Benjy mouse.'

'Hi,' said one of the mice. His whiskers stroked what must have been a touch sensitive panel on the inside of the whisky glass-like affair, and it moved forward slightly.

'And this is Frankie mouse.'

Trillian with the
Point of View gun.

Vogon calculator.

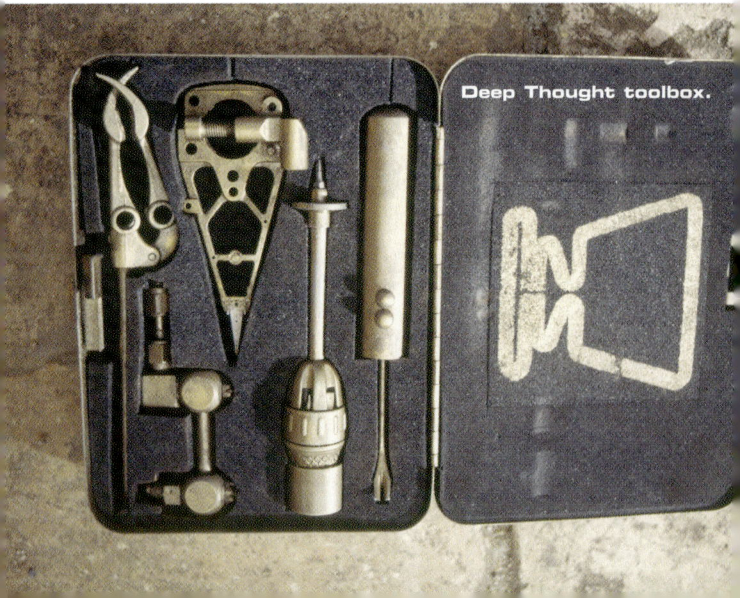

Deep Thought toolbox.

Douglas Adams and Jane Belson on a panel decorating the *Heart of Gold*.

Door handles in the shape of Douglas Adams' nose at Humma Kavula's temple.

Nick and Garth on the Vogon destroyer set.

Mos and Sam in the garden at Arthur's house.

Mos and Martin on a break.

Garth with Anna Chancellor, leaning on the Vogons' map table.

Sam Rockwell with Garth.

Nick with Zooey Deschanel.

Martin Freeman making a point to Garth.

Warwick Davis taking a breather in a quarry in Wales.

Garth and Nick with Roger Birnbaum
and Gary Barber of Spyglass.

Robbie Stamp on set.

The other mouse said, 'Pleased to meet you,' and did likewise.

Arthur gaped.

'But aren't they . . .'

'Yes,' said Trillian, 'they are the mice I brought with me from the Earth.'

She looked him in the eye and Arthur thought he detected the tiniest resigned shrug.

'Could you pass me that bowl of grated Arcturan Megadonkey?' she said.

Slartibartfast coughed politely.

'Er, excuse me,' he said.

'Yes, thank you, Slartibartfast,' said Benjy mouse sharply, 'you may go.'

'What? Oh . . . er, very well,' said the old man, slightly taken aback. 'I'll just go and get on with some of my fjords, then.'

'Ah, well in fact that won't be necessary,' said Frankie mouse. 'It looks very much as if we won't be needing the new Earth any longer.' He swivelled his pink little eyes. 'Not now that we have found a native of the planet who was there seconds before it was destroyed.'

'What?' cried Slartibartfast, aghast. 'You can't mean that! I've got a thousand glaciers poised and ready to roll over Africa!'

'Well, perhaps you can take a quick skiing holiday before you dismantle them,' said Frankie, acidly.

'Skiing holiday!' cried the old man. 'Those glaciers are works of art! Elegantly sculpted contours, soaring pinnacles of ice, deep majestic ravines! It would be sacrilege to go skiing on high art!'

'Thank you, Slartibartfast,' said Benjy firmly. 'That will be all.'

'Yes, sir,' said the old man coldly, 'thank you very much. Well, goodbye, Earthman,' he said to Arthur, 'hope the lifestyle comes together.'

With a brief nod to the rest of the company he turned and walked sadly out of the room.

Arthur stared after him not knowing what to say.

'Now,' said Benjy mouse, 'to business.'

Ford and Zaphod clinked their glasses together.

'To business!' they said.

'I beg your pardon?' said Benjy.

Ford looked round.

'Sorry, I thought you were proposing a toast,' he said.

The two mice scuttled impatiently around in their glass transports. Finally they composed themselves, and Benjy moved forward to address Arthur.

'Now, Earth creature,' he said, 'the situation we have in effect is this. We have, as you know, been more or less running your planet for the last ten million years in order to find this wretched thing called the Ultimate Question.'

'Why?' said Arthur, sharply.

'No – we already thought of that one,' said Frankie interrupting, 'but it doesn't fit the answer. *Why? – Forty-two* . . . you see, it doesn't work.'

'No,' said Arthur, 'I mean why have you been doing it?'

'Oh, I see,' said Frankie. 'Well, eventually just habit, I think, to be brutally honest. And this is more or less the point – we're sick to the teeth with the whole thing, and the prospect of doing it all over again on account of those whinnet-ridden Vogons quite frankly gives me the screaming heeby jeebies, you know what I mean? It was by the merest lucky chance that Benjy and I finished our particular job and left the planet early for a quick holiday, and have since manipulated our way back to Magrathea by the good offices of your friends.'

'Magrathea is a gateway back to our own dimension,' put in Benjy.

'Since when,' continued his murine colleague, 'we have had an offer of a quite enormously fat contract to do the 5D chat show and lecture circuit back in our own dimensional neck of the woods, and we're very much inclined to take it.'

'I would, wouldn't you, Ford?' said Zaphod promptingly.

'Oh, yes,' said Ford, 'jump at it, like a shot.'

Arthur glanced at them, wondering what all this was leading up to.

'But we've got to have *product*, you see,' said Frankie. 'I mean ideally we still need the Ultimate Question in some form or other.'

Zaphod leaned forward to Arthur.

'You see,' he said, 'if they're just sitting there in the studio looking very relaxed and, you know, just mentioning that they happen to know the Answer to Life, the Universe and Everything, and then eventually have to admit that in fact it's Forty-two, then the show's probably quite short. No follow-up, you see.'

'We have to have something that *sounds* good,' said Benjy.

'Something that *sounds* good?' exclaimed Arthur. 'An

Ultimate Question that *sounds* good? From a couple of mice?'

The mice bristled.

'Well, I mean, *yes* idealism, *yes* the dignity of pure research, *yes* the pursuit of truth in all its forms, but there comes a point I'm afraid where you begin to suspect that if there's any *real* truth, it's that the entire multi-dimensional infinity of the Universe is almost certainly being run by a bunch of maniacs. And if it comes to a choice between spending yet another ten million years finding that out, and on the other hand just taking the money and running, then I for one could do with the exercise,' said Frankie.

'But—' started Arthur, hopelessly.

'Hey, will you get this, Earthman,' interrupted Zaphod. 'You are a last-generation product of that computer matrix, right, and you were there right up to the moment your planet got the finger, yeah?'

'Er . . .'

'So your brain was an organic part of the penultimate configuration of the computer program,' said Ford, rather lucidly he thought.

'Right?' said Zaphod.

'Well,' said Arthur doubtfully. He wasn't aware of ever having felt an organic part of anything. He had always seen this as one of his problems.

'In other words,' said Benjy, steering his curious little vehicle right over to Arthur, 'there's a good chance that the structure of the question is encoded in the structure of your brain – so we want to buy it off you.'

'What, the question?' said Arthur.

'Yes,' said Ford and Trillian.

'For lots of money,' said Zaphod.

'No, no,' said Frankie, 'it's the brain we want to buy.'

'What!'

'Well, who would miss it?' enquired Benjy.

'I thought you said you could just read his brain electronically,' protested Ford.

'Oh, yes,' said Frankie, 'but we'd have to get it out first. It's got to be prepared.'

'Treated,' said Benjy.

'Diced.'

'Thank you,' shouted Arthur, tipping up his chair and backing away from the table in horror.

'It could always be replaced,' said Benjy reasonably, 'if you think it's important.'

'Yes, an electronic brain,' said Frankie, 'a simple one would suffice.'

'A simple one!' wailed Arthur.

'Yeah,' said Zaphod with a sudden evil grin, 'you'd just have to program it to say *What?* and *I don't understand* and *Where's the tea?* – who'd know the difference?'

'What?' cried Arthur, backing away still further.

'See what I mean?' said Zaphod and howled with pain because of something Trillian did at that moment.

'*I'd* notice the difference,' said Arthur.

'No, you wouldn't,' said Frankie mouse, 'you'd be programmed not to.'

Ford made for the door.

'Look, I'm sorry, mice old lads,' he said, 'I don't think we've got a deal.'

'I rather think we have to have a deal,' said the mice

in chorus, all the charm vanishing from their piping little voices in an instant. With a tiny whining shriek their two glass transports lifted themselves off the table, and swung through the air towards Arthur, who stumbled further backwards into a blind corner, utterly unable to cope or think of anything.

Trillian grabbed him desperately by the arm and tried to drag him towards the door, which Ford and Zaphod were struggling to open, but Arthur was a dead weight – he seemed hypnotized by the airborne rodents swooping towards him.

She screamed at him, but he just gaped.

With one more yank, Ford and Zaphod got the door open. On the other side of it was a small pack of rather ugly men who they could only assume were the heavy mob of Magrathea. Not only were they ugly themselves, but the medical equipment they carried with them was also far from pretty. They charged.

So – Arthur was about to have his head cut open, Trillian was unable to help him, and Ford and Zaphod were about to be set upon by several thugs a great deal heavier and more sharply armed than they were.

All in all it was extremely fortunate that at that moment every alarm on the planet burst into an ear-splitting din.

'Emergency! Emergency!' blared the klaxons throughout Magrathea. *'Hostile ship has landed on planet. Armed intruders in section 8A. Defence stations, defence stations.'*

The two mice sniffed irritably round the fragments of their glass transports where they lay shattered on the floor.

'Damnation,' muttered Frankie mouse, 'all that fuss over two pounds of Earthling brain.' He scuttled round and about, his pink eyes flashing, his fine white coat bristling with static.

'The only thing we can do now,' said Benjy, crouching and stroking his whiskers in thought, 'is to try and fake a question, invent one that will sound plausible.'

'Difficult,' said Frankie. He thought. 'How about, *What's yellow and dangerous?'*

Benjy considered this for a moment.

'No, no good,' he said. 'Doesn't fit the answer.'

They sank into silence for a few seconds.

'All right,' said Benjy. *'What do you get if you multiply six by seven?'*

'No, no, too literal, too factual,' said Frankie, 'wouldn't sustain the punters' interest.'

Again they thought.

Then Frankie said: 'Here's a thought. *How many roads must a man walk down?*'

'Ah!' said Benjy. 'Aha, now that does sound promising!' He rolled the phrase around a little. 'Yes,' he said, 'that's excellent! Sounds very significant without actually tying you down to meaning anything at all. *How many roads must a man walk down? Forty-two.* Excellent, excellent, that'll fox 'em. Frankie baby, we are made!'

They performed a scampering dance in their excitement.

Near them on the floor lay several rather ugly men who had been hit about the head with some heavy design awards.

Half a mile away, four figures pounded up a corridor looking for a way out. They emerged into a wide open-plan computer bay. They glanced about wildly.

'Which way you reckon, Zaphod?' said Ford.

'At a wild guess, I'd say down here,' said Zaphod, running off down to the right between a computer bank and the wall. As the others started after him he was brought up short by a Kill-O-Zap energy bolt that cracked through the air inches in front of him and fried a small section of adjacent wall.

A voice on a loud hailer said, 'OK, Beeblebrox, hold it right there. We've got you covered.'

'Cops!' hissed Zaphod, and spun around in a crouch. 'You want to try a guess at all, Ford?'

'OK, this way,' said Ford, and the four of them ran down a gangway between two computer banks.

At the end of the gangway appeared a heavily

armoured and space-suited figure waving a vicious Kill-O-Zap gun.

'We don't want to shoot you, Beeblebrox!' shouted the figure.

'Suits me fine!' shouted Zaphod back and dived down a wide gap between two data-processing units.

The others swerved in behind him.

'There are two of them,' said Trillian. 'We're cornered.'

They squeezed themselves down in an angle between a large computer data bank and the wall.

They held their breath and waited.

Suddenly the air exploded with energy bolts as both the cops opened fire on them simultaneously.

'Hey, they're shooting at us,' said Arthur, crouching in a tight ball. 'I thought they said they didn't want to do that.'

'Yeah, *I* thought they said that,' agreed Ford.

Zaphod stuck a head up for a dangerous moment.

'Hey,' he said, 'I thought you said you didn't want to shoot us!' and ducked again.

They waited.

After a moment a voice replied, 'It isn't easy being a cop!'

'What did he say?' whispered Ford in astonishment.

'He said it isn't easy being a cop.'

'Well, surely that's his problem, isn't it?'

'I'd have thought so.'

Ford shouted out, 'Hey, listen! I think we've got enough problems of our own having you shooting at us, so if you could avoid laying *your* problems on us as well, I think we'd all find it easier to cope!'

Another pause, and then the loud hailer again.

'Now see here, guy,' said the voice on the loud hailer, 'you're not dealing with any dumb two-bit trigger-pumping morons with low hairlines, little piggy eyes, and no conversation, we're a couple of intelligent caring guys that you'd probably quite like if you met us socially! I don't go around gratuitously shooting people and then bragging about it afterwards in seedy space-rangers' bars, like some cops I could mention! I go around shooting people gratuitously and then I agonize about it afterwards for hours to my girlfriend!'

'And I write novels!' chimed in the other cop. 'Though I haven't had any of them published yet, so I better warn you, I'm in a *meeeean* mood!'

Ford's eyes popped halfway out of their sockets. 'Who are these guys?' he said.

'Dunno,' said Zaphod. 'I think I preferred it when they were shooting.'

'So are you going to come quietly,' shouted one of the cops again, 'or are you going to let us blast you out?'

'Which would you prefer?' shouted Ford.

A millisecond later the air about them started to fry again, as bolt after bolt of Kill-O-Zap hurled itself into the computer bank in front of them.

The fusillade continued for several seconds at unbearable intensity.

When it stopped, there were a few seconds of near quietness as the echoes die away.

'You still there?' called one of the cops.

'Yes,' they called back.

'We didn't enjoy doing that at all,' shouted the other cop.

'We could tell,' shouted Ford.

'Now, listen to this, Beeblebrox, and you better listen good!'

'Why?' shouted back Zaphod.

'Because,' shouted the cop, 'it's going to be very intelligent, and quite interesting and humane! Now – either you all give yourselves up now and let us beat you up a bit, though not very much of course because we are firmly opposed to needless violence, or we blow up this entire planet and possibly one or two others we noticed on our way out here!'

'But that's crazy!' cried Trillian. 'You wouldn't do that!'

'Oh, yes, we would,' shouted the cop, 'wouldn't we?' he asked the other one.

'Oh, yes, we'd have to, no question,' the other one called back.

'But why?' demanded Trillian.

'Because there are some things you have to do even if you are an enlightened liberal cop who knows all about sensitivity and everything!'

'I just don't believe these guys,' muttered Ford, shaking his head.

One cop shouted to the other, 'Shall we shoot them again for a bit?'

'Yeah, why not?'

They let fly another electric barrage.

The heat and noise were quite fantastic. Slowly the

computer bank was beginning to disintegrate. The front had almost all melted away, and thick rivulets of molten metal were winding their way back towards where they were squatting. They huddled further back and waited for the end.

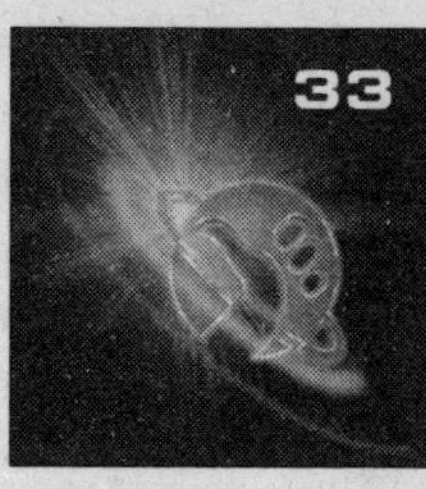

But the end never came, at least not then.

Quite suddenly the barrage stopped, and the sudden silence afterwards was punctuated by a couple of strangled gurgles and thuds.

The four stared at each other.

'What happened?' said Arthur.

'They stopped,' said Zaphod with a shrug.

'Why?'

'Dunno, do you want to go and ask them?'

'No.'

They waited.

'Hello?' called out Ford.

No answer.

'That's odd.'

'Perhaps it's a trap.'

'They haven't the wit.'

'What were those thuds?'

'Dunno.'

They waited for a few more seconds.

'Right,' said Ford, 'I'm going to have a look.'

He glanced round at the others.

'Is no one going to say, *No, you can't possibly, let me go instead?'*

They all shook their heads.

'Oh, well,' he said, and stood up.

For a moment, nothing happened.

Then, after a second or so, nothing continued to happen. Ford peered through the thick smoke that was billowing out of the burning computer.

Cautiously he stepped out into the open.

Still nothing happened.

Twenty yards away he could dimly see through the smoke the space-suited figure of one of the cops. He was lying in a crumpled heap on the ground. Twenty yards in the other direction lay the second man. No one else was anywhere to be seen.

This struck Ford as being extremely odd.

Slowly, nervously, he walked towards the first one. The body lay reassuringly still as he approached it, and continued to lie reassuringly still as he reached it and put his foot down on the Kill-O-Zap gun that still dangled from its limp fingers.

He reached down and picked it up, meeting no resistance.

The cop was quite clearly dead.

A quick examination revealed him to be from Blagulon Kappa – he was a methane-breathing life form, dependent on his space-suit for survival in the thin oxygen atmosphere of Magrathea.

The tiny life-support-system computer on his backpack appeared unexpectedly to have blown up.

Ford poked around in it in considerable astonishment. These miniature suit computers usually had the full back-up of the main computer back on the ship, with which they were directly linked through the sub-etha. Such a system was fail-safe in all circumstances other than total feedback malfunction, which was unheard of.

He hurried over to the other prone figure, and discovered that exactly the same impossible thing had happened to him, presumably simultaneously.

He called the others over to look. They came, shared his astonishment, but not his curiosity.

'Let's get shot of this hole,' said Zaphod. 'If whatever I'm supposed to be looking for is here, I don't want it.' He grabbed the second Kill-O-Zap gun, blasted a perfectly harmless accounting computer, and rushed out into the corridor, followed by the others. He very nearly blasted hell out of an aircar that stood waiting for them a few yards away.

The aircar was empty, but Arthur recognized it as belonging to Slartibartfast.

It had a note from him pinned to part of its sparse instrument panel. The note had an arrow drawn on it, pointing at one of the controls.

It said *This is probably the best button to press.*

The aircar rocketed them at speeds in excess of R17 through the steel tunnels that led out on to the appalling surface of the planet which was now in the grip of yet another drear morning twilight. Ghastly grey light congealed on the land.

R is a velocity measure, defined as a reasonable speed of travel that is consistent with health, mental wellbeing, and not being more than say five minutes late. It is therefore clearly an almost infinitely variable figure according to circumstances, since the first two factors vary not only with speed taken as an absolute, but also with awareness of the third factor. Unless handled with tranquillity this equation can result in considerable stress, ulcers and even death.

R17 is not a fixed velocity, but it is clearly far too fast.

The aircar flung itself through the air at R17 and above, deposited them next to the *Heart of Gold*, which stood starkly on the frozen ground like a bleached bone, and then precipitately hurled itself back in the direction whence they had come, presumably on important business of its own.

Shivering, the four of them stood and looked at the ship.

Beside it stood another one.

It was the Blagulon Kappa policecraft, a bulbous sharklike affair, slate-green in colour and smothered with black stencilled letters of varying degrees of size and unfriendliness. The letters informed anyone who cared to read them where the ship was from, what section of the police it was assigned to, and where the power feeds should be connected.

It seemed somehow unnaturally dark and silent, even for a ship whose two-man crew was at that moment lying asphyxiated in a smoke-filled chamber several miles beneath the ground. It is one of those curious things that is impossible to explain or define, but one can sense when a ship is completely dead.

Ford could sense it and found it most mysterious – a ship and two policemen seemed to have gone spontaneously dead. In his experience the Universe simply didn't work like that.

The other three could sense it too, but they could sense the bitter cold even more and hurried back into the *Heart of Gold* suffering from an acute attack of no curiosity.

Ford stayed, and went to examine the Blagulon ship. As he walked, he nearly tripped over an inert steel figure lying face down in the cold dust.

'Marvin!' he exclaimed. 'What are you doing?'

'Don't feel you have to take any notice of me, please,' came a muffled drone.

'But how are you, metalman?' said Ford.

'Very depressed.'

'What's up?'

'I don't know,' said Marvin, 'I've never been there.'

'Why,' said Ford squatting down beside him and shivering, 'are you lying face down in the dust?'

'It's a very effective way of being wretched,' said Marvin. 'Don't pretend you want to talk to me, I know you hate me.'

'No, I don't.'

'Yes, you do, everybody does. It's part of the shape of the Universe. I only have to talk to somebody and they begin to hate me. Even robots hate me. If you just ignore me I expect I shall probably go away.'

He jacked himself up to his feet and stood resolutely facing the opposite direction.

'That ship hated me,' he said dejectedly, indicating the policecraft.

'That ship?' said Ford in sudden excitement. 'What happened to it? Do you know?'

'It hated me because I talked to it.'

'You *talked* to it?' exclaimed Ford. 'What do you mean, you talked to it?'

'Simple. I got very bored and depressed, so I went and plugged myself in to its external computer feed. I talked to the computer at great length and explained my view of the Universe to it,' said Marvin.

'And what happened?' pressed Ford.

'It committed suicide,' said Marvin and stalked off back to the *Heart of Gold*.

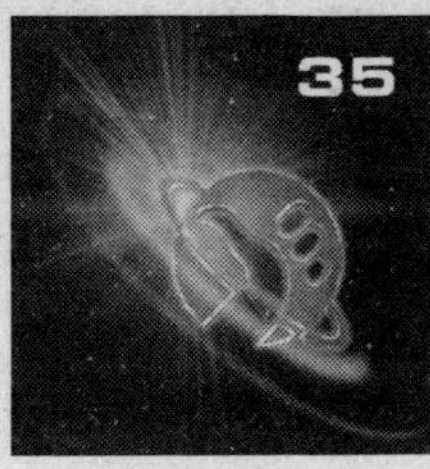

That night, as the *Heart of Gold* was busy putting a few light years between itself and the Horsehead Nebula, Zaphod lounged under the small palm tree on the bridge trying to bang his brains into shape with massive Pan Galactic Gargle Blasters; Ford and Trillian sat in a corner discussing life and matters arising from it; and Arthur took to his bed to flip through Ford's copy of *The Hitchhiker's Guide to the Galaxy*. Since he was going to have to live in the place, he reasoned, he'd better start finding out something about it.

He came across this entry.

It said: '*The history of every major galactic civilization tends to pass through three distinct and recognizable phases, those of Survival, Enquiry, and Sophistication, otherwise known as the How, Why, and Where phases.*

'*For instance, the first phase is characterized by the question* How can we eat?, *the second by the question* Why do we eat?, *and the third by the question* Where shall we have lunch?'

He got no further before the ship's intercom buzzed into life.

'Hey, Earthman? You hungry, kid?' said Zaphod's voice.

'Er, well yes, a little peckish I suppose,' said Arthur.

'OK, baby, hold tight,' said Zaphod. 'We'll take in a quick bite at the Restaurant at the End of the Universe.'

Afterword to the Film Tie-in Edition

by Robbie Stamp

At 9.30 a.m. on 19 April 2004, 'Shoorah, Shoorah' sung by Betty Wright blared out across an 'Islington flat' built on Stage 7 at Elstree Film Studios in Hertfordshire. Under the eyes of the director, Garth Jennings, and the producer, Nick Goldsmith, who together make up the Hammer and Tongs production company, the first assistant director, Richard Whelan, shouted, 'Action!' and finally, just over a quarter of a century since the first radio series was broadcast on Radio 4, a movie based on *The Hitchhiker's Guide to the Galaxy* was under way. Arthur Dent, played by Martin Freeman, stood by himself reading a book, while more than forty actors in fancy dress started dancing. In the midst of the crowd, which included a sugar-pink mouse, a drunk cowboy and an Indian chief, the American actress Zooey Deschanel as Tricia McMillan could be seen bouncing up and down, dressed as Charles Darwin. An edited version of the historic call sheet from that first day is reproduced on pages 320–323.

Douglas Adams once famously described the process of making a film in Hollywood as like 'trying to grill a steak by having a succession of people coming into the room and breathing on it'. Why indeed – despite the phenomenal international appeal of the *Hitchhiker* radio series, TV series and above all the novels – had it taken over twenty-five years to get this movie made? It is a long story.

This afterword to the film tie-in edition of *The Hitchhiker's Guide to the Galaxy* is not an exhaustive account of the two and a half decades it took a senior Hollywood executive to finally say, 'Yes, let's make the *Hitchhiker's* movie.' As Ed Victor, Douglas' personal friend, and literary agent since 1981, has said, 'Many, many people nibbled at it, took a taste and rejected it.' To tell the full tale of all those nibbles would need a book in its own right. But as one of the executive producers, I can tell the story of how the movie finally came to be made, based on conversations with many of the key people involved.

I first met Douglas Adams in 1991 in his house in Islington, where he played Bach to me because there was a point he wanted to make about music and mathematics, and we talked about a television series on evolution he wanted to write and present. My overwhelming impression on that first meeting was of Douglas Adams' powerful intellectual curiosity. We stayed in touch. He introduced me to sushi. We started a company together.* We saw a lot of movies and I was lucky that he became a friend as well as a colleague.

Douglas and I continued to be good friends over the

---

* The Digital Village was designed as a multiple-media company and produced the *Starship Titanic* computer game and the h2g2.com Web site based on the *Guide* itself. The founders were Douglas, me, Richard Creasey (a senior TV executive), Ian Charles Stewart (an investment banker), Mary Glanville (also a TV executive), Richard Harris (a technical expert) and Ed Victor.

years and so it was not surprising that ten years later, when my father died, Douglas was one of the first people I called on returning home from the hospital. He had been compassionate and gently supportive when my father was ill, and we talked at length about the kind of man my father had been. After a while we strayed onto our normal topics of conversation, including new ideas Douglas was hatching, and – for the umpteenth time – talked about our frustrations over the *Hitchhiker's Guide to the Galaxy* movie, which was already well entrenched in Hollywood folklore for its seemingly endless stint in development hell.

The very next day, Friday 11 May 2001, I received a call from Ed Victor and, sitting in my favourite chair in the kitchen, where I had spoken to Douglas just the evening before, I heard the news that he had died of a heart attack less than an hour before in his gym in Montecito, California. I remember my wife calling out in shock as she heard me talking to Ed but I just felt numb and spent the evening fielding and making calls to friends and colleagues.

The outpouring of grief and affection for Douglas on the Web and in the press was a tribute to the enormous impact that *Hitchhiker's* has had on people all over the world. Perhaps, sadly, Douglas's tragically early death and the huge reaction it caused actually were the catalysts that finally got the movie-making process going. If so it is a very cruel irony. Ed Victor remarks on the frustration of trying to get the *Hitchhiker's Guide to the Galaxy* movie made, saying, 'I was always trying to sell *Hitchhiker's*. Douglas always, *always* wanted a film made of this. Four times I sold *Hitchhiker's* and I've described not seeing the movie made for so many years as the single most substantial professional frustration of my life. This was something I'd always felt so sure about. I'd seen the mailbags. I just knew there was an audience out there. I sold it to Don Tafner for ABC to make a TV series. I sold it to Columbia and Ivan Reitman. We did a joint venture deal with Michael Nesmith and finally we sold it to Disney and even then it took seven years to get the movie into production.'

My own relationship with Douglas doesn't go back as far as Ed's, but I have been involved in the film project since the negotiations to sell movie rights to Disney began in 1997 when, following the huge success of the first *Men in Black* film, it seemed that there was interest again in comedy and science fiction. Bob Bookman, Douglas's film agent at the powerful Hollywood talent agency CAA (Creative Artists Agency), organized meetings for Douglas and me with a variety of potential producers. And as a result of those meetings two people really began to drive the *Hitchhiker's Guide to the Galaxy* movie project forward. Roger Birnbaum at independent producer Caravan Pictures (which evolved into Spyglass) had the 'muscle' and enthusiasm to get Disney on board, and via Michael Nesmith, Douglas' friend and former business partner on the movie, we had been introduced to Peter Safran, Nick Reed and Jimmy Miller, who together at that stage represented Jay Roach, then a hot new director coming off the back of his surprise summer hit, *Austin Powers: International Man of Mystery*. Jay also had a strong relationship with Disney. Douglas and Jay struck up a warm creative relationship almost immediately and it looked like a winning triumvirate had been formed.

Hitchhiker's started as a radio series, became a famous novel 'trilogy in five parts', a stage play and a computer game and was at the time being turned into a 'real' guide to the planet Earth by the Digital Village. The rights situation was thus highly complex and concluding a deal took an enormous amount of effort. Ken Kleinberg and Christine Cuddy became the attorneys for the negotiations with Disney. Even with their hard work, the enthusiasm and support of Roger Birnbaum and Jay Roach, and the teams at CAA, Ed Victor's office and the Digital Village all working overtime, negotiations went on for almost eighteen months. The deal was finally done just before Christmas 1998, and stipulated that Douglas and I would be executive producers and that Douglas would write a new script.

Douglas had been working on *Hitchhiker* movie scripts for many years and so, with input from Jay and Shauna Robertson, his business partner at the time, he was quickly able to produce a draft that was full of his extraordinary wit and intelligence; new ideas jostled for space with favourite scenes and characters from the books and the radio series. This early 1999 draft was good but the difficulties of striking the right balance between the episodic nature of *Hitchhiker's* and a narrative drive that made sense had not truly been solved. Indeed this was the issue that had vexed draft after draft of the movie over the years and it continued to be a huge stumbling block. Jay remembers his collaboration with Douglas with great affection but also reflects on the problems they faced.

'Even during the writing time and what became a hellishly frustrating development process, I don't remember ever enjoying a collaboration more. The dinners and the long talks and his laughter. Even later, in the middle of saying "it's not happening", we'd still be making jokes about the absurdity of it all. So the process was extremely pleasurable. It just didn't get anywhere. There was a combination of things built into the struggle to get *Hitchhiker's* made . . . there was always a mismatch between, on the one hand, people's perception of it being a very high-budget sci-fi extravaganza with a lot of spectacle and, on the other, the recognition that it was smarter, more sophisticated, a little more English, a little more ironic than the big money-maker comedies here in the US, and those things didn't synch up, so it was hard to tap into Disney's needs.'

On 19 April 1999, Douglas, frustrated with the pace of progress, sent a fax to David Vogel, then President of Production at Disney, suggesting a meeting. He wrote: 'We seem to have gotten to a place where the problems appear to loom larger than the opportunities. I don't know if I'm right in thinking this, but I only have silence to go on, which is always a poor source of information . . . the fact that we may have different perspectives should be a fertile source of debate and iterative problem solving. It's not clear to me that a one-way traffic of written "notes" interspersed with long dreadful silences is a good substitute for this . . . Why don't we meet and actually have a chat? I've appended a list of numbers you can reach me on. If you manage not to . . . I shall know you're trying not to, very, very hard indeed.' With characteristic humour, he then provided dozens of contact numbers, including those for his own home and mobile, his nanny, his mother, his sister, his next-door neighbour (who he was 'sure would take a message'), a couple of his favourite restaurants and even the number for Sainsbury's, his local supermarket, where he was sure they would page him. It had the desired effect and shortly afterwards Douglas and I flew out to LA for a 'summit' meeting. We talked for hours on that flight about what we both suspected was coming: Disney was going to suggest bringing in a new writer. Roger Birnbaum, who was at the meeting at Disney's Studios in Burbank, remembers it well.

'I knew it would be tricky. I wanted him to know how much we respected him. I admired him a lot and did not want to compromise the material but I also thought that after so many years of working on so many drafts, Douglas was getting bogged down.'

Douglas was faced with an agonizing dilemma. The message was clear. Momentum, that most precious of Hollywood commodities, was slowing dangerously and if the movie was not to stall altogether – again – he was going to have to let another writer into the fold. Disney and Spyglass handled things with considerable tact and respect. In the meeting, David Vogel, a thoughtful man and a former Rabbinical scholar, likened Douglas to the designer of a cathedral, with the next step of the process being akin to hiring the master stonemason – not the man with the vision but a different kind of craftsman, concerned with making sure that the brilliance of the original conception had the right foundations.

An experienced writer was hired and wrote a new draft, which was completed in autumn 1999. There was not much collaborative work possible with Douglas and although it was by no means a bad script it didn't really move the process forward. More ominously it coincided with a regime change at the studio. David Vogel and Joe Roth, who had been in charge when Disney bought the rights, both moved on. Nina Jacobson, now President of Buena Vista Pictures, responsible for developing scripts and overseeing film production for Walt

Disney Pictures, was now in charge. Her biggest concern was budget level and at that stage she was not sure that the material as it was could break out of its fan base to create a movie Disney could get behind.

Frustrated yet again, Douglas decided to write yet another draft and this he delivered in summer 2000. Disney were still not convinced, and in fact were increasingly unsure that this movie was for them. So, with their permission, the script was quietly sent to other studios. The project still had some very powerful supporters. Jay was by now an 'A'-list comedy director and Roger Birnbaum and his partner Gary Barber at Spyglass were extremely influential. Nevertheless, all the studios and the key independents, who were shown the new draft, passed. One call in particular stands out in my mind as summing up everything that was so painful about this tantalizing period. Douglas phoned me from Santa Barbara while I was on a beach in Corsica with my family. He told me that Joe Roth, who was now at Revolution Studios, had passed. I remember the awful sinking feeling as I looked across to my family and saw my wife noticing the anxiety on my face. This call felt to me especially bad news as Joe was a close friend and colleague of Roger Birnbaum's and had, behind the scenes, been very instrumental in bringing *Hitchhiker's* to Disney when he was head of the studios. If he had no appetite for this, who would? Ed Victor also remembers this period all too well: 'It fell into a black hole again. At one point we went to the bar next door to the office here, both ordered huge vodka martinis and Douglas said, "I estimate that I must have spent a total of five years of my professional life on this fucking film, Ed. Never let me do this again."'

But of course Douglas never did really let go of the hope that one day there would be a movie of *Hitchhiker's*.

In spring 2001, with the film still stalled, Jay Roach came to feel that after working on the movie for several years maybe he was simply not the right person to take things further, and very sadly and reluctantly he decided to bow out as director, although as producer he remained as committed as ever. Spyglass too were still determined to find a way forward. Jon Glickman, President of Spyglass Pictures, and Derek Evans, who had first brought *Hitchhiker's* to the attention of Roger Birnbaum when he joined Spyglass as a development executive, had been two of the staunchest supporters of the movie.* Jon remembers seeing the need for realism about the budget and returning to their first instinct, which had been to find a director on the way up, as indeed Jay had been when we first met him back in 1997. But it was a pretty dispiriting time.

And then in May 2001 came the call to say that Douglas had died. In one week I flew out to California for Douglas' funeral and home to England for my father's. It was emotionally and physically exhausting. As friends gathered in the weeks and months after Douglas' death, much of the talk was about the immense frustration Douglas had experienced over all the years of trying to make 'the Movie'. It had almost become an obsession for him and sometime later I asked his widow, Jane Belson, whether, should it prove possible to somehow get the movie made, it would have her approval. She simply said

---

* When the film finally came to be made, Jon Glickman and Derek Evans from Spyglass were producer and executive producer respectively.

yes, and made one comment in particular that given the directing and producing team who finally brought the movie home was very prescient. 'Get a young director, someone who didn't grow up with *Hitchhiker's* in its first flush of success. Remember that Douglas was only in his mid-twenties when he wrote *Hitchhiker's*. Find somebody with a current energy, not trendy, but cool. *Hitchhiker's* was cool when it first came out.'

So I spoke to Roger Birnbaum again and as always he offered his support and continued enthusiasm. He remembers the call well. 'After Douglas' death we froze, and then it was a call from you, saying that the estate were still up for making the movie, that started us going again. We still loved the project and out of respect for Douglas were happy to try and get it made.'

I also spoke to Jay Roach, whose support I knew would be essential. The project needed all the allies we could find and a film like *Hitchhiker's* had to have 'insider' support if it was to stand any chance of being made. Once he knew that Jane Belson wanted the movie made, his deep affection for Douglas meant that Jay also gladly stepped back into the ring as director.

We all knew that without a new draft we would go nowhere; *Hitchhiker's* could be in limbo for years. It was absolutely necessary to hire a new writer, and through Jennifer Perrini (Jay's partner at his production company Everyman Pictures), we were very lucky to find Karey Kirkpatrick. He tells the story of his involvement in his own self-interview (page 300). Karey was not a *Hitchhiker* fan – although he became one – but simply came to the screenplay as an experienced writer who could see where some of the problems lay. His starting point was Douglas's final script, and I was able to make available a lot of material from the hard drive on Douglas's Mac – earlier drafts, back stories and notes on solving problems. And so Karey and Jay, back in the director's chair, set to work on a new 'take', establishing the basic direction in which the screenplay could now go.

Several months later, on an early spring morning in 2002, a meeting was called at Roger Birnbaum's house in Beverly Hills. There, with a log fire in the grate and smoked salmon and bagels on the table, Karey Kirkpatrick pitched the take that he and Jay had worked on to Nina Jacobson, Jay Roach, Jennifer Perrini, Roger Birnbaum, Jon Glickman and Derek Evans. This was the core group of people who could get this movie made. Karey began his pitch with an overview of how the narrative in the movie might work. He just read the 'story so far' from the beginning of *The Restaurant at the End of the Universe,* which summarized the events of *The Hitchhiker's Guide to the Galaxy*.

> In the beginning the Universe was created.
>
> This has made a lot of people very angry and been widely regarded as a bad move.
>
> Many races believe that it was created by some sort of god, though the Jatravartid people of Viltvodle Six believe that the entire Universe was in fact sneezed out of the nose of a being called the Great Green Arkleseizure.
>
> The Jatravartids, who live in perpetual fear of the time they call the Coming of the Great White Handkerchief, are small blue creatures with more than fifty arms each, who are therefore unique in being the only race in history to have invented the aerosol deodorant before the wheel.
>
> However, the Great Green Arkleseizure Theory is not

widely accepted outside Viltvodle Six and so, the Universe being the puzzling place it is, other explanations are constantly being sought.

For instance, a race of hyper-intelligent pan-dimensional beings once built themselves a gigantic supercomputer called Deep Thought to calculate once and for all the Answer to the Ultimate Question of Life, the Universe, and Everything.

For seven and a half million years, Deep Thought computed and calculated, and in the end announced that the answer was in fact Forty-two – and so another, even bigger, computer had to be built to find out what the actual question was.

And this computer, which was called the Earth, was so large that it was frequently mistaken for a planet – especially by the strange ape-like beings who roamed its surface, totally unaware that they were simply part of a gigantic computer program. And this is very odd, because without that fairly simple and obvious piece of knowledge, nothing that ever happened on the Earth could possibly make the slightest bit of sense.

Sadly, however, just before the critical moment of readout, the Earth was unexpectedly demolished by the Vogons to make way – so they claimed – for a new hyperspace bypass, and so all hope of discovering a meaning for life was lost for ever.

Or so it would seem.

Two of these strange, ape-like creatures survived.

Arthur Dent escaped at the very last moment because an old friend of his, Ford Prefect, suddenly turned out to be from a small planet somewhere in the vicinity of Betelgeuse and not from Guildford as he had hitherto claimed; and, more to the point, he knew how to hitch rides on flying saucers.

Tricia McMillan – or Trillian – had skipped the planet six months earlier with Zaphod Beeblebrox, the then President of the Galaxy.

Two survivors.

They are all that remains of the greatest experiment ever conducted – to find the Ultimate Question and the Ultimate Answer of Life, the Universe and Everything.

Nina proclaimed that she got that. We had a broad narrative shape: start with the destruction of Earth, and tell the story of the journey to Magrathea, the fabled planet-building planet. Much of the new material that is now in the movie is about the difficulty of getting to Magrathea and it is here that Douglas invented new plot devices and characters such as the fabulous 'point of view' gun and Humma Kavula the crazed missionary, who preaches about 'the coming of the great white handkerchief'. The other key decision was that the movie would have Arthur as the central character and we would experience the galaxy from his point of view. It sounds very simple, but over the years various drafts had tried placing Zaphod or even the Vogons at the centre of the story; but perhaps feeling less of a creative need to reinvent than Douglas, Karey worked his way towards a narrative structure that worked. He has a very good ear for English humour – its irony and its wariness of sentiment – but also a very good grip on the Hollywood structural sensibility.

Finally there was a sense that we were on the right track. But then barely had it sputtered into life again than the movie nearly faltered again. In the weeks following the 'fireside pitch', Disney, who had already spent considerable sums on rights acquisition and various drafts, balked at paying Karey's rewrite fee and the whole thing looked like it might fall apart. But Roger Birnbaum and his partner Gary Barber saved the project: Spyglass demonstrated their absolute commitment to making the movie by paying for the rewrite themselves. Jon Glickman of Spyglass describes this crucial episode.

'We had this meeting with Disney at which Nina Jacobson – who's a big supporter of the movie now, but at the time still felt the thing was just too weird – said, "I'm not going to pay for Karey." Now Karey's an expensive writer: he'd just had a big hit movie in *Chicken Run* and had written *James and the Giant Peach* and we were all in danger of the *Hitchhiker* movie just slipping away, yet again. I don't know what got into Spyglass at that moment except that we loved the material so much. We'd lived with this for six years and I think a little bit of it for us was the emotional connection to Douglas. It was completely out of synch with how we normally do business. But we picked up the tab for Karey's rewrite. This was extremely risky . . . we were just paying for the draft basically and thinking, "Hopefully Karey will figure this out." That's just what Karey, working with Jay directing the rewrite, set out to achieve.'

Bob Bookman, one of Hollywood's most experienced agents, comments on the phenomenal commitment of so many people to *Hitchhiker's*: 'Movies are a collaborative medium, both getting them to the starting block and actually making them. There were so many people involved over so many years, you, Ed, Jay, Roger, several people you could look at and say "if they weren't involved this wouldn't have happened" and yet the magic of it is that all these people hung in there to the point where we could launch it.'

And the result was that in the late spring of 2002, Karey, continuing to work with Jay and with input from Spyglass and me, started to write. Whenever Karey hit a problem he went back to the radio series, to the books, to *The Salmon of Doubt*,* to the bits of Douglas' hard drive that I had made available, for an insight into Douglas' mind. He delivered his script just before Christmas that year. I came home late one evening and it was sitting in my email. I sat and read it in one go with the hairs rising on the back of my neck. Here was a script that was utterly *Hitchhiker* in its sensibility but had now made the leap and felt like a movie, with a beginning, a middle and an end.

Ed Victor recalls a conversation with Michael Nesmith about the critical importance to a movie of getting the right script. 'Michael said, "If you are a producer of a film, you have a property, and what you are doing is bringing the studio head to the mouth of a dark cave and saying, 'Inside that cave is a golden statue. Just give me 100 million dollars.† You will have that statue. Go in and get that statue.' Well, the studio chief doesn't want to give you 100 million dollars so that he can go into the dark." And then Nesmith pauses and says, "The screenplay is a flashlight and with it you can point into the dark cave and just see the glint, the outlines of a statue. Then he gives you the 100 million dollars and goes in and sees if he can grab the statue . . ." I thought that was a very clever metaphor. You had to see someone

---

* *The Salmon of Doubt* – a collection of Douglas' writings and the beginning of the last novel he was working on before he died, which would have been the third Dirk Gently book.

† Do not assume that is the budget for the *Hitchhiker's* movie!

doing a script of *Hitchhiker's* before you could get it as a movie, for all that it had proved its success in book or radio form.' Now we had a flashlight.

In the New Year, Jay could see that the project was accelerating, and with other movie commitments bearing down on him, decided that he should step aside as director for the last time, although he remained on board as producer. So we needed to find a new director. Disappointing as this was, for the first time we did have a script. In all the long years of trying to make the movie it had always been the other way round – interested directors, but no script. Now there was a currency Hollywood understood and the script was biked around town. Jay knew Spike Jonze, director of *Being John Malkovich* and *Adaptation*, who had once been a leading music-video director, and sent the script to him. There was a general feeling that Spike, who had shown his touch with unusual material, would be a good choice to direct. He was a fan, read the script and liked it but was also committed to other projects. He did, however, play a crucial role in moving us on. He suggested Hammer and Tongs, Garth Jennings and Nick Goldsmith, a very creative and respected music video and commercials partnership, whose collaborations have included work for bands and performers such as REM, Blur, Fat Boy Slim and Ali G.

Initially Hammer and Tongs told their agent Frank Wuliger not to bother even sending them the script. They were working on a movie project of their own and they feared that a *Hitchhiker* script emerging from Hollywood with no Douglas around to fight his corner would be likely to ruin something about which they both cared a great deal. But Frank played another small but vital part in keeping the momentum going: he sent the script anyway. It sat, on a desk, unread for a fortnight until Nick took it home. The next day, with customary understatement, he quietly suggested to Garth that he should take a look. Garth took it home and read almost all of it on the loo, emerging to tell his wife that it actually 'wasn't bad at all'. They could see what a great job Karey had done in letting Douglas' genius breathe.

As Nick and Garth were on my patch in London I was the first to meet them in person. On a fine spring morning, almost a year on from the log fire in Beverly Hills, I found them on their converted canal boat, ironically just ten minutes' walk from Douglas's house in Islington. After all those air miles and moving his family out to California to try and get the movie made, it was about to be 'brought home' by a team who lived in England on Douglas' doorstep. There were chocolate biscuits, a very friendly black dog called Mack and best of all the boat was a homage to the Apple computer. Douglas, as all of his fans know, was a huge Apple devotee – indeed he became an 'Apple Master' – and somehow if Nick and Garth had worked in PC city I would probably have had to make my excuses and leave. But they didn't and I didn't. From the very first meeting it was clear to me that Nick and Garth had the awareness, the vision and the sense of fun to finally take the helm of the *Hitchhiker's* movie.

There was one early meeting that sums up that sense of fun and the phenomenal attention to detail that characterizes Nick and Garth. We had a video conference call with Jay, Spyglass and the team at Disney headed by Nina Jacobson. This was boardroom in LA to boardroom in London but Nick and Garth at our end had arranged for a little theatrical curtain, classic red with gold brocade, to be rigged up in front of the camera. When the team in LA arrived for the conference, there on their screen, instead of the normal view of a big desk in a nondescript room, were the closed curtains. When we were ready to begin, Garth, who had attached the curtain pull to his chair, gradually shifted backwards, the curtains opened and the words 'Don't Panic' rose up on a little board. Nothing sums up Nick and Garth's sense of playfulness, the line they have trodden between freshness and fidelity, and their love of gadgets better than those curtains.

It was also at this meeting that Nina made it clear that if we were going to make this movie, we were going to do it right. She was not going to go down in history as the executive who screwed up *Hitchhiker's*. It *had* to be rooted in Douglas' worldview but to work for Disney it had to reach out to a new audience too.

Through the summer of 2003, Hammer and Tongs worked on the design, story and budget. A crucial part of finally moving into production was finding an approach which could be made to work at a budget level with which Disney were going to be comfortable. This was a challenge Nick and Garth relished. For them invention and problem-solving are worn as a badge of honour. In the autumn Roger Birnbaum decided that the pieces were now lined up. 'We had a script, a director, a vision and a budget. Now was the time to find out if Disney were ready to play.' Under the terms of the agreement concluded when Spyglass had picked up Karey's fee, Roger and Gary were now in control of the project and Disney had first right of refusal to be their financial or distribution partner. Nick and Garth flew out to LA and made their pitch to Nina. It was still by no means certain that Disney would go for it and Jay remembers calling Nina from his car on the Pacific Coast Highway and sensing that there was still some way to go before she was convinced.

On 17 September Nina took the meeting and, as Jay had promised, was bowled over by the energy and vision that Nick and Garth had. The final step was a meeting with Nina's immediate boss, Dick Cook, Chairman of Walt Disney Studios. A kindly and highly respected executive, Dick was the final person who needed convincing, and after an agonizing wait of several days Nick and Garth, the Spyglass team, Jay and Nina gathered in his office on Thursday 25 September 2003 at 4.00 p.m. LA time. Garth, who in a wonderful Hollywood phrase is 'very good in the room', launched into his pitch. Dick heard him out and quietly asked if he could have the movie ready for next summer. Garth heard this to mean was it 'technically' feasible to have it ready for summer 2005 and simply said that that was possible. Dick and Nina had a few whispered words with each other. As everybody was leaving the meeting and Garth was gathering up the designs and story boards he had used during his pitch, Dick said to Garth that if there was anything he needed he should just be in touch. It took Nina following everybody out to the lift to point out that the movie had just been greenlit. Even for experienced Hollywood players such as Roger and Gary and Jay, a greenlit movie with no caveats on cast was unusual and as the doors closed on the lift the whole team literally screamed for joy. I received a call at about 1.00 a.m. my time in London from Nick, who simply said, 'We're making a movie.' Jay came on the phone and was almost in tears. For all those who had worked with Douglas for all those years it was truly a bittersweet moment; he had longed to hear those words, longed to be in a meeting just like that where a senior Hollywood executive said, 'Yes, let's make the *Hitchhiker's* movie.'

Having greenlit the movie, Disney made two very important decisions. The first was to bring the project back in-house. Nina Jacobson's faith in Nick and Garth and her excitement about the material in their hands made her determined to bring it centre stage at Disney in preparation for a major 'live action' summer release. The second was perhaps even more important; having made a very bold creative choice in letting a first-time director and producer loose on a big-budget movie, Nina now also allowed Garth and Nick to hire the core creative team with whom they had worked in their music video and commercial career. The director of photography, Igor Jadue-Lillo, the production designer, Joel Collins, the second unit director, Dominic Leung, and the costume designer, Sammy Sheldon, were all key members of the Hammer and Tongs family. Indeed it was precisely because Garth and Nick had gathered around them a group of highly creative people with whom they had worked for many years that Nina felt confident in allowing them to simply 'get on with it'. Spyglass remained as the movie's producers and in late autumn 2003 we went into 'pre-production', the period in which the film is cast, scheduled and budgeted and the shooting script is prepared.

The story of how the key cast was gathered together is best told in their own words in the interviews that follow, but one theme occurs again and again as they reflect on the experience of working with Garth and Nick – the enormous attention to detail that lies at the heart of their approach. From the outset Garth and Nick were determined that *Hitchhiker's* should not be a totally 'computer-generated' galaxy. Even the most cursory of looks at their body of work shows their love of puppetry, of props that work 'in camera', of real sets. Of course in a movie like *Hitchhiker's* there were always going to be some spectacular computer graphics, but in the end the actors spent very little of their time acting opposite a tennis ball on a stick on a sound stage covered in blue or green cloth. Henson's Creature Shop in Camden, London, was hired to create the Vogons and dozens of 'real' creatures with whom the actors could interact. Over the sixteen-week shooting period at Elstree, Frogmore and Shepperton Studios, and on location in North Hertfordshire, Wales and central London, the production design team created a series of lovingly realized 'real worlds' for the cast to inhabit.

Probably the 'holy of holies' for fans and cast alike was the *Heart of Gold* set. On the famous George Lucas sound stage at Elstree was built a fully realized interior for the ship. It was truly a thing of beauty: gleaming white curves, a magnificent control panel with the Improbability Drive button in the middle, a kitchen and even a bar area for the serving of Pan Galactic Gargle Blasters. And fittingly, on 11 May 2004, the third anniversary of Douglas' death, it was on the set of the *Heart of Gold* that the whole cast and crew gathered for a minute's silence to say thank you to Douglas. Jay Roach, who had his own moment's silence in LA later that day, reflects: 'It all started with Douglas and for all of us it has been about serving what was amazing about the radio plays and the books. The spirit of Douglas united all of us and none of us ever wanted to do anything that did not take it down a path that we hope he would have loved and that his fans will love. It needed to morph itself into this new channel but it didn't need to be essentially anything other than it always was, this amazing prism that you could look at the world through and be inspired and uplifted by, and all of us knew that it would not work without that essence, and when we found Garth and Nick I genuinely thought that they would do a better job at letting that essence breathe than I would have done.'

Roger Birnbaum too considers that 'This has been one of those great adventures in my career. When it takes a long time to get a film off the ground, and then it works, it makes it so much more satisfying . . . everybody has been passionate about this project and has gone the extra mile. We've done it for Douglas' spirit.'

Over the long period of making a film there are many moments that stick in your mind. One such moment for me was when we were filming just outside Tredegar, South Wales, in a disused quarry (keeping alive a long and honourable tradition of British science fiction and quarries), and all day we had been jumping in and out of vans as the rain came in squalls, horizontally down the quarry. The producer from Henson's Creature Shop was wrapped head to toe in Arctic-exploration gear she had borrowed from a friend, whilst in a splendid display of ruggedness some of the film crew remained in their shorts and Timberlands, no matter how cold it got. The rare periods of sunshine necessary for filming had been all too brief. But now in the gentle evening light I could see a very small man, standing all by himself in the middle of the quarry floor, trying to hold a large white head in place against the wind. I could also see the director, with his inexhaustible energy and enthusiasm, testing out a gadget that three of the lead actors were going to have to use the next day. By pushing a little button a paddle flicked up in front of him with alarming speed and stopped just short of his nose. Meanwhile a man in pyjamas and dressing gown, clutching a towel, passed the time of day with the President of the Galaxy. In the distance a Ferrari-red spacecraft, which had gouged out a fifty-metre trench when it had crash-landed, caught the sun on its tail fin.

The date was 1 July 2004, we were filming the exterior shots for the planet Vogsphere and not for the first time I felt a surge of pride and excitement that after so many years we were actually making 'the movie' of *The Hitchhiker's Guide to the Galaxy*. It was something that Douglas had wanted so badly and as usual that pride was mixed straightaway with deep sadness that he was not there to share it with everybody.

Many dozens of times during the pre-production and filming of *The Hitchhiker's Guide to the Galaxy* I was asked things like, 'Do you think Douglas would have approved of the design for the box for the Ravenous Bugblatter Beast of Traal?' or 'Would he have enjoyed the use of a thirty-foot-high sculpt of his nose as the entrance to Humma Kavula's temple?' My answer was pretty much the same each time: it's hard to say on the specifics of the box or the nose (though I can hazard a guess that in both those cases the answer would have been yes), but what I do know is that he would have been delighted by the passion, attention to detail and sheer creative exuberance that everybody involved in the production has brought to making the movie. And there in that tableau in the quarry – with Warwick Davis' stand in, Gerald Staddon,* helping to line up Marvin the Paranoid Android's next shot; Martin Freeman and Sam Rockwell, as Arthur Dent and Zaphod Beeblebrox respectively, making the most of some pretty trying conditions; Garth Jennings putting a prop through its paces; and the crew doggedly climbing in and out of cramped cars – was everything that I hope would have made Douglas proud.

Robbie Stamp
London, December 2004

---

* Stand-ins replace the stars on set while the director of photography and director light the next set up and rehearse camera moves.

For years, while the *Hitchhiker's* movie was still in the pipeline, one of the favourite games for fans was to choose who they would cast in each role. Before he died Douglas Adams had this to say on the matter: 'When it comes down to it, my principle is this – Arthur should be British. The rest of the cast should be decided purely on merit and not on nationality.' – DNA.

The cast that was chosen fulfilled this wish and it was an exciting and unusual collection of actors who came to work on the *Hitchhiker's Guide to the Galaxy* movie in 2004. The full cast was as follows:

Zaphod Beeblebrox **Sam Rockwell**

Ford Prefect **Mos Def**

Trillian (Trisha McMillan) **Zooey Deschanel**

Arthur Dent **Martin Freeman**

Marvin **Warwick Davis**

Slartibartfast **Bill Nighy**

Questular **Anna Chancellor**

Humma Kavula **John Malkovich**

Lunkwill **Jack Stanley**

Fook **Dominique Jackson**

Prosser **Steve Pemberton**

Barman **Albie Woodington**

Gag Halfrunt **Jason Schwartzman**

Ghostly Image **Simon Jones**

Bulldozer Driver **Mark Longhurst**

Pub Customer **Su Elliott**

Technician **Terry Bamber**

Reporter **Kelly Macdonald**

Voices

The Guide **Stephen Fry**

Marvin **Alan Rickman**

Deep Thought **Helen Mirren**

The Whale **Bill Bailey**

Eddie the Shipboard Computer **Tom Lennon**

Kwaltz **Ian McNeice**

Jeltz **Richard Griffiths**

Vogons **Mark Gatiss**

Reece Shearsmith

Steve Pemberton

During filming Robbie Stamp was able to talk extensively with the main human-cast members about how they brought to life Douglas Adams's iconic characters.

In a series of conversations in trailers, on golf buggies, in between takes, and over the odd beer the stars talked about how well they had known *Hitchhiker's* before they were cast and what working on the movie meant to them. Those interviews follow.

Interview with

Martin Freeman

(Arthur Dent)

Credits include *Shaun of the Dead, Love Actually, Ali G Indahouse* and 'Tim' in *The Office.*

Robbie Stamp: Had you ever heard of *Hitchhiker's* before you were approached about the movie?

Martin Freeman: I certainly had heard of *Hitchhiker's*. It was a bit of a favourite in my home growing up, not with me but with one of my brothers and my step-dad. I was very young when the series was on but I do remember watching that. I remember the books being in the house and kind of dipping and delving into those intermittently, but not reading the whole journey from start to end – but yes I was definitely, definitely aware of it, growing up.

And how did you get involved?

By being sent the script and reading the script, thinking I wasn't right for it and then going to meet Garth and Nick and Dom.* I was more concerned with the fact that my girlfriend, Amanda, was on a double yellow line waiting for

---

* Garth and Nick of Hammer and Tongs, and Dominic Leung, second unit director and the third founding partner.

me. I thought, 'I'm only going to be in there fifteen, twenty minutes.' But it was fifteen, twenty minutes before I even saw Garth because I'd been speaking to Nick and then Garth came and was very 'Garthy' and really welcoming so we just chatted for another twenty, twenty-five minutes, then I went to do the reading. All the time I was thinking, 'Christ, Amanda's going to kill me,' so by the time we got in and read it I thought, 'I've got to get out of here, I'm not even right for this! I'm not going to get it.'

Why did you think you weren't right?

Because of my memories of the television series. I'm a very different actor to Simon Jones* and I think Simon Jones *was* Arthur Dent in my mind. And in a lot of people's minds too – or if not Simon Jones then someone very like him, and that's just not me. Anyway it transpired that they were very interested but had to see other people and had to work things out because I'm not a name and I always thought, 'Why would anyone in Hollywood agree to me being the main part in a film?' Well, the main human, anyway. But after a bit of iffing and umming and other people passing and other people coming into the frame I was screen-tested again with Zooey† and that was that.

Your gut instinct that you weren't right was the complete opposite of mine. From the moment I saw that first read I was convinced. While finding the essence of *Hitchhiker's*

---

* Simon Jones played Arthur Dent in the original and new radio series and the television series.

† Zooey Deschanel, who plays Tricia McMillan.

we've all also been keen not to try and recreate what it was like twenty-five years ago.

Part of me would have thought you would go for a recreation of that, and if you didn't go for that, that the approach would be ultra hip and trendy and cool, that you'd go for the exact opposite of past versions and get a nineteen-year-old kid to play Arthur Dent, and make it just really street or really urban, and I thought, 'Well, I'm neither of those things.' That was why I thought at that original read, 'I've got to get out. Amanda's parked.' I think Garth picked up on that. We were very nice to each other and very friendly but I think he must have thought, 'This guy just doesn't care, and he's not interested.' He was aware I was going to get told off, and I was told off! But it all worked out well.

Told off by . . .?

By Amanda, she did indeed remind me that I had said I was only going to be fifteen minutes but I'm really glad that people took a punt on me and I'm very appreciative of it, because I know there are loads of people who in terms of film sense should've been in the queue before me.

So how did you start? When you're thinking, 'Well, I'm not a Simon Jones but I have been asked to play Arthur Dent, and he means a lot to many people,' what starts going through your mind?

Just what I had done in the audition. I thought if they liked that enough to be very interested then that's what I'm going to do. Just trying to infuse it with reality and not playing Arthur Dent as we think we know him. It requires a bit of playing up because it's a light kind of comedy, but I didn't want it to not matter and I didn't want it to not mean anything. I had to approach him as if I'd never heard of *Hitchhiker's*. Because it would be very boring for me and everybody else to try and just do an impression of something that was à la mode twenty-five years ago. If Arthur had been very upper-middle-class with an Uncle Bulgaria dressing gown, if everything had basically been Edwardian, then the contrast with people like Sam and Mos* and Zooey, who are all very contemporary current people and although they're not playing Americans are playing space people with American accents, just would've been another one in the long line of movies where the Americans are hip and the Englishman is a bit dull. It's just not very interesting any more. Take the dressing gown. There were certain points that they had to hit, in terms of my costume especially, that had to be in the film. I wasn't going to say, 'Can I wear a tracksuit or a suit?' It was always going to be a dressing gown, slippers and pyjamas. It was just a question of what kind and to be honest I wasn't going to have too many objections. Sammy† is a good designer, she knows what she wants, and Garth has got his finger in every single pie, how it looks, how it sounds, everything. He's got fantastic people working for and with him, my job is to come in and act. If I'd been presented with something I hated I would've said no, but as long as Arthur looked contemporary and it didn't look like a joke, like we were judging him before he even opened his mouth, that was OK by me. From a make-up and hair point of view I just

---

* Sam Rockwell, who plays Zaphod Beeblebrox, and Mos Def, who plays Ford Prefect.

† Sammy Sheldon, costume designer.

didn't want him to look like a real mummy's boy because that's another thing about lame English men, they're boring. They've got plastered-down hair and look like they've been dressed by their spinster mothers, but as long as he looked like a normal person who lived in the normal world that was all I needed to know because then I could play him as a normal person. I just didn't want to play a caricature.

Very early on in the story we see Arthur lying down in front of a bulldozer: this is a guy who's got something to him.

He has, he has, and I think it would take an enormous amount of balls for him to lie there . . . because that doesn't come easy to him. It doesn't come easy to most people to lie down in front of a bulldozer, but he gets on with it. It's funny because to be honest my own jury is still out on whether I've got Arthur. I'll see when the film comes out, because you never really know when you're doing something, but Christ the world is full of films with people whose instincts are telling them it's great and it ends up being terrible. I don't think the film will be anything like that, I think the film will be really good and I'll be a really feasible Arthur Dent, but we'll wait and see.

Did the responsibility weigh on you?

To be honest I've let other people worry about that because I was never a *Hitchhiking* anorak. I hope I was respectfully aware that it was a big deal for lots and lots of other people, but they're not playing it, I am. You can't take on that responsibility for them and again, because I'm not a rabid *Hitchhiker* fan, it wouldn't be like playing John Lennon, someone who means more to me in my everyday life. Or playing Jesus Christ or just someone who really, really *everybody* knows, and you really know the story and you'd better get it right. This is just an interpretation of a screenplay based on a book and a radio series and I've got as much warrant to play it as anybody else. We'll see if I do it well. I'm just trying my best.

What about the relationship with Trillian? We have worked hard to develop her character.

Absolutely, and I think it's to really good effect. It doesn't look like it's tacked on in a Hollywood way. It still has the essence of the original material. And I think without it, it wouldn't be as good, to be honest.

So the first meeting with Trillian, at the party at the Islington flat; what's happening, why is there a connection made?

Arthur's a fairly intelligent bloke and I think a connection is made because Arthur sees someone . . . well, he sees a woman who is not afraid to come dressed as an old man and who is still physically beautiful. Not only has she come as a scientist, she gets jokes and references, more so than he thinks anyone else would at that party. It's not as if he's exactly outgoing. He's in no position to say these people are idiots. What does he know? He doesn't speak to anybody. He's a typical repressed person, who is able to judge everyone from the comfort of knowing that he's not actually going to find out if he's right because he's too shy. But here's a woman who's showed an interest in him and what a woman she is, she's come as fucking Darwin, she's gorgeous and she's funny, who wouldn't want that?

He was there reading a book by himself.

Absolutely, absolutely and she crossed the room to be with him. He was looking at her but she crossed the room. So all this looks very good until this strange person comes along and nicks her. And once he meets up with her again on the *Heart of Gold,* he goes from being just sad that she's disappeared to being really jealous that she went off with Zaphod. Not only did she go off with someone else but it's someone else who's the total opposite of Arthur, not only not human but just an idiot in Arthur's eyes, all the things Arthur wouldn't want to be and all the things that he kind of would want to be. He wouldn't want to be a moron but he would want to be a bit cooler and he would want to be more confident with women, but he's intelligent enough to know that he can consider Zaphod beneath him because he treats women like objects, which Arthur would never do. But he blows it with her because everything – the world is against him, he's literally lost his planet, he's lost his girl to an absolute idiot and she's not giving him any proper attention. I think it's even worse when you're in a situation where the object of your desire is being nice to you and liking you, but that's not enough, they've got to hate you or love you; anything in between is really upsetting and Arthur finds that very, very difficult. And he knows he's overstepped the mark and he goes through different things with Trillian, being dumbfounded by her and apologetic to her, but by the end they have reached an understanding. He's seen the best in her and she has really seen the best in him because he's finally become a bit of a hero.

One of the finest lines to tread in developing this whole thing into a movie was to develop Arthur without turning him into a mega-sword-welding space hero.

Exactly, I think you only need to see him do a bit and the bit is that he sort of becomes the leader of the group. He doesn't become an action man by Hollywood standards, but by Arthur Dent's standards he becomes more of an action man, you see him come into his own. As the film goes on he becomes more his own person and has more authority and more conviction about what he's doing. I guess there's a point where he realizes, 'I don't have a home any more so whatever this is I've got now I better start living in it, not trying to get home wishing something hadn't happened that did happen.' He's actually starting to take a bit of control and maybe in a way he could only take control in space. He couldn't have taken control in his Earth job. Talking it all through it is a surprising movie. There aren't many movies like this about finding the personal and the ridiculous in the universal. It's not a big epic space adventure. It's full of really ridiculous aliens and stupid fucking creatures – well, not [John] Malkovich. Humma Kavula is genuinely scary but there aren't many like that. The Vogons are ridiculous. You can see they're preposterous and they kill people with poetry, for fuck's sake!

And there's bureaucracy in space and a lot of the things that we've got on Earth, just a bit larger.

Exactly, and with funny heads. It's a very human alien movie.

Talking of human aliens, what about your relationship with Ford?

Ford is my guide, my *Hitchhiker's* guide. I'm not a hitchhiker, I'm a hostage. Arthur would be nowhere without Ford. He'd still be on Earth. In fact he'd be dead but due to a debt that Ford feels he owes Arthur he takes Arthur with him and tells Arthur everything about survival in space, about who the strange creatures are and about what happens on this planet and what happens on that spaceship. So Ford really looks after Arthur.

And he's genuinely affectionate towards him, isn't he?

He is, as affectionate as Ford can be. It's still not very recognizable as human affection; it's slightly odd, and that's kind of cool because Arthur's slightly odd and not a particularly gregarious lovey-dovey person. So in that way they're quite well matched. To begin with Arthur thinks Ford is just a strange human and when he finds out that he's actually from somewhere else entirely I suppose it makes a bit more sense to him why Ford's like he is, but Ford is also totally viable as just an eccentric human being. Arthur certainly hasn't twigged that Ford's an alien before he tells him.

Have there been particular moments that stand out for you?

Yes. The *Heart of Gold* set – it was huge and we all walked round and went, 'Fucking hell, we're in a space movie.' To be honest, without fail all of the settings have been amazing. It was the attention to detail, that's what's really, really impressed me, the design detail and the prop details have blown my mind. To be honest there aren't particular scenes I've enjoyed more, it's more the settings because I like *all* the scenes and some of them are fascinating to play from an acting point of view but it's not like you're doing Chekhov, it's not like, 'Fuck me, I've got a heavy dialogue day today and I've got to talk about how I lost my mother.' On the other hand, there are things to deal with, like how you lost the Earth. Those are the bits I found really hard, where Arthur has to be broken that the Earth has gone. They're hard to play because it's about pitching it at the right level . . . you're not doing a kitchen-sink drama but you also want to make it real, you want to make it real enough that it matters. It's not a tragedy, it is a comedy but you've still got to invest emotion in it. I think you always have to care about the people in films or the fish in films or the Shrek in films, you know? If you don't really believe Arthur gives a damn then why would you give a damn?

Arthur's an iconic character and much of your challenge has been about how you bring depth and richness to him without overloading the whole thing.

Exactly, exactly. Yes, it's very important to me because it mattered to my family and because it was a memory for me and because it's become part of our popular culture over the last twenty-five years. It would have really angered me if it had been ruined, especially if it had been ruined by America. Maybe if I had been a mad fan maybe I couldn't play Arthur. You've got a team of people, all of us doing our job. If everyone was a mad *Hitchhiker's* fan you'd have a terrible film because actually those people aren't practitioners of what we're doing. I really like food but I can't cook it. So I hope people are going to trust us with it. It seems the more I hear the more they are kind of willing to . . .

They are, and I think the trust started with the script. What did you think of that when you first saw it?

I liked it, I liked it, and it works. Given that most of the films I'm asked to read I don't go to the meetings for, there must have been something in it. And as I said before, when I met the boys, I liked them and they seemed to really care about it without being weird – care about bringing it to life as a movie rather than just living in their own little *Hitchhiker's* world. And they just looked like people who could do it. Then when I saw their work I just thought how visually it was amazing and I wanted to be a part of it. And fortunately it has worked really well because Garth's able to communicate with actors and not just his director of photography. Some people are not able to communicate with actors about what your character is doing but Garth is. A lot of people just look through their monitor and wish actors weren't there. But Garth loves human beings as well as toys and puppets and all of that stuff. He's aware that if you don't believe in Arthur and Trillian and Ford and Zaphod their adventures don't matter and nothing else in the film matters. It just becomes academic. Oh, it's good effects or whatever, but who gives a damn because there's nothing carrying you on.

And have you enjoyed working here?

Yes, I really have, I've had a fantastic time, it's been the biggest most sustained thing I've done on the camera and obviously it could have gone any way, I could have had a terrible time or I could have had a great time, and fortunately I've had a great time.

Interview with

Sam Rockwell

(Zaphod Beeblebrox)

Credits include *Matchstick Men, Confessions of a Dangerous Mind, The Green Mile,* and *Galaxy Quest*.

Robbie Stamp: So how do you create a character as wild as Zaphod for the screen?

Sam Rockwell: I started to do a Bill Clinton impersonation but that didn't really work. It was a little too passive. Zaphod has to be more aggressive and so we went rock star, Freddie Mercury, Elvis, a little Brad Pitt.

But there's still politician in there, isn't there?

Definitely. It's as if a rock star has become President of the Galaxy. I tend to get these parts where you really have to be somewhat theatrical and it's a job requirement for Zaphod to be a bit big, a bit theatrical. He's got to be iconic, I guess, and have a certain kind of charm and magnitude. The descriptions of Zaphod in the book really gave me everything. We stayed away from the TV series. We stayed with the book as the source.

What about Zaphod and sex? I remember the original Zaphod, Mark Wing-Davey, talking about that.

Zaphod is very sexy, I mean that's the reason for the Freddie Mercury feel and the nail polish and the eyeliner. He has to be like Tim Curry in *Rocky Horror Picture Show* a little bit. He has to have that effect on people. You don't know which way he goes; he might bend a little, sexually.

There's a lot of species out there.

There's a lot of species out there! Male or female, he's kind of wild, he's David Bowie, he's Freddie Mercury, he's Keith Richards, he's rock and roll, he doesn't care. He's not linear, you know he colours outside of the lines with the crayons . . .

You've worked really hard on a lot of the physical attributes, things like the costume and the gun.

Yes, that's right, that's right. We've worked on the blond hair, the gun, the nail polish, the chain mail, and the gold shirt.

That's your idea?

Well, I liked it because I wanted a shiny spandex shirt and I said silver at first and then Sammy came up with the colour which made sense, *Heart of Gold*: gold! It's given me a lot, that shirt.

How so?

Well, often, wardrobe, clothes will give you a character. The boots before we started were a lot heavier, like big cowboy boots, and I said, 'No, listen, I need them streamlined. I need them to be light on his feet.'

So you could do the dances!

Yes, because I always seem to incorporate a little dancing in each character I do. With Zaphod, he had to be swift, he had to be dextrous. He's a rock star, he's got to move.

He does indeed move! Tell me about the gun. You practised really hard with the gun.

We had to make a smaller gun because the first gun didn't have a trigger guard and you can't spin without a trigger guard. So they put a trigger guard on, made it really streamlined, painted it a beautiful red and white, and they made this amazing holster, which is magnetic. That's something that I've got to take back home. I need that gun!

One of the other things I want to ask you about is the walk.

I don't do a lot of walking actually but I walk on Viltvodle Six and in the snow and I do a little walking and some running on Vogsphere. I *like* the character's walk. [*Sam gets up and does the walk*] Little bit of a strut.

But it's friendly and confident and just 'here I am'.

Yeah, he's affable, but the bottom line is he's a rock star.

So talk to me about the second head.

Yes, the second head is very confusing. I wanted to start doing a New York accent for the second head, like a retro thing, but it didn't work. I wanted a real contrast and we have that now, but it's not so much a vocal contrast or an accent, it's more an emotional contrast between the two heads. One has just had too much sugar, basically. He's ready to kick some ass – a lot of testosterone and just kind of angry. That's what the second head is about. I like the stuff in Douglas Adam's notes you gave me. He was thinking that he has a better memory than the first head, that's great.

When Douglas wrote the book it was just a throwaway line, 'we'll just give the President of the Galaxy two heads', and on the radio and in the book two heads is fine but on screen it's a bit more of a challenge. I know it was one of the things that Douglas and Jay Roach talked about a great deal both from a character point of view, Douglas was keen to develop those possibilities, and also from a technical perspective. When *Men in Black 2* came out, with a character with a second head on a stalk, we thought, 'Well, there's one method we can't use.'

It was a throwaway line having the second head?

Yes, that's right.

Because in the book he never really has the second head talking.

No, there's certainly no serious distinction between the two heads. That's why those notes that I gave you at the beginning were interesting because that's Douglas thinking, 'OK, for a movie what can we do with two heads?'

Yes, for the second head it's a big riff. It is stream-of-consciousness comedy. But I wanted everything to be rooted in the world Douglas created. So I have been referring back to the book a lot and the notes. Ad-libs are fine if they serve the story, propelling it forward, but if they're arbitrary, if it's just the actor playing and it doesn't really help the movie, then don't do them.

Within that world you had a lot of fun with dingoes!

That was fun, and the twelve seasons I got from you, I loved that one. I hope that makes it into the final cut there with the Japanese Groupie on Viltvodle; they were cute.

That was just a reference to Douglas' favourite hotel in LA, the Four Seasons, where we did a lot of talking about the movie on our various trips there to try and move things on. How about Zaphod the politician?

If there's a sequel I'd like to get deeper into some of the political aspects. We touched upon some Bill Clinton and George W. Bush and it is really funny, I think.

I would imagine people would enjoy the line that 'You can't be a president with a whole brain.' I can see that getting a real response in the current political climate.

You can't be a president with a whole brain, that's right, I actually say that. Yes, I didn't even think of that.

Can you tell me how you came to be involved in the movie?

I met with Garth and Nick three times, twice before I got the part, and then after they offered it to me. I asked to meet with them the third time because I had no idea why they had cast me as Zaphod. Originally they were talking to me about Ford! First time, I met with them in New York before even reading the script. But I did quickly get hold of the DVD of the TV series and watched that. I remembered it from my childhood, I'd seen a little bit of it along with *Doctor Who*, so I just wanted a reminder of who Ford Prefect was and I went, 'Oh, that's Ford Prefect, OK, I know what to do,' and actually I liked him. I went in and I had an idea and it wasn't quite right. What they needed was a much more streamlined leading man and I think that's why Mos is so perfect. They talked about Ford as a researcher for the *Guide* being one of these camera guys who go in to Iraq and I thought that was very interesting. At the second meeting, I wasn't supposed to read. One of the fortunate things is, you get to a certain point in your career and you don't have to read that much. But sometimes what I do, which is maybe kind of stupid, is volunteer to read, which they love of course because they're probably getting all these guys who won't even meet them, but I thought, 'Let's read this out loud and see how it feels.' They said, 'Why don't we read a little Ford,' and I said, 'But listen, I haven't prepared this, guys, this is cold,' and that was true, it was cold and so I read Ford and I did a kind of Southern accent thing and it was OK, they started laughing and I kissed Garth on the cheek or something and after I'd done, I said, 'What about this Zaphod guy? He's interesting so why don't we read through some of that?' And I read some of Zaphod and it didn't go well at all, the Ford reading was much better, actually.

What didn't go well in the Zaphod reading?

I had not yet thought about Zaphod. All I remember was that Zaphod's entrance was fantastic and I was picturing Jack Black doing the entrance and I thought, 'Well, how would I do that entrance?' I knew just from skimming the script that Zaphod was a great part, really a great part. But I hadn't read it thoroughly and so we let it go and I thought, 'Well, I kind of blew it because I read Ford OK and I didn't read Zaphod well at all.' So I said to them, 'I was wondering if you guys could consider me for Zaphod. I may not be right, I may be more right for Ford but check out *Galaxy Quest* and check out *The Green Mile*, just skim those two films, because I think there are elements that might lend themselves towards Zaphod, they're much more theatrical.' I didn't hear anything for weeks and then I heard Mos was going to get cast as Ford. I was disappointed but I actually thought, 'That's a pretty good idea. I would cast him as Ford too,' and I'm not just saying that, that's exactly what I thought. So I figured, 'All right, well, that's that.' A long time went by and then out of nowhere, out of fucking nowhere, I'm in London, filming *Piccadilly Jim*, and I get a message from both of my agents and my manager and they all want to talk to me at the same time and when that happens I know there's something up. I get a conference call and I know it's good news but I don't know what the hell it is. Usually when you get a part you know a week before the offer comes in, somebody says, 'It looks good on such and such, they're probably going to offer it to you . . .' But there was none of that. All of a sudden they offered me this really nice salary, it was just one call, 'You got the job and we got a great salary,' and this is it and I was like, 'Wow, what are you talking about? It's all done? Everything? Everything's done?' And my team said, 'Yup, great, congratulations,' but I haven't even thought about this thing for a month and I don't know if I even read the whole thing thoroughly and they said, 'Are you crazy? You've got to do it!' and I said, 'I'm exhausted, I'm working my ass off, let me read it thoroughly and then maybe I should meet with them in a week because I can't read it until next Thursday.' I'm doing this big dance sequence in *Piccadilly Jim*. I was exhausted and I'm in the midst of this heavy love affair with my girlfriend and I need some time to think. So on my two days off, Thursday and Friday, I read it very thoroughly and thought, 'I'll go in and I'll meet with these guys and I'll see if they're open to ideas.' I'd already met them of course but I was confused why they had cast me, I didn't know. So Gina* said, 'Why don't you play it like that Elvis character you do?' I said, 'No, I can't do that, that's silly, that's like a sketch comedy thing,' but basically I went in with that broad idea and they went for it. There's a tape of that meeting. Did they show it to you?

Yes.

Of us in the office?

Yep.

And we were just playing around, but I knew when Garth kept coming up with what I call these 'actor ideas' that I had to do the movie. He's a visual MTV director, who has inventive ideas that are coming from a character's point of view, not a visual point of view. To me that was what was exciting and special about Garth and Nick. Usually directors, especially visual directors, do not cope with actor ideas. It's very rare, it never happens really, the only time I've met it before was Dean Parisot on *Galaxy Quest*. He was really open to ideas. And then of course actors who direct, like George Clooney, are always good. I'd say George Clooney, Ridley Scott, Dean Parisot and Garth Jennings are the four top directors that I've ever worked with.

---

* Gina Bellman.

High praise indeed.

I think he's really something. So I feel lucky to have been on the show. It's been amazing. You've helped with all my stupid ad-libs and it was great working with Martin and Zooey and Mos. I feel like Mos and I came up with some stuff that wasn't even in the original TV series or the movie script, the relationship between Ford and Zaphod. I think we created a whole new bond between those two characters that wouldn't have existed. I mean there are so many places to go with Zaphod. Zaphod's one of the best characters I've ever played.

Are there any moments where you've walked on the set that have stood out?

There are so many. I love Zaphod when he's pleasing the crowd, the moment on the champagne bottle, swinging on the rope, just before he steals the *Heart of Gold*. Just before I went on I found some fudge on set and I just grabbed it and came on stage eating it while I was giving my speech and I just thought that was Zaphod, he just loves life. I think the best moments are when he is very charming and fun and Zaphod's laugh seems to be the key to the character. I always make my characters more physical than they need to be, like that dance sequence, Garth really wanted me to do it. So we got on the Viltvodle set and he said, 'This is where you're going to do your dance, right?' And I said, 'Yeah, sure, what kind of dance?' Because that wasn't in the script at all. Garth said, 'I think it would be great if you were being shot at and you did this operatic rock-concert dance.' It's not like I was twisting his arm. He wanted me to do a dance because he knew I could dance. So they asked me what music I wanted and I went to it, several times! I felt really honoured to do it because it's a great moment for Zaphod.

Garth has always been aware of the danger of slipping into classic action sci-fi moments, so when one of our heroes is under attack from space aliens and gunfire he thinks, 'What can we do to give it a *Hitchhiker* twist?' And it's of course classically Douglas, to give the audience just what they're not expecting, but it works. You've done a lot of running around, haven't you? Running up and down valleys in Wales . . .

Yes, yes – oh my God, the paddle scene, that was the most ridiculous thing I think I've ever done and it was a brand-new Douglas idea. First of all there was the weather. Most of us almost got hypothermia and I had layers and layers on in between takes. But faking the paddles hitting us in the face . . . it's just the bare essentials of acting and really comes down to being a kid and playing cops and robbers and cowboys and Indians. That sequence in particular is about the bare essential, childlike state you're in when you're acting and that scene with Mos and Martin just pretending that there are wooden paddles hitting us in the face coming up from the ground could have been sci-fi acting at its best or at its worst. I remember seeing *Jurassic Park* and I had an argument with my friend, the acting in that movie was very good I thought. He said, 'What are you talking about? That's not acting, it's like bullshit. It's not acting.' I disagree, I think those actors really did well; you don't know how hard it is to do that. That's hard to do, pretending to be terrified of something that's not really there. But acting with those guys was great, it really is an ensemble piece. Originally I thought

Zaphod was strictly a supporting part. But when I really read the script thoroughly I realized it was a lot of screen time and it was going to be hard work and it was. We worked our asses off.

Interview with

Mos Def

(Ford Prefect)

Credits include *The Woodsman, Monster's Ball* and *The Italian Job*. Mos is also a very talented hip-hop artist.

Robbie Stamp: So tell me, had you ever heard of *Hitchhiker's* before you were approached to be in the movie?

Mos Def: Actually I had, although I had never read the book. It was just part of my consciousness. Maybe you've never heard the music of Miles Davis but you sure know the name, and *Hitchhiker's* is one of those things that many people know well and many people don't but everyone is familiar with it somehow.

How did you come to be cast?

I think that Suzie Figgis, the casting director, had seen me in *Topdog/Underdog* at the Royal Court in London and she suggested to Nick and Garth that they should meet with me when they were in New York. So we met and talked about the project and their perspective on what they wanted to see not just in this film but also in films in general. Their taste just hooked me. They're unconventional. They have a great deal of imagination. They've done a video that I was a huge fan of, actually a couple of videos but I didn't know that they had worked on them, Supergrass, 'Moving', and Blur, 'Coffee and TV'. Hammer and Tongs just have great presentation. I liked everything about them, their energy, their enthusiasm and their sense of wonder. You could tell they were very serious but there was also joy.

That sense of wonder – it's absolutely right.

And that's really important to have as a director. I also think that Garth embodies the spirit of the book in a unique way because he's very serious, very thoughtful and yet he's not taking himself so seriously . . . he's aware that this is a mammoth project that it is very ambitious and he's not daunted by any of it. He's up for the task, which is very attractive to an actor. When he sent me the script I was really engaged from the first line – '*It is an important and popular fact that things are not always what they seem.*' It's a great way to open a movie. *Hitchhiker's* is high-minded and big and in the wrong hands it could be so ponderous, it could feel like the work of some smarty pants, but he makes it very, very human and approachable. He also allows space for perspectives and viewpoints other than his own, without discrediting them or ridiculing them, whilst being very steadfast in what his own perspective is. I was really taken aback by the way he dealt with the whole issue of religion, of God. It's clearly individual but it leaves room for perspectives other than his own. It's very rare to work on something with that sort of scope and feeling.

You were telling me that when you were cast kids came up to you to let you know how cool they thought it was that you were going to be in *Hitchhiker's*.

People from all sorts of backgrounds, whenever I mention it, there's only two or three responses: some people have no idea what it means, others go, 'Oh, OK,' and then there are people that are just like, 'What, that's so cool!' They just love it. And I do, too. I really love the humour in it and I really love the sense of awe and wonder, that curiosity about the world around us, it's kind of like the kid looking at the sky and just thinking, 'What's out there?'

I think you're absolutely right, Douglas's curiosity – his intellectual curiosity – was absolutely a defining characteristic.

It's been very satisfying. I like things that have some element of risk, and with the time it's taken to get this movie made, and the mix of ideas and humour, it's going to make people pay attention. It's extraordinary in the literal sense of the word, it's extra and very ordinary, there's this whole universe out there that has been created that is fantastic and mundane at once.

How did you set about finding the character of Ford?

It was really interesting because Ford has gears. He has a gear when he's extremely intense and other gears where he's totally carefree and almost away from it all; not disengaged but outside of things, taking it very relaxed. Before we started rehearsals I was thinking of him as much more aggressive or harsh, a Walter Winchell type of character, a journalist planning the story. There are elements of that and there are heroic Indiana Jones elements to his personality too but rather than make him be any one thing I tried to make him be the sharpest, to have the most honest response to all of his situations and his endeavours; I think that Ford is prepared for anything, the best or the worst, and he sort of embraces it. He accepts things as they are, he doesn't really moan or judge. Another thing I like about Ford is that he's very loyal to his friends; he's very selfless in that way. He believes in the things that his friends want and wants to help them but it's not sentimental. It's like in the airlock when they are about to be thrown into space and Ford asks Arthur if he would like a hug . . . Martin's reaction is funny so it manages to be a tender moment that doesn't get cheapened by something didactic or predictable.

Douglas would have appreciated that, he would have been very wary of the sentimental button, so with a moment like that he would have wanted to twist it, give it an edge. Thinking about helping friends, you played the scene when you explain to Arthur about towels as if it genuinely mattered.

Yes, you're going to need your towel. You have to have it, this is important; it's a tough galaxy out there.

Talk a little bit more abut the relationship with Arthur, because I think I mentioned to you that one of the things that was in an earlier draft of the script, which sent some of the fans crazy, they didn't like it at all, was a running joke whereby Ford was constantly trying to get rid of Arthur and Arthur kept on saving his life and he felt bound to save his life back. Maybe they didn't like that because through all the books the friendship between Ford and Arthur is the most enduring relationship of all.

I like the friendship between them. Often when there are stories about other life forms coming to Earth, it's a hostile attitude they have towards humans, whereas Ford has grown quite fond of the species for all their foibles. As far as Arthur himself is concerned I really like the scene on Magrathea where Ford consoles him, it's almost tender.

Just explain to me what's happening then.

Well, Zaphod finds this portal on Magrathea that he believes is going to take them to Deep Thought and Arthur is apprehensive. Ford is more calculating. He's just assessing the situation and reckoning, 'We can do this.' Arthur is just totally afraid.

It looks pretty scary.

It does. It's the jumping-off place and I like the metaphor that that situation represents: when there's an opportunity to go, go. You know, just go through to the other side because the doors do close. There are points in everyone's life where you have to make a decision, good, bad or otherwise, and you got to just go for it. And Arthur makes his decision just a little too late. He needs to be pushed, to get him outside of himself and be a citizen of the universe. His anxiety and apprehension are internal. He's not wearing them on his sleeve in some predictable way. I love what Martin is doing with his character, man. Arthur is faced with all these urgent situation in a beautiful ludicrous galaxy and in the face of all that how he just buckles down and jumps. Sometimes because he's being dragged kicking and screaming . . .

Literally.

Yes, literally, but he makes the adjustments, he adapts.

And how's it been, working with Martin?

He's got a fantastic ease about himself as an actor that is really nice to work with. This is one of the best casts that I've worked with.

Tell me about your costume.

That was a really involved process because I wanted to do something that was traditional but also a little odd. He is from outer space, he is an alien but he does have to blend in. It was just subtle things – take a normal three-button sports coat, make it four and let's give him a waistcoat. It's all very purposeful. If it's cold I've got a hat, utilitarian but also gentlemanly and straightforward. He's a working man, so he's got a suit and tie, and he's very serious about his work, but not pompous about it. As a researcher he's also totally prepared for head of state or president or a celebrity. He would command a certain level of respect from anyone who he met without seeming unapproachable: and I wanted comfortable shoes!

And what about the inside of the jacket, the colours?

Yeah, the orange, the orange and purple just appealed to me.

They're your colours?

Yeah, I know. I asked Sammy to put purple wherever there could be purple. Wherever there was lining, wherever there was a flap, just small subtle things that she might not necessarily see on clothes from Earth, just small details, small details that could be avant-garde, but that also just blend. I was really, really pleased with the result.

So what's Ford got in his satchel?

Well, the things Douglas described in the book and more. He's got water, the *Guide* of course, peanuts, his towel, his camera, a pen, a pad, his glasses and his shades for moments where sunlight on a planet might be very intense and he needs to cover his eyes or for times when he wants to conceal his identity or assume a character. I love that the satchel has the space-age element; it's this small thing that everything is in. I also love the design of the *Guide* itself. Just sort of simple, straightforward, elegant and streamlined, which I imagine is what it would have to be considering that he's travelling from planet to planet. The idea is that Ford's whole existence is portable and he is ready to go at a moment's notice. He travels light and swift and efficiently, which certainly appealed to me.

Tell me about all the 'stage' business you've developed with the towel.

Well, you want to make it interesting. You want to have it slung over your shoulder, try to make it where it's as much a part of his wardrobe or his identity as anything else that's on him. So he uses it as a weapon, he uses it as a napkin, he uses it to create warmth, he wraps it around his head, I think he has some sort of emotional connection with this towel that's almost able to absorb danger or clean things up or provide comfort. But it's all still real, believable somehow.

It's just a towel and we haven't turned it into some kind of high-tech gadget.

And how's it been, working with Sam's energy?

Oh my God, Sam is actually a great marker for me in terms of my character. I came in to rehearsals thinking that Ford would be more pronounced in his strangeness. I didn't want to make him to be this zany space guy but I did think that there would be things about him that were pronouncedly strange and I think there are still. But seeing Zaphod, I thought, 'Oh, there's somebody already doing that,' and I wanted to be able to provide a contrast. Ford is very matter-of-fact and Zaphod provides a good counterpoint for my character. Working with him just created a very clear place for what it is that Ford has to do in Arthur's story and what his position is in the midst of all four of them. If you have two characters that are both doing zany in a movie it kind of gets silly. You see Ford at the beginning of the movie and kind of think he's crazy but then you meet Zaphod and he almost makes Ford look like another version of Arthur.

He's like a bridge, isn't he?

Yes, Ford is definitely the bridge between Arthur and Zaphod and it's really nice to have them on either side.

And what about Trillian?

Zooey's a wonderful actress and is totally believable, her disaffection, her boredom, her intelligence and her sense for adventure are very clear. It's a fantastic cast all round. It's sometimes nerve-racking because it means a great deal to be in this movie and also the story is complex, very layered. I found myself every week, or every couple of days, discovering something new. Even in the closing stages there are new things that I'm discovering. Starting work on Magrathea was one of those moments. It's the great lost planet and Ford didn't believe that it was real and now he's there, his feet are on the soil, or rather the ice, and after the first day on that set I went back to the book and there was the passage which gave me another clue to Ford's relationship with Zaphod.

> 'OK, so I've bought the fact that it's Magrathea – for the moment. What you have so far said nothing about is how in the Galaxy you found it. You didn't just look it up in a star atlas, that's for sure.'
>
> 'Research. Government archives. Detective work. Few lucky guesses. Easy.'
>
> 'And then you stole the *Heart of Gold* to come and look for it with?'
>
> 'I stole it to look for a lot of things.'
>
> 'A lot of things?' said Ford in surprise. 'Like what?'
>
> 'I don't know.'
>
> 'What?'
>
> 'I don't know what I'm looking for.'
>
> 'Why not?'
>
> 'Because . . . because . . . I think it might be because if I knew I wouldn't be able to look for them.'
>
> 'What are you, crazy?'
>
> 'It's a possibility I haven't ruled out yet,' said Zaphod quietly. 'I only know as much about myself as my mind can work out under its current conditions. And its current conditions are not good.'

I love that *Hitchhiker's* exists in this twilight of fantasy and reality, this inventiveness based in real situations and actors can play off that too. Like the scene when Zaphod and Ford meet up on the *Heart of Gold*. It's just two old friends seeing each other for the first time in years, but we invented a little greeting ritual, which also gave Arthur something to play off. All the time though we were all trying to avoid any of those situations being cartoonish or caricatured.

I think it's been important to take it 'seriously', to avoid those nods and winks to the audience which might pull the audience out of the worlds you are trying to create for them.

Straight ahead, but not too traditional. Garth was very keen on the performance element of all this and it's definitely great to have worked on a science-fiction movie for the last three or four months and not have stood in front of a blue screen or had to act to an imaginary character. Our imaginations were activated by the presence of real things, except for the paddles!

I think that's one of the things that really gives this movie a heart and a charm that some science fiction doesn't have.

Yes, people can detect that too and also it does something for you as an actor. It's interesting because Garth has done a lot of things in this film that you would do in theatre, like the creation of real creatures and sets. The sense of place and environment is very defined and really strong. That's great for us as actors and it's also extremely important for the audience to sense that this is not some fabricated digital world. That it's a world and a place that has been created not only by people's minds but by their hands as well.

Talking about doing things for real, I was impressed with what you and Martin did this afternoon, that was quite a sight!

Ah, the escape hatch of the Vogon ship! Martin and I did that stunt ourselves and it was quite a long way to fall. I love that the role is so physical because it almost brings to mind Laurel and Hardy. I'm a Laurel and Hardy fan, as is Martin. I'm a big Chaplin fan, a Buster Keaton fan and there's a lot of room to incorporate that sort of spirit and that is fun in a science-fiction setting.

How do you make your entrance?

On a shopping trolley full of beer and peanuts coming down a hill towards the bulldozers that Arthur's lying in front of. It's really quite an awesome entrance. As I was reading the script, I could see that Ford was going to be this very way-out sort of guy because when you see him on Earth he does literally look off his trolley. He's excitable and jumping over the fence to Arthur's house, but there's also a very low-key matter-of-fact dimension to him, which makes him seem even dafter. There's a sense of precision to him and having to do physical things, especially on this film, has required a certain sharpness from all of us. I know people always say, 'I'm really excited about this movie.' But I've been working on *Hitchhiker's* for the last eighteen weeks and I'm dying to see it. I feel the same way that I felt when I got here, which is totally enthused, really excited, very open and really pleased and assured that people are going to be floored by this. In a movie with special effects there is a lot you don't get to see as an actor, but I can see from looking at the sets that everything is there for a reason and serves a purpose. In their intelligence and playfulness I think that Garth and Nick have captured the spirit of the book. You have been really helpful as well, because of your enthusiasm, and we've had loads of conversations just about Douglas and small things in the book. I know what it's like to have love for a book and then to see a screen adaptation that doesn't quite do it. I don't think the readers mind it being different and new at all but they want the core of it and that's why I have had the book on set with me every day and in between my naps I'm always dipping in! Ford can be played in so many different ways . . . tender, otherworldly. It's an exciting character to embrace but it's also a character you've got to keep your eye on and pay attention to. That's the type of situation I try to put myself in as an actor and as a singer, where you really have to be paying attention and be involved. Not 'put your back to the seat of the chair and relax' type of work. You should be on the edge of your seat, watching, having to stand up, sometimes getting on top of the seat and it's been very much that experience for me and I'm really happy.

Interview with
Zooey Deschanel
(Tricia McMillan)

Credits include *Elf, All the Real Girls, Good Girl,* and *Almost Famous.*

Robbie Stamp: So to begin, had you ever heard of *Hitchhiker's* before you got involved?

Zooey Deschanel: Yes, I read the first *Hitchhiker's* when I was around eleven. There was like a little *Hitchhiker's* fan club in my class at school. So I read the first one then and I liked it, but I hadn't had a chance to revisit it until I found out that I was up for the movie.

How did you get involved?

I knew about the project and was doing a film in New York with Garth when Nick came to meet me on the set. We had a lunch meeting together and I was very struck by their charm and creativity and their approach to the material. One of the first things that struck me was that even though it was a science-fiction movie, they saw the relationships between the characters as something very important, rather than thinking that the special effects were the most important thing. Garth mentioned Billy Wilder's movie *The Apartment,* with Jack Lemmon, as the sort of movie that he liked and also *Annie Hall*, and those are two of my favourite movies. So right from the first I was intrigued because it seemed unusual to me that someone who was directing a film with a lot of special effects should take a lot of interest in the human relationships and realize that they were really what was going to ground it.

I am frequently asked why the movie was finally greenlit and I think there were a number of steps but I'm sure one of the key reasons that Nina Jacobson finally agreed to go ahead was that we had worked hard to create a real relationship between Trillian and Arthur.

Yes, which is probably the main difference between *Hitchhiker's* in its other incarnations and *Hitchhiker's* the movie. I think that it's going to work very well on the screen. The novel, the radio series and the TV series, they're all totally different things.

Having this 'humanity' in the midst of it lets the whole piece breathe more easily on screen.

Yes, usually there aren't that many intimate moments in large-scale, large-budget, heavy special-effects movies. To have these human relationships juxtaposed with the massiveness of the universe is what makes the material funny. You have these people who are people and aliens who are strangely familiar in the errors they make and in their misconceptions of things and it makes the universe seem smaller and makes the intimate moments seem larger. Douglas seems to have had this core desire to point out that we're smaller than we think we are, that a little humility on the part of the human species would go a long way.

In the other versions of *Hitchhiker's* it is Trillian of all the characters who is the most underwritten, and we have developed her the furthest in the movie, so talk a little bit about finding her and her voice.

From the table read* to now, Trillian has changed a lot, actually, because you always find your character as you do work with them in the film. You just see what works for you and with the other actors and within the context of the film. When we started out Trillian was a bit more passive and we've made her a little bit feistier, a little bit tougher. I think it works, especially to create a foil for Zaphod. The female audience will have somebody that they can relate to and root for because I think it definitely started out a little bit more male-orientated. Trillian is most stimulated by questioning things and by the intellectual, so I think she's most happy when she's reading the manual on the *Heart of Gold*; she's just so excited to figure it out. I think that helps me with the physicality of my approach to Trillian. She's a little nerdy, which is good, she's bookish, and that's great. I wanted to play a character that was strong and sexy and above all intelligent, and when she has to she'll take on certain physical characteristics. When she has to take Zaphod prisoner for the sake of avoiding the Vogons she actually becomes quite tough. I think she's also a little frustrated. It was slightly disappointing for her to go out into space and find people and species like the Vogons, that were just as much idiots as the people on Earth.

---

* British actors call this the 'read through' – the first time the whole cast gets together to simply read the script.

There are now a lot of moments where Trillian takes charge when the boys are faffing around.

Yes, she is very smart, a person who is 'to the point', and I think that there are moments when she does start to grow a little weary of the bickering between the other characters and really does take charge.

She's the one who works out the ship; she's there with the manual. She gets it.

Well, they wouldn't be flying the *Heart of Gold* without Trillian. They all have their own specific things that they do and their own tasks within the story. Without Zaphod there we wouldn't be on the *Heart of Gold* in the first place and his celebrity saves them a few times. Arthur is constantly questioning things and trying to find a way of relating to the girl he met at the party who bowled him over, vanished and turned up again in space. Ford Prefect is very much an observer who isn't phased by too many things and his almost Zen bravery moves the story along. Trillian is very direct, a person-slash-alien who really drives them to get to where they're going.

Did you think at all about being a semi-alien?

I think I am semi-alien myself. All my life, when I was in school, people said I was weird, so now it's paying off! I think that's why a lot of people relate to this story. Everyone feels part alien!

There's a big thread on alt.fan.Douglas-adams, one of the key fan newsgroups, 'Is Trillian human?' What are your thoughts?

When she finds out that she is half alien she is quite happy about it. She's got all these degrees and is so smart that probably the first time she's ever been challenged is when she gets on the ship and has to face the controls and the manual. It's pretty amazing and the designers had certainly come up with a lot of buttons and dials. The Improbability Drive poses a pretty big challenge to the laws of physics as we think we know them on Earth! That was the key for me in the beginning. It's her intellect that explains why she does go with Zaphod Beeblebrox at the party. She has always had this nagging sense that Earth is too small for her really, and the only way to entertain herself is go off on this crazy adventure and see what happens, because she's certainly not being challenged on Earth.

As soon as she gets into space she gets her teeth into the experience in a way that Arthur really doesn't want to . . .

She's led by her intellect, and she first has to see if she can challenge herself before she can really fall in love with anybody.

The scene where you meet Arthur is a seminal moment. He's reading a book and you bounce up to him and say, 'Who are you?'

Yes, basically that's like the start of a different genre of movie and then it gets cut short and really gets interesting, because there's so much more beyond that familiar party scene of boy meets girl. But that 'ordinary' beginning on Earth is so important for the rest of the film. It grounds it before things get pretty wild out in space and we have all these fantastic sets and planets. When it really hit me that this was something special was walking onto the *Heart of Gold* for the first time. Remember, I had read the books when I was at school and it was like all of a sudden rediscovering my youth. It was really a feeling that was completely overwhelming and I just was running around and jumping around and running up and down the stairs. It felt there was scope for the imagination and for the first time it really all came together for me that this whole film was a group of tightly knit people who all wanted to make the best film that we possibly could and I was just completely blown away by all the work that had been done. It's just so inspiring for an actor to see everyone on the set caring so much about what they're doing and I think that there was a tremendous sense of responsibility to the fans and to Douglas Adams and to his family, just to make a good movie and to make a movie that was really worthwhile, where we all put all our creativity and all our intelligence and all our hard work into it.

As you say, we've all felt a deep sense of responsibility for the fans and the family but an equally big responsibility to millions of people who aren't yet fans.

Our new fans! This is an intelligent comedy with a rare undercurrent of philosophical meaning and I think it's a film that you could see over and over again and not get bored. Each time you see it, you will be able to see something new that even I, having worked on the film for four months, haven't seen before or hadn't remembered. It's a movie that I cannot wait to see, and I say that in all sincerity. A lot of the time you're curious about a film you do, but this one is really a special film and I think that there are a lot of people out there who are waiting for an intelligent comedy of this kind. It has a sort of political significance. I just mean you can compare it to a lot that's going on in the world. Yes, it's all aliens and it's the universe but what's really funny about it is that even on this grand scale things don't change. There's still bureaucracy, there are still rash decisions being made on the part of government, there's still corruption, there are still all kinds of things that are frustrating. And I like the emphasis on the human ability to question all the time. Some of the message of the film is that you should cherish your ability to question things. We can question our government, we can question the things around us, we can question the people around us, and that's a great thing. It's interesting that Earth was created to come up with the ultimate question because we are so inclined to come up with questions.

I'd never put those two things together. The Earth is built, designed to answer the Ultimate Question and of course that was very much a part of Douglas' character; he loved questions and had this great ability to provide a new perspective, to make you look at a problem from a different angle. I talked with Mos for a long time and what's been fascinating is how interested both of you have been in the ideas.

I was always interested in philosophy and I found it really interesting to read a novel that's a comedy and a science-fiction novel but so chock-full of ideas. The thing that's made it stick around is the philosophical core and the things that it says about the world and its beauty and its absurdity. That's why it's funny when you hear Jeltz on the loudspeaker talking to the people of Earth when it's about to be blown up:

> 'There's no point in acting all surprised about it. All the planning charts and demolition orders have been on display in your local planning department on Alpha Centauri for fifty of your Earth years, so you've had plenty of time to lodge any formal complaint and it's far too late to start making a fuss about it now.'

I mean in the US it's just like going to the DMV and trying to renew your driver's licence and the person behind the desk goes, 'Oh you have to fill out that form, but you can only fill it out at home with a blue pen and only on a Thursday.' In our imaginations we tend to think of aliens as necessarily greater or smarter than us but to discover that they are actually being as petty as anything else is a really brilliant idea.

I was surprised by how physical the film was for you guys, and your Bugblatter Beast stunt was pretty impressive!

I used to rock-climb when I was a kid and so I was pretty used to harnesses and that sort of thing. So I wasn't nervous about it and I figured the best way to do it was to do it myself. It's better to do a stunt yourself if you can do but if it's really dangerous you want to let a professional do it.

Has the movie been more physical than you thought it was going to be? There are quite a lot of bruises.

I know, actually Jason* keeps laughing because I come home with a spectacular array of bruises, I got hit by a piece of 'bullet' and I *kept* getting hit on the head by flying objects!

---

* Jason Schwartzman, who plays Gag Halfrunt.

And then there was the shaking around in the *Heart of Gold*, when you were being chased by missiles.

That was fun because we were throwing ourselves against things and it was definitely more physical than I ever imagined it. I thought that this was meant to be the intellectual sci-fi action film! But then again at the same time as the physical comedy we're shouting philosophy at each other like on the Magrathea set, that was really funny, Martin yelling over that loud vacuum portal machine.

So what about Trillian's relationship with Zaphod? Was there ever a physical attraction?

I think she thinks he's cute enough; Zaphod's like a summer fling.

But they did have a fling when they got on the *Heart of Gold*?

I want the audience to decide for themselves. Yes, I think she thinks he's attractive but he's not a lasting attraction.

Have you enjoyed working with the others? It's a very unusual mixture.

It really is, I think they did a great job of putting us all together. There's a great moment in the ship when we have all just been tossed around during the missile attack and Arthur says, 'Well, we can talk about normal till the cows come home,' and one by one the characters ask, 'What's normal?' 'What's home?' 'What are cows?' I think that's a really good line, philosophy, character and a joke all in one.

Very *Hitchhiker's*.

It's really perfect for describing the relationship between all of them. Just thinking about that makes me aware how much fun I had working on this movie.

Interview with

Bill Nighy

(Slartibartfast)

Credits include *Love Actually*, *Magic Roundabout* (the voice of Dylan), and *Shaun of the Dead*.

Robbie Stamp: Did you know *Hitchhiker's*?

Bill Nighy: Yes, I was very familiar with *Hitchhiker's Guide to the Galaxy*. I read it when I was a youngish man, as did everybody I knew on the block, because it was a huge book. I enjoyed it enormously, laughed and appreciated it, and then subsequently – almost more satisfyingly – I bought it for my daughter, when she was about thirteen or fourteen. If you wanted to put something on a cover of *Hitchhiker's Guide*, not that anybody should pay particular attention to me and my daughter, you could put 'my daughter fell off her chair', because she did . . . there was a bang behind me and I turned round in a slight panic thinking something terrible had happened. In fact what had happened was that she'd literally fallen off her chair laughing. The other thing which was very appealing and nice about that particular experience was that she found the book so beautiful, funny and kind of funky that she read me almost all of it in order for me to share it. And it was just such a treat to watch her face and see her reading enormous chunks. I bought them all then: *The Restaurant at the End of the Universe* and *So Long, and Thanks for all the Fish*. I think they are a remarkable achievement. I think he was a seriously, seriously gifted man and his books are more than just funny, they're more than just sci-fi. He was a very, very intelligent man and these books are informed by that. I'm very, very glad that they're in the world.

You are absolutely right; they've just got a very rare mixture of humour and intelligence. My daughter, age ten, has just discovered them and she loves them. I think that that bodes well for the movie and I really hope that we will hit a whole new generation of teenagers and that next summer we should be the funny, hip, cool movie to go and see.

Well, that's what I thought when I read the script. I thought I just wanted to be in it because I love the whole thing. It's very superior. The jokes are world-class. It is profoundly amusing and exciting and interesting and thought-provoking – all those little things he throws in like the definition of flying being throwing yourself at the ground and missing, things like that which just tickled me. I think the kids will go mad.

So how did you come to be involved?

First time I knew anything about this was when a mutual friend of Garth Jennings and me was getting married in Scotland. My friend said, 'Oh and by the way he's the director and I think he might want to talk to you about a job on *Hitchhiker's Guide to the Galaxy*.' I nearly got a lift to the wedding with Garth, who I'd never met, but we didn't travel together in the end. We didn't even talk at the wedding. Maybe Garth thought it would be unethical! We probably held hands to Irish music before we ever discussed the project. I received the script shortly afterward and read it immediately and of all the things I've read, and there have been a few, there was absolutely no question in my mind. The minute I put the script down I phoned my agent and said if it was at all possible I would seriously like to be in this movie. I figure also from a practical point of view that it'll be a hit, but who knows? Well, we all think it's going to be a hit otherwise we wouldn't be here. Then again, maybe we would actually. I think I probably would, I'd be here. But I do think it will travel and I think it's got real appeal for everybody and it's got everything, you know, because it operates on every level. The script is very clever, a very good representation of the book. It's a great adventure, it's a fascinating journey, a sweet love story and it's a great resolution and as for an opening, you can't do much better than blowing up the Earth in the first ten minutes. Most movies like this are about stopping that happening. So, yes, I read it and loved it. It was that simple, really. I made the phone call, then as is the way of these things lots of other things happened and we hadn't done any kind of deal and then I remember doing a red carpet in Los Angeles where you had to speak to lots of different microphones and at the end the last question is always 'What will you be doing next?' and you have to waffle because you don't know anything or either you know some stuff but you can't say anything and on the very last one I ran out of waffle and I said, 'Well, I'm hoping to be in *The Hitchhiker's Guide to the Galaxy*,' and it was the BBC and my agent phoned up the next day and said words to the effect of 'What of 'What the flaming hell do you think you're doing?' because we haven't done any kind of deal. It ended up on the front page of the *Independent* newspaper. I wasn't bothered at all. I said, 'Well, you know I want to be in it,' so that was it.

And now we're in Slartibartfast's trailer! One of the things that's intriguing I think is the physical look of Slarti, because we've really moved away from the archetype of man with the white beard.

The thing about beards in the movies, and I'm sure there are a million exceptions to what I'm about to say, is that often they make it slightly difficult for the audience, because you lose an area of expression, you can't read the person's face quite so clearly. That was mostly why we wanted to get away from the 'old man of the west' look. A lot of the design I just went with because Sammy Sheldon and Garth Jennings had come up with a pretty good thing. I didn't feel I needed to fiddle around much. The only thing that we all agreed on was that the beard was probably more obstructive than helpful and the sense of me being a kind of corporate man is just very witty, as are all the costumes. You're not ever going to hit the image that popped into the reader's mind the moment they heard about Slartibartfast or Ford Prefect or Arthur so you can only come up with one that you think works and that is amusing or clever that you feel confident in.

What about your characteristic little snort? It's almost like a compressed laugh, it's just such a lovely little intimate thing to do.

I don't know if this is going to make any sense but it's born of the slightly innocent quality that people sometimes have when they are unaware of themselves to a certain degree. They do make unlikely noises sometimes and it just seemed to fit.

One of the things I've liked most is watching everybody inhabit their characters. We've brought a level of humanity, which I think is quite rare out there in the Galaxy.

That's a large part of the appeal for me and I think probably will be for newcomers to *Hitchhiker's* as well as enthusiasts like me. You don't get heroic behaviour all of the time from everybody. You get mundane human flaws and a kind of intimacy and a kind of colloquialness that you don't associate with the genre. It probably is a kind of genre to itself almost.

Slarti has this nice mix of pride and diffidence. He's happy to be able to talk to Arthur about his job. But there's also a tension there because he is aware that the mice plan to try and take this rather nice Earthman's brain and his job is to deliver him on a platter.

Yes, exactly, I don't suppose he gets out much in terms of meeting folk from other places. The bloody Vogons, literally ten minutes later and he'd have been free and clear and they blow the bloody computer planet up. I love the idea that they needed a race who would do all the boring jobs in the galaxy so they built Vogsphere for the Vogons and some clever clogs put in this mechanism that prevented them from ever having an interesting idea by smacking them in the face with a paddle, which is a very witty reflection on what happens to people who have to do boring jobs.

The paddles were a brand-new idea that Douglas had for the film on a flight coming back from LA. He came into the office the next morning and read it out because he liked to gauge people's reactions. The team who were lucky enough to hear it hot off the press were rolling around laughing.

Well, it's fantastic and several million years of evolution have also turned the Vogons into relentless blighters who do the next thing it says in the manual, which is a funny reflection on bureaucracy generally. By way of contrast, I think Slarti's just a benign figure, a nice man with a healthy compassion, who is proud of what he does. It's like when people who make things, they show you around their workshop, their special-effects shed or model shop, and they don't often get a lot of thanks for what they do but they are quietly proud. It's a very sweet idea of Douglas's, that the makers of the Earth are like this . . . I love the notion that there were men who planted the fields, who pumped the water into the oceans and painted the White Cliffs of Dover and Ayers Rock. In Douglas' world that's how you build Earth. It's so touching, so funky and funny.

And the iconic Norwegian fjords are one of the things people remember best from the whole of *Hitchhiker's*. Such a strange wonderful, idea, somebody winning an award for designing the fjords in Norway, it's a classic moment.

Everyone I've spoken to recently, that's what they recall. Most of them are my age and they haven't read the book for twenty years or something and that's the bit, even before I tell them who I'm playing, which they usually guess anyway, they say, 'Fiddly bits' and 'Norway' and 'Didn't he get an award?' And they remember that bit, everyone remembers that bit – they love it.

I suppose you've worked most with Martin?

Working with Martin is a joy. He is an extremely clever young comic and actor and effortless to deal with both performing and in between times, and when I heard that he'd been cast, I thought, 'Tim from *The Office*, Arthur? Of course, of course.' He has every quality required for Arthur. He has a world-class comic touch. But apart from that he has that kind of appeal you need. He's watchable. You need that because Arthur is receiving an incredible amount of information on behalf of the audience, so they have to experience it through him. You need somebody really very accomplished in order to be able to deliver that kind of performance, you don't get to do all of the party tricks all the time, you have to just be the receptor. He makes it look easy but those central roles where you have to be the audience's eyes and ears are famously difficult.

I agree. And as for your experience, what were the moments that stood out for you during filming?

Yesterday Martin and I were in our cart travelling through the Planet Factory Floor. It was rather good fun, with us trying to act with water cannons and wind machines operating at the same time. Grown men were feeding the water cannon with plastic cups of water, and then this enormously high-pressured cannon would shoot the spray towards us. The director was helping with the water and enjoying himself so enormously that he forgot to hold on to the cup, which got sucked up into the machine and all of a sudden there were plastic cups bouncing off Martin's face! That was quite *Hitchhikery*, in my view, and summed up the fun and the energy that has gone into making this movie.

Self-interview by

Karey Kirkpatrick

Screenwriter

Credits include *The Little Vampire, Chicken Run,* and *James and the Giant Peach.*

A version of this interview was originally written for and published on the *Hitchhiker's Guide to the Galaxy* movie web-log. Karey Kirkpatrick kindly gave his permission for the interview to be reproduced here and added some new questions for himself about the filming period.

HITCHHIKER'S GUIDE TO THE GALAXY INTERVIEW WITH MYSELF

I decided to interview myself because a) I think I'll be harder on myself and know what sort of questions an interviewer might ask and b) no one has asked to interview me. And why should they? Who am I? *Not* Douglas Adams is the answer that concerns most people. So with this in mind let's proceed. Here are some of the questions I imagine most fans of the book (and the radio series and the TV series and the Infocom game) are asking at this point.

Who the hell are you and what gives you the right to muck around with this treasured piece of literature, you American Hollywood hack?

Ah. Good one. Yes, I can see why a lot of people might be wondering this. So let's see . . .

My name's Karey Kirkpatrick. You can Google or IMDB me to find my credits (incidentally, I'm a guy – not the female news anchor in Buffalo, NY). But the short answer is no one has the right to muck around with this treasured piece of literature. I didn't seek it, it found me. The story goes something like this.

Jay Roach was at one point attached to direct the film. He had worked with Douglas for many years on several different drafts of the screenplay, and after Douglas's sudden and tragic death the project ground to a halt for several months. But Jay, along with Robbie Stamp (an executive producer on the film, long-time friend of Douglas's and his partner in the Digital Village), felt an obligation to not let the project die, to honour Douglas's memory, and one day while he was watching *Chicken Run* (with his sons? I don't know. In my head, he watches it weekly) he thought, 'Hey, that writer seemed to create a feature film that worked as a big studio movie while still keeping an existing and uniquely British sensibility.' (I was an avid Monty Python fan growing up, one of those guys who quoted *Holy Grail* to the annoyance of all my friends, except of course for those friends with whom I was quoting Monty Python.) So Jay sought me out. When my agent called and asked if I'd ever heard of *The Hitchhiker's Guide to the Galaxy*, I said, 'Yes, heard of it.' But let's get the first horror out of the way immediately. *I had never read the book or any Douglas Adams* before I was told of this assignment. Now, some of you may have passed out at this point after shouting, 'WHAT?!? BLASPHEMY!', but I've come to believe this gave me a huge advantage in approaching the material. I had no preconceived notions in my head. When I was sent a draft of the script (which was the last draft Douglas worked on before his death) I got to read it as what it was; a blueprint for a movie. And without any knowledge of Babel fish and Ultimate Questions and Vogons, I was able to formulate an opinion of where it worked as a feature film and where it needed work.

You should know that my first reaction – literally, my very first reaction after putting the script down – was, 'I can't write this, this guy's a genius and I'm no genius.' I thought to myself, 'There is no way I'm going to try to write words that blend seamlessly with this guy's words.' It was my *Wayne's World* 'I'm not worthy' moment. I mean, really, this is a guy who wrote '". . . there is an art to flying," said Ford, "or rather a knack. The knack lies in learning how to throw yourself at the ground and miss."' I'm not sure I could ever write a line like that. But I wanted to meet Jay Roach. So I took the meeting to discuss the script thinking, 'Maybe he'll ask me to write *Meet the Fockers*' (yes, I can be that whorish).

I gave Jay some of my thoughts, pointed out some structural and thematic concerns, and much to my surprise, he agreed with most of what I was saying. And when I told him of my 'I'm not worthy' moment, he said, 'I think you're perfect for it and that attitude will probably help you.' And the more we talked about the project, the more excited I became. I mean, how can you not get excited talking about poetry as torture or nuclear missiles that turn into a sperm whale and a bowl of petunias? Assignments like this don't come along every day. Actually they *never* come along. So after pitching my ideas to the Disney and Spyglass executives and Robbie, who was there on behalf of Douglas' estate, I got the job and started writing in September of 2002.

What gives you the right to decide what stays and what goes, you formulaic chicken-writing bastard?

Hey, let's keep it clean. My mother will probably read this.

Keep in mind, I started with Douglas's last draft, so I not only had the new ideas and concepts he had invented specifically for the screenplay (brilliant ideas, too – truly humbling), but also some evidence of what he was prepared to let go of (and in many cases, I thought he had been too hard on himself and put things back in).

To familiarize myself with the material, I thought it best to go back and become acquainted with it in chronological order. It started as a radio play. So I was sent all of the radio plays on CD. I would listen to them in my car, and for those blissful fifteen to twenty hours was actually oblivious to the deeply loathed LA traffic. It was while listening to those radio plays that I first heard what was actually the opening to *The Restaurant at the End of the Universe,* which was a *Guide* entry that started 'The story so far . . .' It goes on to summarize what happened in *The Hitchhiker's Guide to the Galaxy* and I realized that was what the script needed. That one summary expressed some ideas and themes more clearly than the screenplay did. And suddenly, it became clearer to me what the script was missing, and I suddenly had some hope that I might be able to fill in some of the missing pieces.

Next, I read the book with pen and highlighter in hand, underlining passages that had been left out that I wanted to try to get back in and making notes on characters and themes that were present in the book but not really playing as well as they could in the screenplay. I was going to watch the TV show, but Jay suggested that I not do that, just so that I wouldn't have any of those images in my head. The idea was to try to *create* something rather than recreate. I did, however, buy a book that had the scripts for the *radio* plays.* When I started writing, I had the novel on one side of my G4 laptop and the radio playscripts on the other side. They are both well worn.

I was also given another invaluable piece of source material. Robbie Stamp, who became an integral ally in my writing process on this film as he was able to answer the 'What would Douglas have wanted?' questions, forwarded to me electronic copies of *Hitchhiker's Guide to the Galaxy* files from Douglas's hard drive; notes on his drafts, notes from him to the studio, random ideas and bits of dialogue exchanges, etc. Receiving this was a real thrill. I felt like Moses at the burning bush when I opened these files, a sort of 'take the sandals off, you're on holy ground' moment. It also gave me a peek into his process. There were unfinished scenes, character back stories and notes to himself on areas where he was having problems. I loved reading Douglas's

---

* *The Hitchhiker's Guide to the Galaxy: The Original Radio Scripts* (Pan Books, 1985 and 2003).

unedited musings and tried to put as many of them into the screenplay as I could.

My goal in the writing was to be like an editor on a feature film. If an editor has done his job well, you don't feel his or her presence. That was my aim here. I thought, if people read this script – especially people who knew Douglas or knew the material well – and can't tell the difference between what I created and what Douglas did, then I will have succeeded. I was never trying to put my stamp on this material or bring my 'voice' to it (whatever the hell that elusive thing is).

I started reading his other works, reading biographies, watching documentaries (graciously sent to me by Joel Greengrass), and I found myself feeling an odd connection to the man I had never met. There were some eerie similarities between us: mutual love of Macs, wannabe rock guitarists, world-class procrastinators, avoidance a huge part of the writing process, love of satire, belief that nothing is so sacred it can't be poked fun at – to name a few. The biggest difference, however, was that Douglas was an amazing conceptual thinker and I tend to be stronger with structure. This, as it turns out, was a stroke of good luck because many of the concepts were already there, they just needed a tighter structure in which to exist and thrive.

So . . . what exactly did you change? More importantly, what did you think was worthy enough to add?

That's a hard question to answer because it depends on whether you are comparing the final shooting script to the book or to the screenplay that I inherited from Douglas. If you compare it to the screenplay, then the answer is that

I added very little. One of the things I really admire about Douglas is that he was willing to keep *The Hitchhiker's Guide to the Galaxy* an organic evolving entity. While reading the various drafts and familiarizing myself with the history of *Hitchhiker's*, I noticed that most of the incarnations seemed to contradict themselves. Douglas had a very refreshing lack of faithfulness to himself, so since *Hitchhiker's Guide to the Galaxy* was in a constant state of revision by its creator, I felt a certain amount of freedom to continue carrying that torch, mostly with the new concepts, characters and plot devices that Douglas had already created. Naturally, there were holes that needed to be filled so some new material and dialogue was required. But I was always going to the source material to find the right voice and tone.

Was this a tough adaptation?

Douglas had a famous quote about deadlines and how he loved the whooshing sound they made as they rushed past. One of my favourite quotes about writing is 'I hate writing, I love having written'. This seems to be my mantra, and I have hated, loathed or dreaded writing just about every draft I've ever been involved with, mostly because writing is such a lonely and demoralizing process (with the exception of *Chicken Run* – I did have an unusually good time on that one). And people have said to me, 'Wow, adapting *Hitchhiker's* must have been hard.' But I can honestly say I have never enjoyed writing a script more. And it is all because I had such amazing source material (and collaborators). Whenever I would get the least bit hung up on something, I would simply open up one of the books and either find what

I was looking for or find the spark of inspiration I needed to create something new. I loved writing this movie, love having written it, and am still loving the writing I am doing today.

I finished my first draft just before Christmas 2002. It was 152 pages long.

152 pages!? What did you do next?

I played dumb to the studio. 'What? You think that's long? Compared to *Lord of the Rings* it's a short!' They weren't buying it. So I started the painful process of cutting. And I didn't want to cut any of it. Didn't know *what* to cut. Sent it to a couple of writer friends and asked 'What *should* I cut?' And they each said, 'I understand your dilemma. IT'S ALL GOOD!' And it was. I give a huge chunk of the credit to Douglas, obviously, because I was mostly rearranging, tightening and enhancing his existing concepts. And the studio was very excited about the first draft. They felt I had created a structure that finally worked. It was just too long.

First drafts for a screenwriter are usually the easiest because you don't have any notes from the studio and there is nothing but hope and possibility ahead of you. And in this case, I didn't have the blank-page problem because, as I mentioned, I had such excellent source material.

But second drafts are tough and third drafts are the toughest, mostly because you now know what *doesn't* work and your choices are becoming more and more limited. But I knew it was too long. And as Jay rightfully pointed out, you can't have a two-and-a-half-hour comedy. So I got Draft 2 down to 122 pages. Maybe one day, after the movie comes out, they'll let me post my first draft on the Web so I can say to all the fans who want to drag me to the nearest stake and set it ablaze, 'See! I wanted this in the movie, too! But they wouldn't let me put it in, I tell you! They wouldn't let me!'

It was during the trimming-down phase that I found myself facing what had been the dilemma that prevented *Hitchhiker's Guide to the Galaxy* from becoming a feature film for the last twenty years, and this dilemma can be summed up in the words of an executive on the project (who shall remain nameless because . . . well, because I'm not that stupid). He said, 'We aren't going to make a $90 million cult film.' And I get that. I understand. If I had turned in a draft that could be made for $15 million, they would have more or less let us do what we wanted. But everyone knew the budget for this movie was going to be, at the very least, $50 million. And when that kind of money is on the line, those who are putting up the money tend to want a film that will appeal to as wide an audience as possible to ensure some return on their investment (and rightfully so). But it put me in the position of being the servant of two masters because on the one hand I desperately wanted to make sure that the integrity and distinctive sensibility of the book was being maintained, but on the other I wanted to be fiscally responsible to those signing my cheques.

There is an intelligence at work in these books that I was trying to preserve. Douglas was a great satirist because he possessed a very real understanding of the incredibly heady concepts he was satirizing. In one interview he said that if they had had computers when he was in school and had taught computer science, that's probably what he would have pursued. He also could have been a theoretical physicist; he was that knowledgeable on the subject. So it was important to me that that intelligence remains at the epicentre of the piece. It's what I love about Python's *Life of Brian*. That movie is just a hair's breadth away from being viable theology. So the goal was to create something that had pace and narrative structure and an emotional storyline that an audience would care about and put all of that in the context of this very intellectual, irreverent, satirical world.

Again, I found myself going back to Douglas's drafts, which were much shorter than mine. He cut much more mercilessly than I did, so I felt I had some leeway there. Mostly I had to cut a few of the *Guide* entries with the assurance that they would end up on a DVD someday in the future. And what's great about the *Guide* entries is that they are somewhat modular, so final decisions regarding them can be made after filming is complete and the movie is assembled.

What did you do when Jay Roach decided not to direct and who the hell are those Hammer and Tongs guys?

I'll be honest. One of the main reasons I got into the project was to have a chance to work with Jay. Mutual friends had told me we had similar temperaments and sensibilities and that it would be a good match, and they were right. Jay was an invaluable collaborator on the outline and first two drafts. He put in a lot of time with me, and the script wouldn't be the success it is without his involvement. So I'd be lying if I didn't say I was feeling a bit gutted when he decided this wasn't the best film to make his next.

But what followed was an interesting process because several names were bandied about and I even met with one of them (and we're talking A-list directors here). And the general sentiment from all of them was: 'No, thank you, I don't want to be known as the guy who screwed this one up.' And part of me understood and another part of me was saying, 'Oh, God, does that mean *I'm* going to be known as the guy who screwed this up?'

But Jay gave the script to Spike Jonze and Spike said he couldn't do it but he knew the perfect guys and he suggested Hammer and Tongs. And when I got the call that I was to have a conference call with said Hammer and said Tong, I asked the question everyone seems to be asking – 'Who are they and what have they done?' Needless to say, it wasn't of much comfort to find out they had never directed a feature. And I didn't get a chance to watch their commercial and music video reel before the call (because my DVD player wouldn't play UK Region 2, but I digress), but when I heard that they wanted to talk to the writer before talking to anyone else, I thought, 'Hey, these guys are either very cool or *very* naive. Don't they know screenwriters are but a fly on the ass of this business?'

Let me just say of my experience with Hammer and Tongs that not since working with Nick Park and Peter Lord at Aardman have I worked with someone with more creative spark and inspiration. Each conversation I had with either of them improved the script in some way. In retrospect, it feels like it was meant to be. I now can't imagine this movie in anyone else's hands. I didn't think anything could inspire me on *Hitchhiker's* more than the source material, and I am happy to say I was wrong. So in May of 2003, Nick Goldsmith and Garth Jennings came on board. I flew to London with Derek Evans from Spyglass to have three days of intense meetings at their office which, as it turned out, was a converted barge sitting in a river somewhere in Islington. They had 'some ideas' for the third draft, and I'll admit at the time I was very apprehensive and guarded. It's always a bit of a nail-biting moment when directors come on board, especially ones from the world of commercials and music video. But their ideas were inspired and showed not only that they were incredible visual thinkers but also that they had a very strong sense of narrative structure. I left London with an outline and a feeling that the script would improve and the movie was in very good hands.

To this day, however, I am embarrassed to say I still don't know which one is Hammer and which one is Tongs.

Quit being so vague! Give us specifics, damn it! What's in the movie and what isn't?

Sorry to say, I will continue to be vague. I really don't want this to turn into a 'what Karey did versus what Douglas did' situation. By Douglas's own admission, *The Hitchhiker's Guide to the Galaxy* is a story with a long beginning and then an ending. There isn't much middle. And movies need a middle. So most of the new material comes in the middle. Douglas created much of it. I took what he did and enhanced, expanded and connected (much like a Wonderbra – and this wouldn't be the first time I've been compared to that miraculous contraption).

More has been made of the Arthur–Trillian relationship and the Arthur–Trillian–Zaphod triangle. Douglas knew, as I know, that in order to make a feature film bankrolled by an American studio that is to play on the global stage there needs to be a certain amount of attention paid to character,

character relationships and emotion. The trick here is doing that while staying true to the spirit of the book, which is what I hope we've done. It's fine if there's a bit of a love story, it just can't be sentimental and sappy.

But I think people, especially diehard *Hitchhiker's Guide to the Galaxy* fans, will be happy to see that it is very much the same story as the radio play, the book and the TV series with all the well-known and beloved scenes, characters and concepts. Arthur, Ford, Trillian, Zaphod, Marvin, Eddie, Vogons, Slartibartfast, Deep Thought, Lunkwill & Fook, the mice, whales, petunias, dolphins, 42, even Gag Halfrunt; all present and accounted for.

Do you consider yourself to be in the Mister Friggin' Lucky Club?

Yes. Definitely. This was a unique assignment for me because it became more than just a job. Actually, all of them are more than just a job because as one famous quote goes, 'Writing is easy, you just open a vein and let it pour onto the page'. I always feel I do a bit of that on each project (yes, even *Honey We Shrunk Ourselves* – a small vein maybe, but a vein nonetheless). But this one was different. This became a quest: a quest to do the memory of Douglas Adams proud. And that has been the attitude of essentially every person who has joined this production (except for the accountants, who say they want to do the memory of Douglas's accountants proud, but hey – whatever works). Never before have I been involved with a project where everyone seems to be aiming for a higher cause, which is great because it means egos get checked at the door. Each time the film enjoys some form of success along its way (getting a director, getting the green light, attaching cast, etc.) it is always bittersweet because we're happy to see what was Douglas's lifelong hope becoming a reality, but deeply saddened that he can't be here to enjoy it with us.

Before turning in our third draft to the studio, Garth, Nick, Robbie and I gave the script to Douglas's wife, Jane, and then went over to her house (ironically a ten-minute walk from the Hammer and Tongs barge) for a chat and, of course, tea (this was England, after all, and whenever two or more people assemble in England, it is national law that tea must be served. I'm from Louisiana and we have a similar law that involves Dr Pepper and Cheetos). We were so relieved and delighted to hear that she was very happy with the script. She gave us some of her thoughts, but most importantly – her blessing.

I think fans will be pleased and I trust new fans will be created in the summer of 2005.

What is your favourite line from the book?

Tough question. So many great ones. Many of my favourites from the book are actually in the prose, like easter really meaning small, flat and light brown or the passage about Hooloovoos, which are super-intelligent shades of the colour blue. How did this guy think up this stuff? Amazing. I read lines like that and I am humbled and awed.

Most of my favourite lines of dialogue, however, are said by the Voice of the *Guide* or the narrator. I love the passage about Vogon poetry and the Azgoths of Kria and how, during a recitation of a poem by Grunthos the Flatulent, four of his audience died of internal haemorrhaging, and the President of the Mid-Galactic Arts Nobbling Council survived by gnawing one of his own legs off. That just cracks me up every time I read it (and as of this date, it's still in the movie). I also love the Babel fish entry and how it proves the non-existence of God and I love all the Oolon Colluphid titles (*Where God Went Wrong, Some More of God's Greatest Mistakes* and *Who Is This God Person, Anyway?*).

Mostly what I love are Douglas's subtle word choices. He's a wordsmith. There's a line (I think this one is actually in *The Restaurant at the End of the Universe*) that talks about someone being 'nibbled to death by an okapi'. I crack up every time I hear it. The word 'nibbled' is the first thing that gets me, and the fact that it is an okapi doing the nibbling is just icing on the cake.

In *The Hitchhiker's Guide to the Galaxy*, there's a passage about the Vl'hurgs and their commander being 'resplendent in his black jewelled battle shorts'. Black jewelled battle shorts? Who thinks up this sort of thing? I love it.

What was the hardest part about adapting the script?

One day, I found myself addressing a note from the studio to 'clarify the concept of the Infinite Improbability Drive'. As if it was something that actually existed and thus needed clarification. And sadder still, I tried to clarify it and soon discovered how little I knew about laws of probability.

Actually, Garth and Nick and I spent an entire day sitting poolside at the Four Seasons Hotel in Los Angeles discussing the Infinite Improbability Drive and how to make more sense of it and better use of it as a plot-driving device. This was tough because what I always assumed about the IID was that it was basically a plot-contrivance machine. Writers are always struggling with contrived plots; the old 'would this really happen?' problem. And I thought this was yet another stroke of brilliance from Douglas to create something that allows a finite probability to become an infinite improbability – all at the touch of a button. It's a contrivance-justifier machine.

Each time we tried to clarify the IID, we'd look through the script and say, 'It's in there, isn't it?' By lunch, we moved from coffee to wine and the IID concept was gaining clarity. By late afternoon, when we moved from wine to more wine, we had deduced that we were, in fact, brilliant and that the script was flawless. So we decided to go with the 'less is more' theory and left the script alone. And then we had more wine.

What is the strangest note you received?

Garth Jennings (Hammer? Tongs? Your guess is as good as mine) sent me a note once that said, 'When Zaphod first comes out of the temple and is approached by well-wishers, the banana alien on the mole-horse needs to replace the multi-headed groupie.'

You just don't get notes like this every day.

You've established you can write for chickens, but can you write for real people?

We'll see. Fortunately there aren't many 'real people' in this movie.

Give it to us straight; is the movie in good hands?

Yes. Very. From the top down. Everyone has been very supportive. From Nina Jacobson and Dick Cook at Disney to Roger Birnbaum and Gary Barber, Jon Glickman, Derek Evans and all the folks at Spyglass – to Jay Roach (now producing) to Robbie to the directors to the crew – everyone is just really excited about how unique and wonderful this film can be. This is one of those rare films where everyone seems to be on the same page. Even the agents! From Douglas's long-time agent in London, Ed Victor, to his film agent in LA, Bob Bookman, who has seen this film through many an incarnation. I recently saw Ed at a party and he said to me three simple words that made my day, actually made my last two years. 'You nailed it.' I could see the relief in his eyes because people like him have been waiting a long, long time for this to finally come to fruition.

Any last words?

I've recently returned from London where I spent two weeks rehearsing with the actors and making last-minute script tweaks (they were so great, so accommodating and so very enthusiastic about the material). I had to return home just before shooting started but have been told the first week was a blazing success.

I started knowing little about this wholly remarkable book and have become a devoted fan. In my dreams, everyone will be happy with it. I know this isn't possible, but I feel really confident about the work we're all doing.

Most importantly, I think Douglas would be pleased.

If he isn't, may I be nibbled to death by an okapi.

AMENDMENT TO INTERVIEW WITH SELF

So, Karey, now that filming on *The Hitchhiker's Guide to the Galaxy* is complete, is there anything you'd like to add about your thoughts and experiences during production?

Oh, I would love to, Karey. Thank you for asking. Actually, I can sum up my feelings about how the production went in three simple words.

I wasn't there.

What?? Shocking!! A big-time Hollywood writer such as you wasn't allowed on set??? Do I smell scandal?

No, no, no. Nothing like that. Garth and Nick were happy to have me on set. And I was all set to come back to England mid-July, but my passport was refused by the British authorities. They said that since I have already been given some of the UK's most valued titles to work with in motion pictures (*James and the Giant Peach*, Aardman, *Thunderbirds* and now *Hitchhiker's*) they figured the best way to keep me from getting my American tainted hands on any more treasured material is to keep me off the island.

So I stayed home and adapted *Charlotte's Web*. But I have a contact in England who's shipping me bootlegged copies of *EastEnders*.

How did it feel when those actors wanted to change your lines?

Alfred Hitchcock once said that actors are like cattle. To me, actors are more like the North American woodchuck. Perky, excellent climbers, good teeth. They're also quite good with dialogue (I'm talking actors now, not woodchucks), so when ean actor suggests a line change, I welcome it with open arms. Unless, of course, the line sucks.

None of these actors suggested sucky line changes. Sam Rockwell seemed to want to add 'all right' to every second line. And not as a question, more as a sort of nervous addendum. Example: 'Let's go to Magrathea. All right.' 'Hit that drive button. All right.' Sort of an Elvis additive. And that worked out . . . all right. Martin Freeman kept saying, 'You know, if Ricky Gervais were here, he'd write the line like this' – and that just wasn't necessary. So I told him Tim in the American version would probably be better than him. Mos kept wanting things to be more 'poetic'. Curse you, Russel Simmons! Zooey told me I was really in touch with my feminine side and ever since I've been watching more football and have sold all my Bette Midler CDs.

OK, honestly – the script got better the two weeks we worked on it together. They're a great cast and they were all very collaborative. I hated that I had to leave.

How many hours of rewrites did you have to do?

Not many. The read-through revealed the script to be in pretty good shape. Most rewrites were done on the spot while we were working the various scenes.

I did do one fun exercise. For all of the scenes between Arthur and Trillian, I wrote two different versions. In one I replaced the dialogue with the subtext dialogue. In another, I wrote (in dialogue form) exactly what the characters were thinking, which they spoke out loud before delivering their actual lines. It actually turned out to be very helpful.

Isn't that fascinating? I think it's absolutely riveting. I asked Garth and Nick to include that on the DVD. Their response? 'Hmm. Let us get back to you on that.' So I wrote out the subtext of their response and here it is.

'Dream on, wanker.'

So, how's it looking now?

I think – and I say this with all humility – that it may very well be one of the best films ever created. It is beautifully shot, masterfully directed, and exquisitely acted.

Then again, I haven't actually seen it so I might not be the best person to ask.

The Hitchhiker's Guide to the Galaxy

MONDAY 19TH APRIL 2004 CALLSHEET:1

Producer: Nick Goldsmith
Executive Producers: Robbie Stamp & Derek Evans
Co-Producers: Todd Arnow, Caroline Hewitt

Director: Garth Jennings
Unit Call: 0730
Breakfast: 0645

Locn	Scene Description	Sc	D/N	Pgs	Cast #s
Elstree Stage 7	INT Islington flat Arthur & Tricia (Trillian) meet & hit it off	10pt	FB N2	1 2/8	1,4
Elstree Stage 7	INT Islington flat Montage of party dancing	10pt	FB N2	1/8	1,4
Stby Scene					
Elstree Stage 7	INT Islington flat Zaphod interrupts Tricia & Arthur	12pt	FB N2	2 4/8	1,3,4

#	Artiste	Character	Car	P/up	Call	Costume	Hair/M.Up	Reh	On Set
1	Martin Freeman	Arthur	2	0645	0730	0900	0800	0730	0930
4	Zooey Deschanel	Trillian	5	0600	0630	0800	0630	0730	0830
On Stby									
3	Sam Rockwell	Zaphod	4	TBC Stby @ Hotel from 1200					

Supporting Artistes	Call	Costume	Hair/M.Up	On Set	Remarks
22 x Fancy Dress Party Goers	0630	0630	0630	0800	

Stand in		Call	On Set	Remarks
Brian Carrol	Arthur	0700	0730	
Nadia Silva	Trillian	0700	0730	
TBC	Zaphod	Stby	Stby	

Requirements	
Art Department:	As per: Joel Collins:
Props:	As per: Bruce Bigg: Books, CD Cases, Arthur's Mobile Phone, Flash Machine, Drinks to include wine, Cane/Walking Stick for Trillian, Record Players — Practical, Records, Stuffed Beagle, wheelchair, herbal cigarettes for crowd please
Construction:	As per: Steve Bohan. Standby to put in additional flooring for Rooftop area from 1500 please
Camera:	As per: Igor Jadue-Lillo.
Grip:	As per: John Arnold
Lighting:	As per: Eddie Knight
Sound:	As per: Mark Holding: Music Playback today please
Video:	As per: Demetri Jagger
Creatures:	As per: Jamie Courtier — Hensons: Elstree Crew for Rehearsals Stage 8
Costume:	As per: Sammy Sheldon: Fancy dress today please. Additional Costume Assistant: Annette Allen in today please.
Make up:	As per: Liz Tagg: 6 Additional Make up Assistants: Rebecca Cole, Claire Ford, Lizzie Yanni, Christine Greenwood, Renata Gilbert & A.N Other.
VFX:	As per: Angus Bickerton: Stby Blackscreen for EXT Rooftop Sc12pt.

SFX:	As per: Paul Dunn: 2 x SFX Assistants today, Atmos Smoke for Party Scene today please
Asylum:	As per: Mark Mason: Pre Rig Bugblatter Beast Box set today please.
Stills:	As per: Laurie Sparham: Still of Trillian & Trillian with Arthur for Mobile phone to be taken today please
Medical:	As per: Mary Price Radio Ch1
Publicity:	As per: Deborah Simmrin
Catering:	As per: Premiere Catering: Peter Titterrell/Caroline Moore Breakfast from 0645, Am Break 1000, Lunch Stby from 1230, PM Break 1630. Tea & Coffee available throughout the day. Crowd Breakfast with Crew, Tea & Coffee in Crowd area from 0630 please. All for 110 Cast, Crew & Crowd please
Facilities:	As per: Elstree Studios: Cast Dressing Rooms — George Lucas Building. Catering Marquee up & running for 0630 AD Office Room 8, Ground Floor, George Lucas Building. Crowd Costume & sign in area Marquee Nr Security, Crowd Make up Rooms 4 & 7 Ground Floor George Lucas Building please
Production:	Additional Runner: Rani Creevey, Additional 3rd AD: Ollie Kersey in today please. Golf Buggy for Cast TBC.
Health & Safety:	Health & Safety Officer C/o David Deane Call: 0730. Please see today's risk assessment attached to Callsheet.

For more information on the *Hitchhiker's Guide to the Galaxy* movie, please visit **www.hitchhikersmovie.com**.

For more information on Douglas Adams and his creations, please visit **www.douglasadams.com**, the official Web site.

You may wish to join ZZ9 Plural Z Alpha, the official Hitchhiker's Guide to the Galaxy Appreciation Society. For details, please visit **www.zz9.org**.

Douglas Adams was a patron of the following two charities: The Dian Fossey Gorilla Fund (**www.gorillas.org**) and Save the Rhino International (**www.savetherhino.org**).

DOUGLAS ADAMS

The Salmon of Doubt

PAN BOOKS

You are on the verge of entering the wise, provoking, benevolent, hilarious and addictive world of Douglas Adams . . .

The Salmon of Doubt comprises eleven chapters of the novel on which Douglas Adams was working at the time of his death, in which Dirk Gently is on the trail of half a cat and a mysteriously easy to track actor. Co-starring with the pizza-addicted detective are Thor, Norse God of Thunder, and a highly confused rhinoceros called Desmond. Alongside this is an astonishing collection of short stories and non-fiction pieces recovered from Adams's beloved Macintosh, including: 'Young Zaphod Plays it Safe', featuring the intergalactic star of the Hitchhiker series; an earnest twelve-year-old Douglas's letter to *Eagle* magazine; and insights into a teenage mind full of adoration for the Beatles and loathing for short trousers. There are also lectures and articles on subjects as diverse as religion, the letter Y and Adams's love affair with two dogs in New Mexico.

The Salmon of Doubt is the ultimate smorgasbord of the insanities, urbanities and wonders of life, the universe and everything.

'One of the world's sanest, smartest, kindest, funniest voices'
Independent on Sunday